I0739323

Duel Realms

Duel Realms

RACHEL E. HUNT

Rachel E. Hunt UNITED STATES
* MMXV *

ISBN 978-0-9890264-4-4

Printed in the United States of America

"For I know the plans I have for you," declares the LORD,
"plans to prosper you and not to harm you,
plans to give you hope and a future.
Then you will call upon me and come and pray to me,
and I will listen to you.
You will seek me and find me when you seek me
with all your heart."
— Jeremiah 29:11-13 NIV

Duel Realms

Along the fissure of time and eternity,
two opposing worlds collide.

PROLOGUE

The path weaved through shadowed bends and dark trees. *This forest is old.* Luke could sense the age in the breeze that swept across his skin. The air was musty and damp, smelling of sodden earth and wet leaves, but unbearably humid. The muggy stickiness of it all clung to his face as if he was walking through an invisible curtain of steam.

Ancient, giant trees pressed close. *Too close.* He could smell the moist bark on their rugged trunks, and he traced their branches as they twisted up into the canopy. He stood pensively, waiting. Watching.

The longer Luke peered into the dark canopy, the stronger his uneasiness became. Though the branches seemed to reach desperately for the sun, which was hidden somewhere beyond the leafy labyrinth overhead, he was certain that these branches wanted something else too.

Me. They reach for me.

A cruel laugh startled him. He immediately looked at the man ahead of him.

He finds my hesitance amusing. "Quiet yourself," Luke said harshly. "I was—"

"You were what?" the man asked. "Frightened?"

Luke stiffened at the word. "No. It's these trees, I tell you. They're unlike any I've seen. Strange."

"Aye, no doubt. Strange." The man watched him and laughed again. "Strange as you are."

The man may have been called Edward early on in his life, but he was not known by that name now. He'd been dubbed Eddie the Rat by those who knew him best yet hated him most.

Eddie was a tall young man, far too skinny for his height, whose overall weight depended on how wet he was. But like a wet rat, he reeked not of beauty. His body was long and gangly, and the combination of his stretched nose, narrow eyes, and gaunt cheekbones created the face behind the name. A thin line of whiskers beneath his nose served as a mustache, and a clump of matted brown hair capped his rodent-like appearance.

Eddie stood but a few paces ahead on the trodden path, and his laughter suddenly turned to gagging.

"Poor Luke! So lost—" Eddie coughed and spit to the side. "And alone. Are those tears I see? Come now, don't weep."

Wheezing fool. Luke glared at him. "I can't help but weep, since the ugliness of your face pains me so." He felt a smile forming on his lips. "Your name truly does suit you."

The amused coughing abruptly stopped.

"I warned you never to speak of that." Eddie took two long strides back down the path, cutting the distance between the men in half. "It would serve you well to remember."

Luke resisted the urge to laugh in Eddie's face, which was flushed so deeply as to nearly be purple. *It would serve you well to remember, rat.* He pushed past Eddie, striding ahead in spite of the trees which barred his view around the bend.

"Well, are you coming?" Luke hollered over his shoulder. "Or are you frightened?" When he heard the scuffling of footfalls behind him, he stopped and whirled.

Eddie halted before him. "Your arrogance will be the death of you." He crossed his arms and spit to the ground. "I ought to leave you out here."

"Do as you will," Luke said. "I can find my way."

Eddie laughed. "Do as I will?" He looked Luke in the eye then and moved closer. "As you say," he said lowly. "Mayhaps I will."

Luke stepped back and wrinkled his nose. *His breath smells like rotten eggs.*

"Aye," Eddie said, "you ought to be scared. There's things out in this forest. Foul things you don't want to meet in the night...in the dark, if you get my meaning. I've heard stories," he scanned the trees warily, "about a creature. A beast—"

"Malfera," said Luke, rolling his eyes. "I know the tales. Stories from the mind of a drunken fool."

Eddie grinned slyly. "So you think." The few teeth he had were loose and brown.

I think it is you who are foul. Luke turned away and began walking again. "How much farther must we go?"

"Not far." Eddie came up beside him and nodded ahead. "Right around this bend. He'll give us what we came for, and we'll be home before nightfall."

"You've no reason to doubt him then?" Luke asked.

"No. I've dealt with him many times," Eddie said. "He'll do as he promised. All the Veneos are true to their word. Trust me."

Trust you? Or trust the Veneos? Luke looked ahead but felt for the dagger hanging from the leather sheath at his side. He wrapped his fingers around the hilt.

"You truly think that little sword will protect you from the Veneos?" Eddie asked. "Nothing can shield you from them. This has been known for ages. For your sake, I pray you don't learn it the hard way."

Luke wrenched his hand from the hilt and tightened it into a fist.

"Anything I may yet not know, experience will grant me. And I'll be all the stronger for it." He looked at Eddie then. "Unlike some."

Eddie laughed. "Then you're a bigger fool than I thought!" He hacked suddenly and spit. "Your courage will fail you the moment you see him, that I swear. Only then will you truly know how little you know. This world isn't what it—"

Luke stopped Eddie with his arm but stared ahead.

Eddie cursed and shoved his arm away. "What are you—"

"This was a mistake." Luke watched uneasily. "We should go."

It turned its head and looked their way.

"Calm yourself," Eddie said sternly. "We're nearly there. Come."

Luke saw him walk ahead, but he did not follow.

Eddie stopped and turned around. "*Come.* He doesn't have all night, and neither do we."

Luke took a step forward. And another. Eddie grabbed his upper arm and yanked him closer.

"Don't make a fool of yourself," Eddie said lowly. "And do not stare at him. He will sense your fear."

"Release me!" Luke wrenched from Eddie's grasp and stormed up the path.

But the farther he strode, the more his courage evaporated, and he was left with only his growing fear to spur him on. Even the forest itself seemed to mirror his decaying strength. With every step he took, each tree became a little more deformed than the last. The leaves darkened and withered. The dirt path became soggier, so much so that the surrounding terrain looked more like a swamp than a forest.

Worst of all was the suffocating humidity. An unbearable heat radiated from this place, and the atmosphere was clogged with moisture. The salty sweat poured from his face, stung his eyes, and dripped from his beard. He struggled to breathe.

His pace deteriorated, and Eddie quickly overcame him.

"Let me do the talking," Eddie said. "And don't stare."

Luke nodded and bent over, pressing his palms just above his knees. He could not find the breath to speak.

Eddie slapped him on the back. "Do try not to retch on him."

Luke raised his head weakly as Eddie walked away. He saw him stop a short distance ahead.

"Is this the one you spoke of?"

The words themselves had little impact. Luke barely felt them. It was the mighty clap, the deep boom of the unfamiliar voice that struck him squarely in the face, as if demanding his immediate attention. He lurched to his full height at the sound.

Eddie kneeled before it and bowed his head. "Yes, m'lord. He's the one. His name is Luke."

It raised its eyes and looked at him.

Red eyes. Fiery red eyes which seemed to sear right through him. Luke cringed. He could almost feel the heat inside of him.

"Luke," it commanded, "come here."

He tried to move, but his feet seemed chained to the ground.

"Do not be afraid," it said calmly. "I will not harm you. I will give you what you desire, but first you must come to me. It is normal to fear at first. I too was just like you once. But you must trust me. Come."

"Who...who are you?" Luke asked. He stepped closer but stopped behind Eddie.

"Luke!" Eddie stood up quickly. "Do not ask—"

"Eddie," it chuckled, "leave him be. He does not understand. But soon, he will."

Luke waited while it placed its pale hand on Eddie's shoulder and focused its red eyes back on him.

"The true question, Luke, is not so much who I am but what I am," it said. "I am Veneo. And we, my kind, all share this one name. We were once like you—men of low stature, unable to withstand the sweltering humidity and foul air of this place. But because of our loyalty and service to the Prince, he imbued us with his power. We are the only ones who can live in this forest. Our power enables us to thrive here, and to do many, many other things as well."

If Veneo was telling the truth and he truly was once a man, Luke could see no evidence of that person remaining. Veneo's body was indeed built like a man's, but nothing about it was human.

Veneo wore a long hooded cloak, black as obsidian and shiny like silk. The cloak draped his entire frame and tumbled in layers upon the ground, hiding his feet from sight. Two bony hands protruded from the cloak's drooping sleeves, and the skin was ashen white, a striking contrast to the black cloak. The fingernails, though, were jagged and bruised. Each one resembled a dead claw that was on the verge of detaching from the finger.

"Are you prone to staring, Luke? Do you find me hideous?" Veneo held out his arms, as if inviting Luke to embrace him, and smiled.

Or at least Luke thought the sinister sneer was a smile.

Veneo watched him from under the hood of his cloak, but even the hooded shroud could not hide the face framed within its shadows. For within the dark, round hole, waves of long white hair fell over his head and dangled about his neck. The color of the skin on his face matched the paleness of his hands, and if his eyes had not moved now and then, Luke might have mistaken Veneo for a corpse that was somehow standing erect. His lips were shriveled and extremely thin, almost to the point of not being there at all. And his nose, unlike his lips, truly was nonexistent. A triangular hole in the center of his face served as his only way to breathe.

But even faced with the multitude of cadaverous features, Luke might have been able to steady himself if it had not been for the demonic eyes. Two blazing red dots, like gleaming rubies, burned within the dark eye sockets. They watched Luke now, followed his every move, read his every thought.

Luke looked at the ground. "Forgive me. I did not mean to stare.

You look...you look well."

The shriek of amusement which burst from within Veneo knocked Luke a step backwards.

"I look well?" Veneo asked sharply. "Considering the centuries of no sleep and no rest, I suppose *well* will have to serve! After years of standing in this place, breathing in the fetid fumes, dealing with people like you...well, one might expect that my features should not be what they used to."

"Forgive me, Lord Veneo." Luke brought himself beside Eddie and bowed his head. "Please, forgive me."

"Lord?" Veneo asked. His voice sounded oddly amused. "Yes. You will soon know that I am Lord."

Luke felt a bony finger press beneath his chin. The finger was like an icicle gouging into the soft skin under his jaw, but he raised his head obediently and forced his eyes to meet Veneo's wicked gaze.

"You are forgiven," Veneo said. He lowered his sickly finger. "Now, before I can give you what you came for, you must give me what I desire. Has Eddie explained this to you?"

"Yes, m'lord," Eddie replied. "He knows."

Luke watched as Eddie unbuckled the wide leather belt from around his waist and tugged the brown tunic over his head.

Eddie looked like a giant boy as he stood bare-chested before Lord Veneo. His ribs protruded from his hairless chest and stomach, while his slender collarbones held his narrow shoulders in place. His baggy brown breeches sagged about his waist and hung loosely down to his shins, barely long enough to be tucked into his black boots.

Luke grimaced. *Where is his skin?*

"Luke, you must remove your tunic as well."

Eddie looked as though he'd been attacked by a black-clawed beast. Swirling black tattoos covered his stomach, chest, and back, and each stroke appeared to have been branded into his flesh. Many of the markings looked like jagged flames which wrapped around him and exploded in every direction. All the tattoos were painfully enflamed around the edges, as if they were deep lacerations which would never completely heal.

"Luke," Veneo said. "Now is the time. Remove your tunic."

Feeling for his own belt, Luke glanced from Eddie to Veneo, and back again. Eddie nodded.

Luke unbuckled and removed the wide black belt which held the dagger's sheath against his side. His gray tunic drifted loosely about his chest, and he pulled the garment over his head. He tossed his things to the ground.

"How...smooth." Veneo gazed at his naked chest. "Ah, I see you already have one. Not one of mine, but you have one nonetheless."

Luke followed the red eyes' stare to his left upper arm, where the image of an ancient stone cross was tattooed. The crossbeam and upper half of the cross were ringed crookedly by a halo of twisted vines, which bore dangerously sharp thorns.

"Why did you choose it?" Veneo asked eagerly.

Luke looked down his shoulder, where the muscle curved into his arm then bulged through the tattoo. He covered the tattoo with his hand and rubbed it gently, trying to evoke a memory.

"To brandish my defiance," Luke said. He lowered his hand to his side and looked at the ground. "I meant for it to be...to be a mockery."

"Excellent," Veneo hissed.

Luke looked up. "M'lord? I—"

Veneo lunged with his bony forefinger extended and locked at the joint, while his eyes flared a vicious crimson.

Luke gasped as the jagged claw sank into the flesh above his left breast. Searing pain exploded within his chest. He felt the claw tear across his skin, like a dull blade ripping through cloth, and he fell to his knees. His chest was on fire.

Veneo stabbed again.

Luke cried out and clamped both hands around Veneo's wrist,

which had once appeared so frail but was now suddenly stronger than he. He felt the claw wrench again, lurching inside him as his flesh burst open.

When Veneo at last withdrew his claw, Luke fell onto his side. He lay in the mud, writhing as the blaze festered within him. Every frantic heartbeat sent jolts of fire through his veins. He clutched his chest desperately.

Though blinded with fever, Luke felt the shadow wash over him and imagined it glided towards Eddie. He saw it stop, then fling itself violently at Eddie, who did not appear to move.

Luke moaned. Mud and sweat coated his hair and blurred his vision. The band which held back his hair had fallen out, and he pushed the strands from his eyes and gingerly rolled onto his back. The green canopy above him seemed utterly black now.

"Eddie." His voice choked in a whisper.

The rampant stinging within his chest slowly abated as he lay still, but the constant burning within the wound did not. He could still feel Veneo's claw lodged inside his breast, twisting and ripping.

He heard footsteps marching steadily through the brush. They stopped near his head.

"I have it, Luke. Sit up."

Luke recognized Eddie's voice but made no effort to move. "Leave me be. It hurts too much...to move." He pressed his fingers around the wound and squeezed gently. "Let me rest for—"

"You whimpering wench." Eddie bent down and heaved Luke's shoulders from the ground. "I said sit up!"

Luke groaned as his world flew upright. He brought his knees into his chest and held them there, rocking back and forth steadily as the pain pulsated through him.

"Not so arrogant now, are we?" Eddie asked. He nudged Luke with his boot. "I tried to warn you, that I did. But look here, I've something that will perk you right up. Give me your hand."

Luke raised his head. Eddie was holding his fist out to him, and it was covered in chalk.

"Is that what we came for?" Luke asked.

"Aye, 'tis," Eddie said. "The white powder of bliss. They call it sordes."

"So you said before." Luke cupped his hands beneath Eddie's fist and watched the powder stream down. "Did you bring a pipe?"

"No, not this time." Eddie dusted his hands together and wiped them on his breeches. "Just put your nose in it and take a good whiff."

Luke gazed at the powder but looked up, suddenly distracted. He watched the trees, followed the path until it disappeared into the brush. All was still and silent.

"Veneo is gone," Eddie said. "He left us to our pleasure."

Luke looked at Eddie. "You told me—" *What's wrong with him? He looks like he hasn't slept in days.*

"Aye?" Eddie peered at him through bloodshot eyes. "Told you what?"

Luke steeled his gaze. "You told me there would be no pain. You lied."

"So I did. What of it?" Eddie asked. "A little pleasure is worth a little pain. And the pain will lessen the more you come here, this I know. So go on. Try it."

Luke looked at the powder in his hands. *A little pain and then the pleasure comes.* He pressed one nostril shut with his finger and held his powdered palm directly beneath his nose. With one quick inhale, the white dust flew into his nose and vanished.

"Well?" Eddie asked. "Do you feel anything?"

Luke felt his muscles relaxing all at once. He shivered. A pleasant fog crept into his mind, while the burning in his chest gradually numbed as well.

"*Aye,*" Luke sighed. He glanced up at Eddie and grinned mischievously. "May I have some more?"

"Seems I had you pegged right!" Eddie laughed. "Aye, you may have as much as you wish, and more. I'll give you your share, soon as we reach home."

Luke rose from the ground drowsily. He lost his balance and stumbled a little, but then stood steady.

"Yours looks worse than mine." Eddie spit to the ground then nodded towards Luke. "Your mark, I mean."

Luke looked down at his chest and saw the wound clearly for the first time. The crisscrossed gashes formed a deep, black *X* directly over his heart. The edges of the wound looked angry and enflamed.

"Reminds me of my first one," Eddie said. He glanced at his own blackened chest and brushed his fingers along the claw marks. "Well, wherever it might be. Been awhile since my first." He grinned and picked up his things from the ground.

Luke gathered his own tunic and belt from the mud and wiped the dagger's sheath on his breeches. He glimpsed Eddie pulling his tunic over his head and walking away from him.

"Slow your pace, Eddie!" said Luke. "I don't want left out here alone."

Eddie buckled his belt about his waist and looked over his shoulder. "Oh, is the poor boy frightened again?"

Luke laughed loudly, almost crazily. "So frightened I may wet myself! Eddie, wait while I—"

Luke.

"What?" Luke asked.

Eddie stopped and turned around.

Luke.

Luke whirled and looked behind him. Nothing was there.

"What are you doing?" Eddie shouted.

Luke tightened his grip on his tunic and clenched his belt in his hand. He pulled the dagger from its sheath and scanned the trees. Nothing moved.

Luke.

The wound in his chest burned.

"Hurry up, Luke!" Eddie called out behind him. "If you need to relieve yourself, get on with it."

Luke turned slightly. "Eddie, something's not—"

An unnatural roar resounded through the forest as the black beast sprang from the trees. It pounced upon Eddie and threw him back against the ground, planting its paw squarely on his chest. Though Eddie flailed and screamed, the beast lowered its mouth around his head, and his shrieks became muffled cries. Then the beast snapped it jaws shut and twisted. The cries ceased.

Luke froze. The tunic and belt fell from his hands. The dagger plummeted and staked in the ground. He stared.

Malfera.

The monstrous lion raised its head, chewing a fleshy morsel. Bloody drool seeped from its jaws. Eddie's body lay on the ground, unmoving. Headless.

Where are you going, Luke?

His heart shuddered in terror. His chest seared with pain. He planted his foot and turned.

There is nothing you can do to escape, Luke.

The lion's red eyes peered at him, as if daring him to run.

And so, he did.

Luke lurched into the forest. Distorted trees blurred past him while their branches clawed at his face and gouged at his eyes. He stumbled over broken limbs and mangled roots. Briars tore his flesh. The swampy murk sucked at his boots, slowing his escape and pulling him back.

All the while, his pounding heart pumped the burning poison through his veins, and the fiery sting returned to his lungs.

Luke.

Limbs snapped and leaves exploded behind him.

Luke.

He did not see the root until it was too late.

The earth flew up to meet him, and he slammed into the ground. The impact knocked the wind from his lungs, and he rolled onto his back as he gasped for breath.

A terrible galloping through the underbrush thundered closer.

The wound in his chest flared with torment. He sat up, clutching his heart as his chest heaved and his hair stuck to his face.

Two red eyes glared at him from behind a patch of withered leaves.

You're mine. Forever.

CHAPTER 1

The pungent smell of grilled hamburger meat saturated the air almost as much as the perpetual chaos engulfed the room.

Shrill timers whined for her attention, blaring that the French fries needed removed from the sizzling vat. She pressed the buttons and jerked the wired basket out of the bubbling grease. Someone yelled her name. She glanced in that direction. The coffee pot was overflowing. Two swift strides and she reached the volcanic surge and switched out the full pot with an empty one. She could hear people chuckling behind her. She whirled and ran back.

The screens were still full and flashing, a never-ending confusion of colorful lines and complicated orders. She yanked a medium-sized paper bag from the metal canister. The phone rang.

It'll have to wait.

She whipped the bag down and away from her, while her fingers clasped the edge of the bag's mouth. The bag flicked open in one angry snap, a time-saving trick she had mastered over the years.

"Park it, Brian!" she yelled above the hysteria.

The scurrying worker in the cramped drive-thru niche looked up at her, helpless panic written all over his face.

"But Sarah, I've already parked two cars—"

"Park it!"

Brian scrambled to the drive-thru window, whisked it open, and leaned out to the waiting car.

Sarah could hear the familiar speech rambling from his lips.

"I'm sorry, your food's not quite ready yet. If you could pull forward, we'll bring it right out to you."

The window rattled and whooshed along its track, sliding back and clattering shut.

"Well, *he* wasn't happy!" Brian said. "Have fun runnin' that order out."

Sarah twisted her mouth and glared at the ceiling. *If I hear that one more time today—*

"Sarah!"

A petite teenaged girl ran up to her. "Sarah, this guy's sandwich is messed up. He wanted no pickles and extra onions, but he got no onions and extra pickles. What do I do?"

Sarah looked at the sloppy burger in the ketchup smeared wrapper, which was delicately cupped in the young girl's hands like a fragile gift. The mangled burger had a big bite mark in it.

"Throw it in the waste trashcan, Jenny," Sarah said, a little too harshly. "I'll have them make a new one. Tell him it'll be just a sec."

Jenny bit her lower lip and nodded quickly. She flung the messy bun into the trash and hurried back to the front counter.

"I need a double cheeseburger *no* pickles and *extra* onions, please!" Sarah shouted to the workers in the kitchen.

"Got it!" a young man shouted back.

"Thank you!" Sarah grabbed a sandwich from the warming area and thrust it into her bag. Next came the fries, then the napkins, some extra salt packets, and finally the receipt. She glanced over her shoulder. The dining room was clearing out, and only a few customers were in line now.

Almost there.

She grabbed two more bags and whipped each of them open like before, scanning the flashing screens for the next orders. One bag got chicken tenders, and the other got a bacon burger and fries. Napkins tossed inside with a receipt, the bags were ready to go.

"Jenny!" Sarah rolled down the tops of the three bags. "I need you to take these outside for me. There's three cars. The receipts are in the bags. Make sure they get to the right cars."

"Okay." Jenny fumbled with the bags as Sarah handed them to her. "But don't forget about my guy...the one with the messed up sandwich."

"Oh!" Sarah said. *I did forget.* "I'm glad you said something. I'll get him."

Jenny grinned. "I knew you wouldn't remember."

"Yup, you were right," Sarah exhaled. She shook her head lightly. "Hurry, Jenny. Those guys have been waiting awhile."

"Aw man, they better not be grouchy." Jenny shuffled around the counter to the door. She adjusted the bags in her arms as she backed into the door and pushed. "If they're mean, I'm comin' to get you."

Sarah chuckled as she watched. *Those bags are almost as big as she is.* "You'll be fine. Don't forget to smile!"

Jenny grinned as she scooted out into the vestibule, backside first. The glass door drifted shut behind her, but she kept smiling as she bumped the second door open and approached the first parked car.

Sarah turned back to the flashing screens. "Is this my double cheeseburger no pickles an' extra onions?" She picked up a sandwich from the warming area.

"Yup, double no onions extra pickles!"

"Okay, thanks!" Sarah took two steps and halted. *Shoot.* She turned back. "Hey, you mean no pickles extra onions, right?"

A young man stepped out from the kitchen and wiped his forehead on his sleeve. His black pants and green shirt were splotched with grease stains. "Yeah. No pickles extra onions. What you said, yup."

"Greg," Sarah said, "this guy's been waiting and we already messed his food up once. You're sure it's—"

"No pickles. Extra onions." Greg smiled and tipped his chin confidently. "I got this, Sarah. No worries."

How many times have I heard that before? Sarah looked from Greg's smirk to the carelessly wrapped sandwich in her hand. One side of the yellow plastic wrap was mushy and red. Several onions peeked out from the bottom of the wrap, where the corners folded together, and fell into her hand.

Well, at least he got the extra onions right. That's a good sign.

Her gut told her to have Greg remake the sandwich, but the customer had been waiting so long already. He would be even more upset if he had to wait any longer.

It'll just be a few seconds, though. Surely he can wait a few seconds.

Sarah turned around and glanced at the customer.

Then again, maybe not.

The man must have been in his late twenties, but the sorely peeved look on his face reminded Sarah of a grouchy senior citizen. His hair was thick and black, and it probably would have brushed his shoulders if had it not been pulled back into a ponytail. His beard looked more like several days' worth of unshaved stubble than an actual beard. His mouth was hard, jaw set and lips pressed together.

Sarah forced a smile and walked towards him. He uncrossed his arms and stood tall from his lazy stance against the wall.

She had not noticed how big he was until that moment.

Broad shoulders bound his rugged frame, which was close to a foot taller than she was, and she could see the outline of his chest beneath his gray cutoff T-shirt. The baggy blue jeans he wore were faded, holey, and stringy, but a black leather belt held the pants to his waist, where the sleeveless tee was tucked into his jeans.

"Hi there," Sarah said cheerfully. She held the sandwich out to him. "I'm sorry about your wait. Thanks for—"

"You might wanna teach those idiots back there how to read." The man yanked the sandwich out of her hand. "No pickles extra onions, right?"

His voice was much deeper and more forceful than she'd expected, and Sarah felt her chest tighten at his rude tone. She met his gaze. His eyes were gray and unhappy, like an overcast sky or a stormy sea.

And they watched her now, intently.

Sarah tried to remain friendly. "Yup, no pickles extra onions. I made sure—"

"Thanks," the man said. He walked through the lobby and vanished out the door, without so much as one look back at her.

She'd caught sight of his tattoo, though, just as he'd turned to leave. It was on his left arm, just below the shoulder, and seemed to bulge with the muscles beneath his skin. It was a medieval cross, or at least looked like one. *What were those around it? Vines? And thorns? Ugly thorns.*

"So was he mad, Sarah?"

Sarah blinked and looked away from the door. "Yeah, Jenny. He was mad."

"Aw, what'd he say? I thought he was cute!" Jenny grinned as she looked around the lobby. "Is he still out there?"

"Cute!" Sarah made a face. "No, he wasn't cute. You always think the ugliest guys are—"

"Oh, but did you see his muscles? And that tattoo." Jenny hugged her shoulders and sighed. "It was scrumptious, Sarah."

Sarah rolled her eyes as she walked away. "A scrumptious tattoo? Now that's something I've never heard of."

"Scrumptious and...more scrumptious," Jenny said. She skipped to the counter where the coffee pots were. "I think you should go out with him, Sarah. He looked like he was about your age."

Sarah guffawed. "Yeah right, Jenny." She bent down to stock the bag canister. "I would never—"

"Who's Sarah goin' out with?" Brian asked from the drive-thru.

Great. Here we go. Sarah muttered to herself when a few bags slipped through her hands and fell on the floor. "No, Brian. I am not—"

"Sarah's got a date?" Greg poked his head around the prep table. "Who's the lucky guy?"

Sarah quickly grabbed the bags from the floor and stood up. "I guess the lucky guy is some dude—" She forced the lopsided pile of bags into the canister. "Who needs a haircut and an attitude adjustment!"

Greg grinned at her. "Oh really? That's neat." He stepped back and wiped the prep table off. "Does this dude have black hair? And a ponytail?"

"Yeah, why?" Sarah asked. "Did you see him earlier?"

"I think so," Greg said. "Was he wearin' a gray cutoff?"

"Yeah, and these really holey jeans," said Sarah. "And he had a weird tattoo on his arm too." She wrinkled her nose at the memory.

"Oh yup, that's the guy I saw then." Greg pushed some crumbs into his hand and tossed them in the trash. "Actually, there's a guy that looks just like him standing right behind you."

Sarah felt the embarrassment rush through her. She stared at Greg, irritated he thought it was funny and hoping it was a joke.

"What?" she asked.

Greg scooted closer to the prep table. He nodded at something over her shoulder and continued to wipe the table off.

Sarah twisted her mouth. *I'm going to kill you.*

Greg kept smiling.

Sarah took a deep breath and tried to keep her cool. *This guy's going to be super mad. It'll be even worse if he sees what I'm thinking.* She put on a pleasant face and turned around.

"Oh! I'm sorry, sir. What can I do for—"

"I hate pickles," the man said. He dropped the half-wrapped sandwich onto the counter. Gobs of juicy, green wedges hung over the sides of the ketchup soaked bun.

Greg, you idiot! Sarah feigned remorse. "I'm so sorry, sir. I'll get that fixed—"

"Extra onions...*no* pickles," the man said. "Do I need to draw a picture? Or do you think this piece of crap is enough of a picture?" He smacked the sandwich right at her.

Sarah caught the bun just as it slid off the counter's edge. "It'll be just a moment. Sir." She felt her cheeks flushing and quickly walked away.

"Yeah, that's what you all said last time, and I waited like ten minutes."

Sarah dropped the sandwich into the trashcan, resisting the urge to fling it. She could feel the man watching her.

"Greg!" she shouted. "I need a—"

Greg popped around the table and stood in front of her. "No worries, Sarah. I got this." He held out a neatly wrapped sandwich to her.

Sarah took the sandwich but looked at him doubtfully. "You made it that fast?"

"Yup, no pickles extra onions. Booyah!" Greg whipped his arms out and crossed them triumphantly.

"If this isn't right, Greg, I'm—"

"Sarah." Greg leaned closer. "No worries. I—"

"Yes," Sarah rolled her eyes, "I know." *Here we go again.* She turned around.

The man pushed off from the wall and came toward her.

"Well? Is it right this time?" he asked.

Sarah smiled and handed him the sandwich. "Yes, no pickles extra onions, just like you ordered. I apologize for your wait, sir. If you want, I can write your name down, and you can have a free sandwich of your choice the next time you come in."

The man snorted. "Luke. Luke Porter."

"Okay," Sarah said, "I'll write—"

"Or better yet," Luke said, "you could just call me the dude with the weird tattoo who needs a haircut." He smiled then. "You'd probably remember me better that way."

Sarah felt the heat sweep across her cheeks.

"Have a great day." Luke smirked. "Ma'am."

She gaped at him as he walked away, flustered by the smug smile that seemed to stay on his face. When he disappeared out the door, she whirled on her heel and stomped over to bag a customer's order.

"Why that—" Sarah snapped a bag open furiously. "Rude stupid grump!" She grabbed a sandwich and stuffed it into the bag. "Arrogant." She crammed a second sandwich into the bag. "Cocky." A third sandwich plopped into the bag. "Sarcastic—"

"Sarah," said Greg.

"Gray-eyed grouch!" Sarah threw the French fries into the bag. "Mr. Muscles—"

"Sar*ah*!"

"What!" Sarah slammed the bag on the cart in the drive-thru.

Greg pointed over her shoulder.

Sarah caught her breath. *He's standing right behind me, isn't he?* She felt a tug on her shirtsleeve.

"Sarah, there's a guy that wants to talk to you," Jenny said. "We messed up again on his sandwich."

Great. Just great. Sarah laid her hand on her forehead and rubbed her eyes. She exhaled. *I can only imagine—*

"Sarah?"

"Yes, Jenny," Sarah said. "Thanks. I'll talk to him."

"Okay."

Did he hear all those things I said? Sarah looked up and forced her feet to swivel on the greasy tiles. *What do I say to him now?* She winced as she faced the man. "I'm so sorry, I—"

He smiled at her.

Oh.

"Hey there, um…I don't mean to be a pain, but I think I'm missing a medium fry." The man rummaged through his crumpled bag. "I came through the drive-thru a little bit ago…probably ten minutes ago, maybe…and they parked me outside. But they forgot a fry when they brought my bag out."

What did he say? Sarah watched his lips move and listened to the sound of his voice, but the words themselves did not matter.

He was not quite six feet tall, and his eyes were the color of a cloudless sky. His hair was blonde and cut short in a burr, and a neatly trimmed goatee framed his mouth. His shoulders were broad but lean, and the turquoise polo he wore was tucked into a pair of tan slacks, with a brown woven leather belt winding around his waist.

Most distracting of all was the way the bright blue shirt reflected into his eyes and made them even bluer, almost angelically so.

"Um, Miss?" he asked. "Can I have my fry?"

Jenny giggled.

"Oh, yes!" Sarah said. "Let me get that for you." She dashed to the fry station and shoveled the freshest fries into a large fry box. Then she strode back to the counter. "Here you go."

"Whoa, is that a medium?" he asked. "I think you gave me too much."

Sarah handed him the fry eagerly. "It's on us this time." She smiled when she felt his hand brush against hers. "Since we messed up and you had to come back."

"Oh." He glanced from the fry to Sarah. "Thanks."

"Is there anything else I can get for you?" Sarah asked. "Ketchup, salt, napkins?"

He laughed a little. "No, I think that's all. Thanks though."

"You're welcome." Sarah gave him her most flirty smile. "Have a great day."

He smiled back. "You too."

She watched him tuck the bag under his arm as he walked away. When he reached the door, he pushed it open and stepped into the vestibule, but stopped.

Sarah felt her heart stop too. *He's coming back!*

"On second thought," he said as he walked over to her, "there is something else you can get me."

"Yes?" Sarah asked excitedly. She felt something stir within her.

"Well, it *is* Friday...and I don't have any plans tonight," he said. "Would you wanna go out?"

"Yes."

"Yes?"

"Yes."

"Ookay." He ran his hand over his hair. "So, uh, could I get your phone number so I can call you?" He chuckled. "Or maybe your name?"

"Yes!" Sarah thrust out her hand. "It's Sarah! Sarah Ryans."

"I'm Damon." He took her hand in his. "Damon Jefferies."

Sarah smiled. "Nice to meet you, Damon."

Damon laughed. "Nice to meet you too, Sarah."

Firm but gentle. Sarah traced the lines on his hand as she held it. *His hand makes mine feel so small.*

"Um, could you write your number down for me, Sarah?"

Sarah quickly let go of his hand. "Sure, yes! Just let me grab a napkin." She jogged to the drive-thru, scribbled some numbers on a napkin, and came back. "Here you go! I get off at five, so you can call me after that."

Damon took the napkin and looked it over. "Okay, I will." He looked up at her then. "See you tonight, Sarah."

"See you tonight," Sarah said.

Damon walked through the lobby and out the door, but Sarah kept watching long after he was gone.

"See Sarah?" Greg said behind her. "It's a good thing we messed up after all, 'cause now you got yourself a date. I told you—"

"No worries." Sarah smiled mischievously as she turned around. "I got this."

CHAPTER 2

The coarse bread was a bit stale and a little thicker than usual, but the cinnamon spiced ale masked the chalky flavor and washed the dry crumbs down his throat.

Luke wiped his mouth with the back of his hand and devoured the last bite of the veal trencher, chewing methodically as the meat's juices filled his mouth and soaked the parched bread. He swallowed, ran his tongue along his teeth and gums, and drank some more ale from his tankard.

He leaned back in his chair then, pitching it on its hind legs, and pressed the tankard's wide mouth around his lips. A few drops of the warm ale trickled through his beard and streamed down his chin.

When the ale was nearly gone, he lowered the tankard from his mouth and exhaled a satisfied sigh. Tipping forward, he slammed the tankard on the table as the chair's legs hit the floor. A few leftover onions bounced from the table and scattered onto his lap. He scowled and brushed them to the floor.

I wouldn't have been angry if those fools had made it right the first time.

Leone's Inn was one of the most prominent taverns in the

kingdom, and Luke frequented the place daily. The upper half of the inn was built of timber logs and housed ten bedrooms, five on either side of a center hallway, and each was fitted with a small bed, oak nightstand, and washing basin and pitcher. The inn's lower half was a patchwork of variously shaped stones, and this ground floor was where the tavern was located.

From wall to wall, the tavern's rustic interior abounded with antlers, animal hides, and weaponry. A great stone fireplace and chimney consumed the right wall of the room, while a splendid bear rug covered the floor just in front of the fireplace. On the opposite side of the tavern, the kitchen itself was hidden from sight behind the bar, where a waist-high wooden counter traversed its front. Four log tables ran side by side along the length of the room, from the bar to the fireplace, and fifty men could be seated comfortably upon each table's two benches.

Luke had sat upon those benches many times over the years. And yet, every time he went to the tavern to get himself something to eat, he could always count on the workers to muddle his order.

The veal trencher I requested today was simple enough. He had not wanted beef, pork, or mutton. He preferred veal, meat from the young cattle, and liked it on dry bread with a slice of cheese. He'd told the young girl to put a little of that tomato sauce on it too and a few slivered onions, with a slice of dry bread on each side of the veal to form the trencher. He would wrap the food himself in a linen handkerchief and take it home with him, retreating to the privacy of his own house to enjoy his meal.

My request was simple enough. Luke shook his head as he swirled the ale in his tankard. *But still too complicated for the simpleminded, it would seem.*

He'd been halfway out the door before he'd thought to check the breaded veal, and why he'd not examined the food before departing remained a mystery to him. *I shouldn't have to check my order. The fools should've made it as I requested.* But he'd never seen so many pickles as he had when he'd peeked beneath that upper slice of bread.

I hate pickles. And he'd told the girl as much.

Luke shuddered at the memory. *What did I say to her? Something about fools and needing to draw them a picture?*

But those fools had muddled his trencher twice, and he'd had to bring it back a second time. *So the girl deserved to feel my spite.*

Luke propped his elbow on the table and pressed his fingers to his forehead. *No. She did not deserve to be spoken to like that. And over a few pickles, no less.* He pursed his lips and stared down at the table. *No wonder people think me cold and callous.*

She'd smiled when she'd greeted him, or at least tried to smile as best as she could. He'd seen the timidity in her blue eyes, though, and sensed the uneasiness in her demeanor as she'd approached him. She'd tucked a strand of hair around her ear when she'd looked at him, and he'd noticed when her cheeks had flushed red. He must have seemed terribly intimidating, with his huge frame towering over her, although he'd not realized it at the time.

Sarah. That was her name.

He'd heard the little girl say it when he'd been standing there waiting. He'd seen Sarah many times before. She was always running around and directing her workers and talking to patrons. But she'd never seen him, not until today. And what an impression he'd left with her.

See if she ever speaks to you again.

Sarah looked to be of an age with him, and she was a beauty to behold. Black tights hugged her slender legs, and a loose-fitting red tunic draped her shoulders. A black belt embraced her waist and held the rosy cloth snugly against her, revealing her delicate figure. No buttons or lace decorated the half-sleeved tunic, but the split-necked collar was embroidered with black filigree, which weaved a flowery design all around her neck. Her hair was a reddish brown and was loosely clipped behind her head, but many of the strands dangled about her cheeks and neck.

If the clip were removed, her hair would fall in waves all about her shoulders, softly caressing her cheeks and framing her face.

Or so he'd imagined.

Luke exhaled as he looked around his one-roomed shanty. *I have nothing to offer her. Nothing but pain and unhappiness.*

He had not been able to find work since he'd been removed from the builder's guild several months ago. Ultimately, his drunkenness had cost him his livelihood, but his ale was the only thing which got him through the day. When he was sober, all he could feel was the pain and the overwhelming emptiness of his life. *I'd rather feel nothing at all.* The ale allowed him to do just that.

But I was happy here once, long ago. Terra Caligines was a beautiful place to live, and it was his home.

The kingdom was encircled by Lake Solardens to the north and the Lumbrai Forest to the south, and its climate was pleasantly warm and summer-like year round. Its village was dispersed throughout a lush plain between the lake and the forest, and the meandering Dedanima River, which flowed from east to west, formed the village's southern border. Nospero's Bridge provided the only crossing of the river to the forest, while the Prince's castle towered upon a rock outcropping at the northwesternmost point of the plain and overlooked Lake Solardens.

Luke could not remember coming to Terra Caligines. The memories of his childhood were hazy, like scenes from a forgotten dream. His memories did not become clear until he was a teenager, or maybe just a few years before. It was as though he'd always lived here, whether he knew it or not, but still did not really belong.

And perhaps this realization was what bothered him so. Without his memories, a part of him was missing. Not knowing where he came from and why he was here rendered his whole life incredibly meaningless. He needed to remember in order to feel whole again.

But I want to forget in order to feel nothing.

He'd been eighteen years old when his family had abandoned him for Rovenia, the kingdom beyond the Abyss. They'd asked him to come with them, begged him in fact, but he would have nothing to do with that place.

An unseen place which, if Luke believed the talk of crazed villagers, lay somewhere beyond the empty, abyssal sea that surrounded the mountainous island of Terra Caligines.

The colossal Abyss, infinitely deep and miles wide, forever separated the land of Terra Caligines from Rovenia. To the east and west of Terra Caligines, the Dedanima River cascaded into the Abyss like two giant waterfalls, disappearing into the misty darkness below. The Lumbrai Forest to the south stopped along the rim of the rocky cliffs, while tree roots jutted from the sheer rock wall and searched for something to cling to. And Lake Solardens to the north went on as far as the eye could see, but it too could not escape the Abyss and tumbled forever beyond the horizon.

No man-made bridge could span the heinous chasm, and no rigging of any kind could traverse the bottomless pit. The few people who attempted to cross on their own fell to their deaths. There was only one way to cross the monstrous Abyss, and those who found the way could not guide other people across. The impossible feat could be accomplished only by a leap of faith—an abrupt thrusting of one's foot out over the emptiness and a held breath that the extended foot would not land on air.

The fatal step required mountains of faith. *But faith in what or who?* Luke shook his head.

Come with us! His family had pleaded with him to make the journey himself, but he had refused. Terra Caligines was his home, and Rovenia was a foreign land. He had no reason to leave. Here, he could eat, drink, and be merry after a hard day's work. In Rovenia, such flamboyancy was forbidden. Only mad desperation could propel a person over the Abyss and into a land like Rovenia.

Terra Caligines is burning, Luke! If only you could see what we see!

On and on his family had raved about the fire. The fire which consumed every tree, engulfed every building, and raged all around him was utterly invisible. The insane pull of Rovenia had taken his family from him, and they were now cursed with the fiery delusion which had misled so many others.

Afflicted with hallucinations of flames and ash, many Rovenians returned to Terra Caligines to work at their trades, but they continually spread their demented warning of blazing destruction. Other Rovenians came back silent, as if they knew nothing about a fire, but continued with their daily affairs while going back to Rovenia for rest. Nevertheless, anyone who dared to cross the Abyss and actually succeeded was never the same afterwards.

Nine years had passed since his mother and father had left him, and Luke communicated very little with either of them now. His father was yet a stonemason in Terra Caligines and his mother still a seamstress, but foreigners were despised and ridiculed in Terra Caligines. The Prince had established that precedent long ago.

Once a Rovenian himself, Prince Leone Mortuo had been banished across the Abyss for leading a rebellion against King Omnideus of Rovenia. It was during this time of exile that Prince Leone had founded Terra Caligines and invited any man or woman to be free from the tyranny of the Rovenian King.

Hundreds of people had flocked to Terra Caligines, captivated by the freedom and prosperity of the land. And as time had gone by, the population of the Prince's kingdom had quickly grown to outnumber that of Rovenia.

But King Omnideus had watched Terra Caligines with jealous eyes from across the Abyss. And so, he had warred with Prince Leone and battled him for the right to take back the villagers.

The War of Citizenship had ended in Prince Leone's defeat, but King Omnideus had not claimed the villagers of Terra Caligines for himself. Not wanting to force the villagers into submission, King Omnideus had made a way of faith across the Abyss and invited the villagers to seek him voluntarily. Any person who did so would become a citizen of Rovenia forever but an outcast eternally in Terra Caligines.

Fools. A leap of faith across the Abyss to a kingdom I've never seen. Aye. Desperate, ignorant fools. King Omnideus seemed so distant that Luke doubted if he even existed. *This world is much more pleasing. And real. I can find my own sort of peace right here.*

The white powder from the leaves of the sordes plant was his newfound hope. With one swift inhale, the powder's vigor had raced through his veins. His worries had faded, his pain had dwindled away, and his troubles had evaporated. All his body had relaxed as the tingling rush took hold, and he had felt at rest.

You're mine. Forever.

His chest suddenly seared with heat, as if someone had pressed a hot iron against his skin. He rubbed the front of his tunic and massaged the blackened scar that branded his heart.

If a scar is the price of a little happiness, then so be it. Luke wanted more. Needed more sordes. *But I'll have to get it myself this time.*

Eddie was dead. Luke should have been dead too, but the beast had let him live, had watched him run away.

Malfera. The demon lion. It had stared at him with its red eyes, caustic and focused and burning. *I can still see them. And feel them. Why didn't—*

The sudden pounding against his door startled him. He stood partway from the chair.

"Who's there?" he asked gruffly.

The only response was the sound of three more firm knocks.

Luke cursed and kicked the chair, slamming it into the table, and stomped to the door.

He yanked the door open. "Who —"

"Are you Luke Porter?"

The man kept his head bowed. Only his nose and lips showed from beneath the hood of his cloak.

What sort of man knocks but refuses to show his face? Luke scowled at him. "I'll have your name first."

The man raised his head, took the hood in both hands, and gently lowered it onto his shoulders.

Luke stepped back from him. Chunks of his beard were missing, revealing ugly sores upon his cheeks and jawline, while leathery splotches of pink skin marred his forehead.

"I am Christoph." He bowed at the waist then stood tall. "Many people call me Christoph the Scarred."

It's as though someone's gone and ripped his beard out. Luke kept his hand firmly upon the door as he looked him over. "What is it you want?"

Christoph watched him but spoke not a word.

"I am not a patient man." Luke started to close the door. "If you'll not—"

A gleam of silver flashed from within the cloak, and Christoph thrust his arm upwards in one blinding motion.

Luke did not see the dagger until it was inches from his face.

CHAPTER 3

Shafts of light glinted along the edge of the blade as the man turned his wrist this way and that.

Luke watched, stunned and silent. The threat of imminent peril filled the small space between himself and the man, but Luke dare not move. He stood rigidly, holding his breath, while he stared at the shimmering blade. His hand throbbed from its grip on the door, but he could not let go.

The scarred man suddenly looked at him.

"Is this yours?"

Luke narrowed his eyes. He said nothing.

"You're Luke, right?" the scarred man asked. "Luke Porter?"

"Might be," Luke said carefully. "Why?"

"Well, this knife...dagger, whatever you wanna call it. Is it yours?" The scarred man lowered the knife and turned it over. "It's got your name engraved on the blade."

The golden letters glistened upon the silver blade, and Luke immediately recognized the knife as his own. "Yeah. It is mine," he said. He took the dagger from the man's hand. *I thought I'd lost it for good.* "Where did you...I mean, how...what did you say your name was again?"

"Chris," the scarred man said jovially. He held out his hand. "Chris Scarlett. And you're Luke, right?"

His hand is scarred too. Luke shook it uneasily. "Uh, yeah...I'm Luke. Luke Porter." He let go and wiped his hand on his jeans. "Just like it says on the knife."

"That is a nice knife you got there," Chris said. He nodded towards the blade. "I couldn't believe it when I found it."

Luke watched him carefully. *Who is this guy?*

The brown hooded sweatshirt Chris wore was plain and a little faded, and his jeans were neither baggy nor tight but fit his legs and fell over a pair of black work boots. He was of an average height, a little shorter than Luke, but he looked older, possibly in his thirties. His brown hair was cropped short on top but buzzed around his ears, and his closely trimmed beard covered his cheeks, save for the raw splotches where the hair did not grow.

Luke cleared his throat and looked down at the knife in his hands. "Yeah, it is a nice knife. Where did you find it? Or better yet," he looked back up at Chris, "how did you find me?"

"Well, I tell ya." Chris slid his hands into his pants pockets. "I was hikin' over in Powhite Park early this morning—you know where Powhite is, right? Just south of the James River?"

"Yeah, I go there a lot," Luke said. "I was there last night for...a little while. That's when I lost my knife. I like goin' to Powhite when I wanna be by myself. It's so secluded that you don't know the highways of Richmond, Virginia run all around it. There's not too many forests like it so close to the city."

"Yup, I know what you mean," Chris said, nodding. "I just moved here from South Carolina a couple of months ago, and I found that park one day when I was explorin' Richmond. But yeah, I was out there hikin' early this morning, and I found your dagger off one of the trails. I saw somethin' shiny layin' in the leaves, just after I walked around a long bend in the trail, and there it was. I thought maybe it was a piece of trash or somethin'. Sure wasn't expectin' to find that!"

You can tell he's not from around here by the way he talks. He shouldn't be in this part of this city. "So how'd you find me?" Luke wiped either side of the blade on his jeans. "My name's on the knife but my address isn't."

"That's true," Chris laughed. "I'm pretty good with computers, so I ran your name through a search online. Out of the three Luke Porters living near Richmond, you were the closest one to Powhite Park. So I figured I'd try you first."

"That's kinda scary," said Luke. "It's amazing what you can find on the Internet these days. Did they have anything else on there 'bout me?"

"Mmm, no. Not that I noticed. Why? You a secret spy or somethin'?"

Luke chuckled. "No, not a spy. Just got a few things on my record is all. Nothing bad, you know. Just puny stuff."

"Oh. Puny stuff?"

"Yeah. Anyways, thanks for bringin' this to me. You coulda kept it, but you didn't. I appreciate that. This knife means a lot to me."

Chris nodded. "Yup, not a problem. I couldn't have kept a knife like that, knowin' it belonged to someone else and had the name right on the blade an' everything. Where'd you get it?"

Luke held the knife to the light and swiveled his wrist. The curved hilt was raven black and wrapped with golden wiring, and the stainless steel blade rippled in the shadows. He watched the golden lettering flicker as his wrist moved.

"My mom and dad," he said. "They gave it to me as a graduation present almost ten years ago. I collected knives back then, and my parents had my name engraved on the blade. It was the last present they gave me before...well, we haven't really spoken since I was eighteen. Long story short."

Chris frowned and shook his head. "Oh. Yeah, that happens some-times. Too bad. Just based on the detail and thought that went into that gift...well, I'd say your mom and dad cared about you a whole lot."

"Yeah...maybe," Luke said bitterly. He slid the knife into the leather sheath on his belt. "What about you? You said you're from South Carolina. Is that where your family is?"

"Actually," said Chris, "my family lives overseas and does missionary work in different countries around the world. I've been overseas too, but I came back to South Carolina a few years ago and became a fireman. That's why I'm in Virginia. They transferred me up here to work in Richmond's fire department. Said the department was short a couple of firefighters, so I agreed to go."

Luke stared at the scars on Chris's hands and face as if he was seeing them for the first time. He suddenly understood.

"Yup, you're right," Chris said. "I got these from a fire I was fightin' back in South Carolina. But I'm proud to say the fire lost."

Luke blinked and averted his eyes. "Ah man, I'm...I'm sorry. I didn't mean to—"

"Hey now, that's alright. I'm used to people starin' at me." Chris looked at his maimed hands and slid them back in his pockets. "To be honest, I don't mind. Gives me an opportunity to stand out from the crowd and tell my story, ya know? Speakin' of stories...what's yours, Mr. Luke Porter? I know you collect knives, but that's about it. Where do you work?"

Luke shifted his weight uncomfortably. "Actually...um, I'm not really workin' right now. I used to work for a construction company in Richmond, but that sorta fell through, I guess you could say."

Chris nodded slowly. "I see...so are you—"

"This dude botherin' you, Luke?"

Chris turned and Luke gasped. The tall, lanky man stood in the hallway and peered at them through bloodshot eyes.

"Eddie?" Luke stepped around Chris into the hallway. "Man, you're alive? But I thought you—"

"Well yeah, I'm alive. Just 'cause one of us is a wuss and decides to run doesn't mean—" Eddie glanced at Chris and tipped his chin. "So who's the Amish guy? Bet his last name's Yoder, isn't it?"

Chris held out his hand towards Eddie. "I'm Chris. Chris Scar—"

"Dude!" Eddie pointed wildly at Chris's hand. "Look at those scars! And they're all over his face too! He looks like Quasimodo with all them marks. Hey now, that's funny." He sniggered. "Quasimodo the Amish man. I like it."

"Eddie, knock it off," Luke said. "His name's Chris Scarlett. He brought back my knife, the one I lost last night. Chris, this is Eddie Ratcliffe. He's a buddy of mine—"

"Nope." Eddie held up his hands and stepped back. "I don't shake hands with Amish people, 'specially ugly ones. Luke, I don't like this guy." He looked at Chris suspiciously. "Somethin's different about him. I can feel it. Get rid of him."

Luke cursed. "Eddie, shut the—"

"Whoa Luke, it's alright." Chris laid his hand on Luke's arm. "I've got to get goin' anyways. I'll be on my way now."

Luke looked from Eddie to Chris and quietly unclenched his fist.

"Yeah, that's right," Eddie said, grinning. "Go on now, Quasi. Git."

Chris smiled a little. "It was nice meetin' you, Eddie. Behave yourself."

Eddie made a face. "What do you mean *behave*? You don't know me, you—"

"And Luke," Chris said, "behave yourself too, alright?"

"Alright," said Luke. "Sorry for...well, thanks again for bringin' my knife back. Like I said, I appreciate it."

He grasped Chris's hand and gave it a firm shake. But this time, he did not let go so quickly.

"You're welcome." Chris nodded kindly. "I'll see you later, Luke."

Yeah, I kinda doubt that. Luke nodded back. "Okay. See ya."

Chris strode down the hallway, and Eddie seemed to watch him until he finally disappeared down a flight of stairs.

"Who in the world was that retard?" Eddie asked. "And why the heck were you talkin' to him?"

Luke rolled his eyes. "Eddie, you're a real jerk, you know that? The guy wasn't bad. He came all the way over here just to return my knife. I lost it last night—"

"And whose fault was that?" Eddie asked, jabbing Luke in the chest. "I didn't tell you to drop the thing and run. You acted like a scared little girl."

Luke clenched his fists again. "Eddie, you were convulsing. And I saw...I thought you were dead—"

"And you just left me there!" said Eddie. "Some friend you are!"

You're not my friend. You're my drug connection. Luke tried to control his anger. "Why are you here anyways?"

Eddie smiled. "Wouldn't you like to know?" He walked past Luke into the apartment.

Luke slammed the door and followed him. "Eddie, I'm not in the mood—"

"Dude, you need to get yourself a maid! Or a woman or somethin'." Eddie looked around the room and wrinkled his nose. "It's a mess in here."

The tiny, one-roomed apartment was dim and stuffy, with only one window above the kitchen sink that looked out over an alley. The combined kitchen and dining room was made up of a stove, refrigerator, and sink against the back wall, and the bathroom in the back corner of the room and was just big enough to hold a toilet, shower, and sink. A worn leather couch sat along the left wall, and an unmade bed lay opposite it against the right wall. A small wooden table with one chair sat in the center of the room.

Luke did not have a closet or a dresser for his clothes, so the floor and bed served in their place. Dirty dishes were scattered all over the kitchen sink, and old food molded on some of the crusty plates. The once gray carpet was stained brown and ripped in places, and one of the couch cushions leaked its stuffing. Most noticeable of all was the sea of empty beer bottles surrounding the little table.

Does he think I don't know how it looks? Luke glared at him. "Eddie, either tell me why you're here or get—"

"I brought you something," Eddie said. "I think you'll like it."

Luke felt a twinge of excitement. "What? Did you bring my—"

"Whoa!" Eddie laughed. "You're addicted already!"

"No. I'm not," Luke said lowly. "I just...how'd you get it? I thought—"

"You sure think a lot of things," said Eddie. "First you thought I was dead. Then you thought I'd forget your share of the drugs. Somewhere in there you were seein' things. Maybe you shouldn't do this stuff. It's potent. Takes a man to handle it."

Luke smirked as he looked at him. In his flimsily strapped sandals, faded blue jeans that almost made it to his ankles, and baggy AC/DC T-shirt, Eddie looked more like a teenage boy than a man himself.

"So how'd you get outta there then?" Luke asked. "I saw you lyin' on the ground. You were shakin' all over the place."

Eddie shrugged. "Honestly man, I really don't know. I snorted the stuff before I gave it to you, and I was feelin' great. But then all of a sudden, I couldn't feel a thing, like my whole body went numb. I dropped to the ground and don't remember much after that, 'cept wakin' up alone in the dirt in the forest. I hiked outta Powhite to my car and drove home. I remember seein' you run when I dropped...but nothin' else. Why'd you run anyways? 'Cause I was shakin'?"

"No, Eddie," said Luke. "I saw somethin' out there before I ran home. I think I musta hallucinated. There was this beast. Dark like a panther but built like a lion. It attacked you—"

Eddie laughed so hard that he spewed little beads of spit into the air. "A beast? A lion? So what, did it bite my head off and rip my arms and legs off too? Luke, you're a re—"

"*Don't* call me a retard," Luke said angrily. "I know what I saw. That guy gave us some bad stuff. I knew we shouldn't have gone to him. Why'd we haveta meet in the woods? We shoulda—"

"Because Powhite is secluded and there's no cops, duh. And it's not his fault the batch was bad. He's just my supplier. His people don't make it."

"Yeah, I guess. But you don't even know his name. Doesn't that make you wonder how legit he is?"

Eddie exhaled loudly. "No, 'cause I don't need to know his name. People just call him Ven. Maybe it's short for...well, I dunno what it's short for. All I know is he's good, and he sets a fair price. That's all I care about." He reached into his pants pocket then and pulled out a clear, plastic baggy. "Here. This is your stash. I woulda given it to you last night, but you ran off before I could."

The sealed, pint-sized baggy bulged with its white powdery contents. *And it's all mine.* Luke swiped the baggy from Eddie's hand. "Dang! I didn't expect this much. I only paid the guy a hundred bucks."

"Told ya," Eddie said. "And it's good stuff. Just don't do too much or you'll start seein' unicorns dancin' on the ceiling."

"No doubt!" Luke said. "Thanks man."

"No prob." Eddie walked to the door. "I'll leave you alone with your new friends now."

"Alright. Sounds good to me." Luke pinched the top of the baggy between his thumbs and separated the seal.

"I'll catch ya later, Luke. Don't have too much fun."

Luke did not move his eyes from the powder. "I will."

The door creaked open and slammed shut.

With the open baggy cupped in his hand, Luke rushed to the table and flipped the bag upside down. A tumbling white waterfall fell from the bag's mouth and formed a powdery mountain on the table.

Luke tossed the empty baggy on the floor and sat down in the chair. Using just his forefinger, he scraped some of the powder towards himself, closer to the edge of the table, while a few loose grains of powder avalanched down the little mountain's side.

He pinched the clump of powder into a small straight line and scooted his chair back. He lowered his face to the table.

He exhaled lightly as he hovered above the white line, and pressed his left nostril shut with his forefinger.

With one swift inhale, Luke followed the trail of powder with his nose and sucked the drug from the table.

He flew back in the chair and blinked, crinkling his nose and sniffing steadily. The powder needed to stay in his nasal passages and not drip into his throat in order to have the greatest effect. Eddie had told him so.

He waited.

The fog seeped into his mind as the powder absorbed into his bloodstream, and his senses gradually became heightened and euphoric. The wooden chair he sat on was suddenly soft and cushioned, and the silence in the room cooed in his ears. He could feel his muscles relaxing as an unnatural energy coursed through his body. The air itself tingled around him.

The numb delirium ravaged his body. *Don't stop. Please don't stop.* His heart pounded with pleasure, and his body warmed from the increased blood flow.

Yes.

He felt the room floating away.

Yes.

He closed his eyes and inhaled deeply.

Yes, Luke.

He shivered as the ecstasy took hold.

Luke.

Two red eyes flamed in the darkness.

You're mine. Forever.

Acidic fire exploded in his chest and blazed through his body. Luke screamed as his eyes flew open, and he dug his fingers into the flesh above his heart. He fell to the floor, writhing in pain.

The crackling of flames shrieked in his ears. He could smell his flesh burning.

All the while his heart pounded relentlessly, accelerating the fiery flux through his veins.

He cried out again and lurched onto his other side.

"*Help me!* Please, hel—"

And suddenly, nothing.

The invisible flames died. The stench of singed meat evaporated. The scorching heat faded.

Luke lay motionless on the floor as the fever left him. His back was slick with sweat, and his hand remained clamped around his heart.

"*Stop,*" he gasped. "Please stop."

He forced himself to sit up and hugged his knees tightly to his chest. He rocked back and forth like a lost child, staring across the room at nothing.

Desperation took hold of him as the fleeting euphoria carried away his pleasure, leaving behind an empty hole in its place.

"I can't...this isn't worth—" He coughed and winced. *I can't do this anymore.*

His numb delirium vanished completely, and he could feel everything again. The anger, the hopelessness, the misery—everything swelled within him.

He squeezed his heart. The burning pain was still there.

It will always be there. Forever. As long as his heart beat, the pain would throb within him.

Luke pushed himself from the floor and stumbled across the room. He fumbled for the door handle and wrenched the door open.

He knew what he had to do.

CHAPTER 4

Her auburn waves swayed just above her shoulders, forming the perfect oval frame for her rosy cheeks.

Sarah had struggled for nearly thirty minutes to angle the part just right, so that the shorter layers of hair curved around her cheekbones and dangled even with her chin. The reddish-brown hairs swished when she turned her head from side to side, but the natural wave which flowed through the strands helped her hair keep its shape.

She leaned over the sink and examined her hairline in the mirror, meticulously tugging a few stray hairs into their proper places. *Now if only I can get it to stay this way for the whole night.*

Damon had called her at 5:15 exactly, just as she'd unlocked her front door and stepped inside her house. She'd gotten off work at five and rushed home, eager for his phone call but a little scared too. She'd feared that he might have changed his mind. That maybe, after he'd had time to think, he would not want to go out with the greasy girl behind the counter after all.

But when she'd heard her cell phone ringing and seen the unfamiliar numbers illuminating the screen, all her girlish anxieties had vanished, and a swarm of butterflies had replaced them.

"Hey Sarah." The deep, sultry voice had crooned the words into her ear, and she'd melted right then and there. For the past hour, she'd heard the phrase over and over again in her head and imagined him smiling at her.

They'd talked for about fifteen minutes, but to Sarah the conversation had lasted only a few seconds. Damon had asked her how work went, they'd chatted about this and that, and finally he'd asked her what she'd wanted to do tonight. She'd responded with something like *oh, it doesn't matter to me as long we can hang out together.* He'd laughed. She'd realized how dumb she'd sounded.

After he'd called her crazy, Damon had asked her if she'd ever been to the Night's River, a bar and grille pub on the James River. She'd said no but that she'd heard of the place. It was south of Richmond, right? He'd said yes, due south from the heart of the city. He went there a lot and knew the place well—loved the pub's grilled chicken and rice platter. She'd said sure, she would love to go, and he'd said he would pick her up at seven.

Sarah glanced down at the sink counter and pressed a button on her cell phone to light up the screen. Seven o'clock was just twenty minutes away.

She reached for the jar of foundation and twisted the lid off. Patting her makeup wedge into the tan powder, she brushed the powdered sponge all around her forehead and hairline, working her way down her face and blending the makeup as she neared her throat.

The whole process was tedious and time-consuming. Sarah rarely wore makeup and was picky about how it looked when she did wear it, which was typically on special occasions only. She always felt more comfortable in jeans and a girly T-shirt, wearing no makeup whatsoever, than she did all done up and in heels.

But that's exactly what tonight is. A special occasion. How often do I go out? She usually got ready in thirty minutes or less, shower time included, but she'd taken nearly three times as long tonight to get herself organized.

After several minutes of rummaging through her closet, holding various shirts against her, and posing in front of the mirror, she'd finally decided to go with her favorite blue blouse. The shiny silk material hugged her form and showed off her petite figure, and the button-up front and lacey collar gave her outfit a dressy edge. She'd matched the blouse with a pair of dark jeans and finished off the look with a pair of black open-toed heels. One silver bracelet and two dangly earrings later, her outfit had been complete.

Laying the makeup wedge in the jar of foundation, Sarah twisted the cap back on and grabbed her black eyeliner pencil. She leaned over the sink to the mirror, being careful not to get her shirt wet, and closed her right eye. After a few light strokes above her eyelashes, she blinked and turned her head to do her left eye.

I can't believe I told Damon where I lived. And I didn't even hesitate. She never gave her address out to people she did not know. She lived by herself in a small duplex in Lakeview, a suburb of Richmond, and she always kept her door locked, just to be careful. But Lakeview was a good area. Its streets were lined with houses and duplexes, so she felt safe with all the neighbors around her.

Still though, her willingness to trust Damon made her nervous. *I promised myself I would never trust a man again until he proved himself worthy of that trust.* Most men wanted more from her than she was willing to give, so she'd practically given up on finding the right guy.

Until this afternoon, when she'd seen *him.*

All of her stubborn rules, heartfelt promises, and emotional walls had been blown away by his smile. He'd seen her at her ugliest, and still he'd wanted to go out with her.

Sarah had been sweaty and stressed when Damon had first seen her behind the counter at Leon's Grille. Her hair had been falling down from its clip, and the oil had been slick on her forehead, not to mention the coffee stain that splotched the lower part of her work shirt had been brown and obvious. She had been a mess, but Damon had seen it all and still asked her out.

Sarah set the eyeliner pencil on the counter and picked up the eyeshadow palette. *Well, I wouldn't have been so stressed in the first place if it hadn't been for that Luke Porter guy.* She flipped the palette open. *I can't believe I even remember his name.* She pinched the little brush from its groove and swept it through the eyeshadow. *It still makes me mad! He was so...so....*

"So rude!" She stroked the powder onto her eyelid. *Luke is a jerk. And a host of other things too. He had no right to talk to me the way he did.* She turned her head and did her other eyelid. *And to think Jenny thought he was cute.*

"Ha!" She snapped the palette closed. *He might have been handsome if he wasn't so mean...and ugly!*

Sarah grabbed her cell phone from the counter and pressed the same button as before. She had five minutes exactly.

Running her fingers through her hair, she took one last look in the mirror and aligned the strands perfectly around her face. *I hope Damon notices. I hope he sees me.* She quietly tucked a strand of hair behind her ear.

Sarah smiled at her reflection and flipped the light switch excitedly. She hurried down the stairs to the living room.

She whisked her purse from the couch and swung the leather handbag over her shoulder. As she dropped her phone inside, she took out her keys and walked to the front window.

She'd already shut the blinds and drawn the curtains, so she slipped her hand between the curtains and separated two of the slats with her fingers. She stood on her tiptoes and peeked through.

The driveway was empty.

Sarah let the slats spring back together and guided the curtains as they drifted into place. She was relieved that Damon was not waiting on her.

But her heart sank a little as she closed the curtains. *What if he's not coming?*

She glanced at the luminous numbers on the DVD player beneath her TV.

It was 7:03. Damon was late.

Her excitement began to fade, and an anxious uncertainty took its place. *Maybe I should call him.*

Sarah pursed her lips. *No, he's only three minutes late.*

The digital numbers suddenly changed. Now it was 7:04.

Okay, four minutes then.

Sarah quickly turned off the lamp and walked to the front door. She grabbed her jacket from the coat rack and threw it over her arm. She laid her hand on the doorknob.

He won't stand you up. He won't. She gave the doorknob a firm, determined twist. She pulled the door open and stepped out into the night air, and then closed the door behind her. She locked it securely.

Sarah sat down on the concrete step in front of her duplex, stuffing her purse into her lap and laying her jacket over her knees. She fumbled through the handbag and found her cell phone.

The screen lit up in her hand.

7:08 PM.

Sarah exhaled. *I'll wait all night if I have to.*

An over-sized truck barreled down the street and rumbled past her driveway. She watched it shudder and slow as it rolled through the intersection farther up the street. *I wonder what kind of car Damon drives?*

The usually sporadic traffic was steady since it was Friday evening, and Sarah watched each vehicle expectantly as it sped by. Each time her anticipation soared as the headlights brightened and the engines roared closer, but her hope plummeted when she saw the taillights and listened to the engines' waning hum.

She wanted to check the time again. *No, be patient. He's on his way.*

She fiddled with her jacket's zipper. She rolled her phone in her hand and tapped it on her knee. Another car went by. Then another from the opposite direction. She frowned. Her finger wandered to the button.

7:18 PM.

Disappointment flooded her chest. Her worries were coming true with each passing minute, but one fear cut deeper than the rest.

Damon was not coming.

Sarah moved her finger to another button and scrolled through her contacts. She glanced up at the street. Pairs of security lights illuminated the way to her drive, like lights on a runway strip, but no cars were coming or going. The street was completely still.

She looked at her phone and pressed the name *Damon*. Ten digits glowed on the screen. She laid her finger on the *SEND* button.

The distant hum of an engine suddenly came from her right. She looked up. A vapor of light reflected onto the power lines, while a misty glow illuminated the street. Two radiant beams appeared over the street's incline and sped down the road, bathing the bushes, sidewalks, and houses in golden light as the car passed by.

Sarah instantly perked up and sat tall. She could feel her hope returning.

Black as night and sleek as steel, the powerful sports car cruised nearer to her driveway. The security lights reflected from its glossy surface and rippled along its doors, while its spinning rims sparkled like faces of a diamond. Its tinted windows were so dark that Sarah could not see inside, but she could hear the steady thump of the bass booming within the car.

Sarah waited excitedly. *I get to ride in that!*

The car approached, headlights sweeping over her yard and just touching the drive.

But the car did not slow. It raced by without so much as a tap of the brakes. She could have cried.

That's. It.

Sarah threw her phone into her purse and yanked the coat from her legs. She stood and stomped to the door, trying to dig for her keys in her purse as she walked. *I just threw them in here. They should be right on top.* She heard them jingle. *Really?* She moved her hand around roughly. *Why can't I—*

A bright red light suddenly shined beside her. She turned.

And her hope came soaring back. The black sports car had stopped just beyond her drive and was reversing.

Sarah practically leaped onto the sidewalk. She reached the driveway just as the car was backing in.

The sporty coupe stopped and parked, its two red brake lights glowing against the black bumper. Sarah recognized the galloping horse insignia branded onto the trunk lid. She had never ridden in a Mustang before.

She paused a few feet from the car when the driver's side door opened.

"Sarah!" Damon exited the car and looked over the roof at her. "I am *so* sorry. I made a wrong turn and...wow."

Sarah watched him look her up and down.

She smiled. He was forgiven.

Damon grinned and laid his hand on the open door. "So, are ya ready?"

Sarah kept smiling as she strolled to the passenger door, heels clicking confidently on the cement driveway.

She had never been more ready.

CHAPTER 5

Night had fallen over the kingdom of Terra Caligines, and with the night came the darkness.

The twilight sun had traveled beneath the horizon, stealing the last few streaks of purple and burgundy. All color was gone from the sky now, as if the sun had absorbed the blues and pinks and reds within itself and was saving them for tomorrow. What hue was left behind in the sky was not a color, but a shadow. A dark expansive shadow, with no stars and no moon, clouded the domed firmament and shrouded the land below.

The shadow moved and watched, hovering over the man as he stumbled through the village. It confounded his steps and pressed close around him. The shadow draped his head in a dark fog and blinded him. The man breathed the shadow and it seeped into him, mixing with the blood in his veins and flowing directly into his heart. The shadow consumed him.

Luke could not see through the darkness, but the shadow in his heart guided his footsteps. He knew where he was going this night.

The stale air smothered Luke as he lurched out of his one-room shanty onto the raucous village street. He staggered to his left, tipping forward and struggling to keep his balance, while his mind reeled from the haze of the sordes powder. He bumped into a rain barrel beneath the spouting of an old tavern and ricocheted into the path of an oncoming horse.

The horse reared and whinnied, pawing the air with its hooves and snorting steam from its nostrils. He spun and dodged while the horse's rider cursed and waved a clenched fist.

Luke heard the rider's incensed ravings, but he did not listen. He recognized the panic in the horse's wild eyes, but he did not see. He felt the ground shudder beneath his boots when the horse thundered back to earth, but his feet did not react. A reckless stupor had taken hold of him, and his mind was possessed by one thought and one thought alone.

I must end this. Tonight.

"Fool boy!" the rider yelled, tugging the reins and jerking the horse back onto course. "Get out of the way or I'll run ya o'er! Drunken halfwit!"

The rider spurred his horse and the horse raced forward, charging in a frenzied rage directly at Luke.

Somewhere within himself, an instinctive rush of fear jolted his body to move, and Luke felt his feet scrambling away from the horse's attack. The galloping fury blurred by, a billowy cloud of dust and horse and curses, while Luke pressed his back against a shop stall for support.

Chest heaving and heart pounding, he doubled over and slammed his palms onto his knees, suddenly and painfully aware of his ragged breathing. The adrenaline had sucked the air right out of him, and he struggled to catch his breath as he fought the urge to retch.

The street spun around him, and the earth rocked beneath his boots. He squeezed his eyes shut and opened them. He pitched forward, off balance and still bent over, and blinked again.

"Sir? Are you well?"

The concerned voice vibrated incoherently within his skull, and Luke squinted and looked in the direction the sound had come from.

A woman wearing a brown woolen dress watched him worriedly from a distance. One of her hands clasped a frayed shawl around her shoulders.

"Sir? Do you need help?"

He heard the garbled utterance, but his vision would not focus, and the woman transformed as he stared at her. Her eyes reddened and her mouth grinned savagely, while her hair turned gray as ash and grew unnaturally long, crawling over her shoulders and down her back. Her thin figure swelled and expanded, mutating into a burly, hulking beast which ripped the dress from its furry pelt.

Luke sprang in terror and flew back against a shanty. His fingers groped at the wall while his feet scratched at the ground to get away.

The monster growled something and held out a deformed, clawed hand.

"Get away from me!" Luke fled down the street like a madman.

He rubbed his eyes as he careened onto a side street, and vaulted over a lopsided cart. He was vaguely aware that he was going the wrong direction, but the madman within him drove him away from the village's crowded main street, and he chose the quickest escape.

But he must get to the river, and the river was due south.

Luke kept up his frantic pace, jogging through the street and desperately hoping for an intersection. Decrepit wooden shanties walled either side of the cobblestone road, and the small huts were built right next to each other, with hardly a gap in-between. Torches speckled the shanties, illuminating the street in an orange glow, while the flames' shadows danced on the walls. A few people milled about in the street and stared at him as he reeled by, but he did not care.

He lunged ahead through the night, boots scuffing on the stone street and arms pumping through the air. His loosely bound hair bounced and whirled behind his head as he ran, but several wild strands stuck to his face. The sweat beaded above his brow and slid down his stubbled face, gathering in a stream and dripping from his chin. His gray tunic was drenched with sweat, and his breeches flapped haphazardly from the tops of his boots. The dagger slapped against his thigh with every thud of his foot.

A narrow intersection suddenly emerged from the shadows, and Luke veered to his right, stretching out his left foot and pivoting into the cross-street. He bolted forward, never once slowing his frenzied gait.

Now he could see the curving southerly border of the village, where the torches ceased and the dark plain began. Each hurried step brought him closer to the street's end and the river's beginning. *It will all be over soon.*

A horse-drawn wagon rumbled onto the street from the road that wound through the plain. Luke slowed and shimmied against a wall as the wagon navigated between the stalls and shanties. He could smell the wagon's sweet load and see the colorful mounds when the wagon clamored by. No doubt the fruit had been gathered from the trees in the plain and would be sold on the morrow in the village market.

Luke jogged to the center of the street and walked the last few steps to the muddy road. The cobblestones gradually scattered and finally disappeared altogether as his boots stopped clicking and started squishing. The light from the torches dimmed behind him as he stepped beyond their reach into the grassy plain. He found the wagon's ruts and walked in the middle of the path, where the grass was not completely trodden into the muddy ground.

He inhaled deeply, relieved to have the village at his back but still looking ahead. The Dedanima River was a hundred yards away, flowing from east to west across his path, and Nospero's Bridge provided the only way to the other side. Once across the river, the dirt path meandered through the plain and around the fruit trees, lazily sloping through the fields, until the trail vanished into the Lumbrai Forest due south of the village.

But Luke would not be crossing the river today. Once to the river, he would turn right at its banks and head west, to the place where the Lumbrai Forest circled northwards and met the river as it flowed through the plain. He would follow the river into the forest for a short distance, hiking along the muddy trail that began at Nospero's Bridge and ultimately ended at his destination.

I must end this. Tonight.

The plain was peaceful and quiet compared to the bustling village, and Luke felt his heartbeat calm and his breathing slow as he neared the river. But somewhere inside of him, even out here amongst the orchard trees and planted fields, he sensed the fear and desperation surrounding him, tormenting him, like an unseen evil that pursued him wherever he went.

His mind had cleared a little from the sordes, and he was no longer stricken with the urge to run for his life, but he could feel the woman's red eyes burning behind him, watching from the village.

That beast of woman with her rotting hair and monstrous claws had reached out to him, tried to grab him. She'd even spoken to him, though he could not understand her snarling. *She was just a hallucination. A figment of my drugged mind.* But she'd seemed so real as well. *So horrifyingly real.*

The wet *plop* on his forehead splattered into his eye and dribbled down his nose. He glanced up just as the rain gushed from the shadows overhead and pummeled the ground. A startling flash of white brightened the plain, and he glimpsed the river rushing and rippling in the instant light. The darkness returned just as quickly, followed by a distant rumbling to the north behind him.

Luke was soaked by the time he reached the Dedanima and turned west onto a new but familiarly muddy trail. The sound of the river's crashing blended with the steady downpour as it peppered the ground, and he marched silently while the wet orchestra thundered around him. He lowered his head and hunched his shoulders when the wind howled and blew the stinging droplets into his face. His boots became caked with mud, and he could feel the sucking *splosh* as he plodded through the muck along the river bank.

The storm pelted him, harassing him on all sides and obscuring his steps. The lightning blinded him, while the thunder laughed at him. The wind snickered through the fields, and the rain beat him with pleasure. The rain matted his hair and streamed down his face in chaotic rivulets, and it drenched his tunic and breeches until they clung to him like pinesap. The air grew muggy and damp, and a steamy fog floated up from the cool ground, clouding the plain in a ghostly mist.

But Luke was not hindered by the storm's persecution. He was determined to reach his journey's end, and he felt settled and assured. A sense of resignation had washed over him with the rain, and he was relieved that he no longer had to fight. He felt comforted by the knowledge that he had made his decision, and he knew without a doubt where he was going.

A burst of lightning painted the land in white brilliance, and he saw the glossy walkway arching over the river. Nospero's Bridge glistened in the rain. The black bridge was over ten feet wide, with two walls on either side that came up to a grown man's waist, and arched some thirty feet over the Dedanima River.

He paused in front of the bridge, watching the sodden plain and the Lumbrai Forest ignite in pale green when the lightning exploded overhead. *This is the last time I'll ever see the bridge and the forest beyond.* He shivered and kept going.

The soggy trail wandered beside the river at all times, and the constant crashing of the waters upon the rocks quieted as Luke became accustomed to the sound. The downpour gradually weakened, and the pounding rain became a soft drizzle. He trudged through the swampy field while the lightning continued to flicker.

He glanced to his right just as he moved beyond the village's western border, where the two-story houses of the wealthy folk embellished the landscape. The wealthiest people had always sought residence on the north and west sides of the village for one simple yet obvious reason.

Prince Leone's lofty castle was located on the northwesternmost point of the kingdom, positioned a half of a mile away from the exact northwesternmost point of the village, and all the rich lords and ladies strove to be as close to Prince Leone and the castle as possible.

Proudly erected against the backdrop of the shimmering waters of Lake Solardens, the black castle crept into view as Luke moved beyond the extravagant mansions. Four walls of colossal granite stones surrounded the castle on all sides, while four watchtowers rounded the corners of the towering walls. Black crenellations ran along the top of the walls like large gapped teeth, and several torches flickered in the arrow slits which dotted the rounded towers.

The red flames watched him like hundreds of tiny eyes in a pitch-black face. Lightning flared behind the castle, illuminating the vast lake and wet stones in a ghostly glare.

The dark castle itself soared above the outer walls, looming over the bluffs of Lake Solardens. Steepled turrets decorated the keep, where most of the castle rooms were located, and several tall towers rose like spears behind the walls. A noticeably square gap just behind the keep was where the courtyard sat, and the stables were tucked away in a corner to the north of the courtyard. The main gate stood within the east outer wall, and the cobblestone road sloped and curved from its entry to the village below, where the plain gently met the lake to the north and river to the south.

Luke had been in the castle once long ago. Eddie had introduced him to Prince Leone, who had eagerly greeted Luke and welcomed him to the kingdom. The Prince's friendly demeanor and charming personality had seemed completely out of place in the eerie castle, but Luke often thought back to that day and wished things could be the same.

In his heart, though, he knew they never would be.

The wispy mist thickened into a dense fog which engulfed the riverbed and the plain. Luke did not realize how close he was to the forest's circling perimeter until a row of trees suddenly materialized before him.

Not much longer now.

The rain continued to patter his skin, and he took one last look at the plain behind him. He could see the village faintly, a distant orange glow of shadowed shanties, bustling taverns, and crowded streets. The muddy trail leading from the back of the village sloped slightly to the river, where Nospero's Bridge still gleamed in the falling rain. Another muddy path intersected the first and ran east and west along the riverbank, crossing the crop-laden fields and weaving through the fruit trees.

Luke traced the path's wandering, sodden course until his gaze stopped at his own mud encrusted boots.

Never did I dream I'd be standing here now. Like this.

He looked up.

The castle gleamed upon its rocky outcropping, while the bright torches pierced the fog that drifted about the castle's walls. Lightning flickered far to the north, somewhere over the lake near the horizon.

Luke took a deep breath and exhaled slowly, wiping the moisture from his brow as he looked on. The fog brushed against him. He dug his heel into the mud and turned. Without a second glance behind him, he strode into the forest.

The fog obscured his every step, and the forest canopy darkened the already bleak landscape, but a renewed sense of determination surged through his body. His steady march grew into a brisk jog, and the brisk jog accelerated into a final desperate run.

Luke sprinted alongside the river, leaping over fallen trees and dodging gnarled limbs. Leaves slapped his face and the mud sucked at his boots, but he did not miss a step. The fog swirled around him, wisping and billowing as he plowed through it. Twigs snapped and briars scratched. The river gushed and roared and foamed beside him, racing him to his destination.

The mud suddenly turned to gravel, and the sodden path became solid rock. His boots scuffed against the new stony turf. The fog began to dissipate and slowly evaporated. The trees dispersed and scattered, and a lighter shade of darkness radiated through the clearing.

Luke mindlessly sped forward, arms pumping and lungs swelling and legs burning.

The river jetted around boulders and spouted over rotting driftwood, surging headlong and matching his frenzied pace.

One fallen tree barred his path and stretched across the river, damming the river's course as well. Neither Luke nor the river slowed.

Together with one final thrust, Luke and the river flew over the collapsed trunk and burst into the empty clearing.

The river exploded over the rocky ledge, diving into the air and tumbling into the Abyss.

Luke slid to a halt upon the wet stone, his boots inches from the airy threshold and his shoulders heaving over the edge. He flailed his arms desperately for balance and gaped into the pit.

Down into nothing.

Blackness consumed the Abyss and plunged down, down, down into nothing. Into nothing but air and darkness. Into nothing but death and hopelessness.

I must end this. Now.

The hopelessness latched onto his heart and pulled him down, beckoning him to jump as he teetered on the edge. The wound in his heart burned from the painful tug, and his shoulders drooped from the weight.

He had no hope, no future, nothing. The family he loved had left him, and the friends in his life were no friends at all. He had no trade, and he lived in a shack. No one cared. The ale and sordes numbed his pain but only temporarily. He wanted more, more than this wretched existence, but he knew he would never find it in this place.

Luke swayed on the balls of his feet, his heels raised dangerously off the ground. The river thundered beside him, drowning his hesitation and spurring him onward.

No one would miss him. Not his family, not his friends, and not even Sarah. She would probably be glad if he was dead, after the way he'd treated her earlier that day.

The world would be better off without me.

He closed his eyes.

Lightning flashed across the Abyss, bathing the kingdom of Rovenia in radiance upon a distant mountain. But Luke did not see.

He leaned, tipping precariously.

And finally let go.

His upper body dove forward while his legs gave out from under him. He tumbled, weightless, dropping into nothing as the darkness soared upwards, eager to claim another victim.

An iron jerk wrenched his shoulder backwards.

Luke lurched away from the cliff, too shocked to recognize the scarred hand clamped around his shoulder and too dazed to understand the voice speaking in the darkness.

"Long way down, isn't it?"

CHAPTER 6

Squeezed between the walls of an abandoned office building and a run-down mechanic's garage was the Night's River, a dingy pub on the banks of the James River. Claiming to be a bar and grille, the pub had duly provided two food-stained menus to Sarah and Damon when they'd sat down at one of its many stool tables.

After taking Damon's advice and ordering a margarita to wash down her chicken and rice platter, Sarah inadvertently discovered an overt quality of the crowded pub.

By the bland taste of the food and the alcoholic potency of the margarita, the Night's River was far more *bar* than *grille*.

Damon looked at her from across the table and said something. Sarah saw his lips move but could not make out the words.

"What?" she shouted above the music. "I can't hear you! It's so loud—"

The reverberating bass stopped.

"In here."

Another song immediately blasted over the ceiling's speakers, picking up where the previous song left off, but at least this song's bass did not throb within her chest.

Damon laughed. "I know! I'm sorry! It's usually not this loud. Must be 'cause it's Friday night. More young people out, I guess."

"Young people!" Sarah snorted. "I must be an old woman then!"

"Yup, me too!" Damon reached for his beer. "Well, an old man anyways, not an old woman."

Sarah giggled as Damon downed the rest of his beer. His red, button-down shirt tightened around his chest as he tipped his head back, and she could see how brawny his body was. The short sleeves showed off his lean arms and tanned skin, and a few veins bulged within the toned muscles. His dark carpenter jeans were a little baggy but fit him nicely, and he wore a black belt to keep his shirt tucked in. The black, steel toe boots he wore made him seem even stronger.

She could not stop staring at him.

"What?" Damon asked. He set his glass on the table and met her gaze.

Sarah quickly looked at her plate and plunged her fork into her food.

"What? Yeah! It's good, isn't it?" She stuffed a mound of chicken and rice into her mouth, but did not realize her mistake until she tried to chew the dry morsel.

Damon grinned at her. "So you like it then? The food, I mean?"

He knows I was staring at him! Sarah felt the blush warming her cheeks. "Um yeah," she said between chews. She forced the overcooked chunk of food down her throat. "It's good."

Damon leaned back in his chair. "You're sure about that now, right? Not too dry?"

Actually, it's the worst chicken and rice I've ever had. Sarah wiped her mouth on her napkin and nodded enthusiastically. "Yeah, it's great! Maybe a little dry, like you said, but not bad!" She reached for her knife and sawed through the chicken, trying not to slop the rice into her lap as she struggled.

"It's usually a little overcooked, but I like it that way. Brings out the grilled flavor." Damon leaned his elbows on the table. "How's the margarita? What flavor was it?"

Sarah scooted some rice onto her fork and skewered another piece of chicken. "I think it's cherry watermelon. I like it," she said, glancing at the red slush in the bowled glass. "Kinda strong though. I can taste the alcohol every time I take a sip."

"They do make the drinks strong here," Damon said. "I'm impressed though. You've drank half of it! I thought you said you didn't drink much?"

"Mm mm." Sarah swallowed again. "I don't."

"Bet you're a lightweight then, huh?"

Sarah shrugged. "Yeah, I guess you could say that. But maybe since this chicken is so dry, it'll soak some of the alcohol up."

Damon laughed. "Hey, I hadn't thought about that!"

His blue eyes twinkled whenever he laughed, and Sarah watched his whole face light up. Perfectly white teeth gleamed when he smiled, or at least she imagined they did, and his blonde goatee enhanced his charming mouth. Something inside her fluttered knowing that she was the one who aroused that smile.

"So, are you going to get anything else?" Sarah asked. "I can't believe you ate so fast! I feel like I've been working on this chicken for hours."

Damon laid his silverware and napkin on his empty plate. "Nope! I'm stuffed. But you take your time. I don't mind waiting."

Great. I love being stared at when I eat. Not awkward at all. "Okay, great! I'm almost done." Sarah took a sip of her margarita.

Damon just smiled and watched her.

Sarah gulped and forced a smile, casually looking down at her plate as she cut another slice of chicken. She popped it in her mouth and chewed slowly, grinding the stringy chicken into something she could digest.

The leathery mass rolled around in her mouth for what seemed like hours, but she focused on her plate, hoping that Damon had gotten distracted and was looking elsewhere.

With her head bowed and fork in hand, Sarah raised her eyes and looked across the table.

And made eye contact with Damon's baby blues.

He smiled.

She smiled and hurriedly looked away, while the music continued to dance and thump throughout the room.

They were seated in the back of the pub, in a dusty corner next to a window overlooking the river. Sarah had noticed the window when she'd first entered the bar and had begged Damon to sit by it, at the tall table with the two empty stools. The gigantic window extended from the ceiling to about two feet from the floor and ran the entire length of the back wall. As the only window in the room, it was utterly breathtaking compared to the rest of the dimly lit pub.

The pub was rectangular in shape, with the shorter walls positioned parallel to the river and the longer walls running north and south. With a low ceiling and several tables bunched together, the room felt cramped and stuffy and smothering. The air was stagnant and moist, smelling of sweaty people and warm bodies. Decorative neon signs flickered all around the room, and a wall of colorful glass bottles embellished the frame around the entrance. The kitchen was somewhere to the right of the entrance, behind a swinging door in the wall.

Sarah watched the bartenders and waitresses as they scurried out the door, to the tables, and back into the kitchen. She glanced at a TV hanging from the ceiling in the center of the room.

Football. I wonder if Damon likes football? "Damon, do you watch—"

"You don't come to places like this very often, do you?"

Sarah glanced from the TV to Damon, unsure of his meaning. With the pounding music, chattering people, and blaring football game, she couldn't be certain if she'd heard him right anyway.

"What now?" Sarah asked, leaning forward a little. "What did you say?"

Damon scooted forward too, always smiling. "I just wondered if you came to bars a lot, since you don't drink much. You seem like you're really studyin' the place."

"Oh, no...I mean, not really," Sarah said. *I hope he doesn't think I'm sheltered.* "It's just so crowded and noisy. But that's alright. The food was great, so that makes up for it."

"Well, I'm glad you liked it," Damon said. "It's one of my favorite dishes. If you don't mind me asking, why don't you drink more? Are you religious or somethin'?"

"Uh, religious?" The question made Sarah uncomfortable. "Like, do I go to church?"

"Yeah, exactly. Do you go to church?" Damon asked. "It's cool if you do. I was just curious."

Sarah lowered her gaze and sipped the margarita. She bobbed her head between a nod and shake, while she uncrossed her legs and re-crossed them in the opposite direction. Despite the deafening noise in the room, her stool screeched against the hardwood flooring when she fidgeted.

"I don't anymore," she finally said. "When I was a kid, I'd go with my family, but everyone was so fake." She shrugged. "I guess I didn't really like it all that much."

Damon nodded. "I know what you mean. People act a certain way on Sunday mornings when they're sittin' in the pew, but Monday through Saturday they're acting however they want."

"Yeah, that's how my family was. Especially my dad." Sarah rolled her eyes. "He'd drag us all to church on Sunday morning, but he'd be the last one leaving the bar every Friday and Saturday night. Most of the people in our neighborhood went to church because it's just what everyone did on Sunday, like a tradition or something. So, I think that's why we went...to keep up appearances and be social and what not."

"So, is that why you don't drink?" Damon asked. "Because of your dad?"

Sarah pursed her lips. "Um, I guess that's mostly why, yeah. I see what alcohol does to other people, like my dad, and I don't want to be like them. Plus, I really don't like the taste of alcohol anyway, so it's easy not to drink. And I'm not against church or anything. I learned a lot of things there, and some stuff has stuck with me. But I can't be fake like those people. Seems like the word *Christian* is just a label anymore."

"Definitely, yeah." Damon shook his head. "And it's a very general label. One that includes things that probably aren't so upright and righteous. So what's the point really? I say be true to yourself and try to be a good person. It's your life. Do what feels right as long as it doesn't hurt someone else."

"Yeah...I guess so," Sarah said. "But don't you think there should be a standard for right and wrong? I mean, if everyone does what they feel is right, then doesn't that mean that my right way could be wrong to you and your right way could be wrong to me?"

"Wow, I'm not confused at all now." Damon laughed. "Say that again? If my wrong way is right and your right way is left...."

"Noo," Sarah giggled, "I *said* if your way is wrong to me, and my way is wrong to you, then do we really know what *right* is? Since there's no standard?"

"Ooh," said Damon, "now I get it. So if there's no standard, how do we truly know what's right. That's your question?"

"Yes, very good," said Sarah. "That's my question."

"Okay then. Here's my answer." Damon tapped the table with his finger. "Don't judge."

Sarah made a face. "What?"

"Don't judge. Just think about it for a sec," Damon said lightly. "When the standard of right and wrong is relative, and each person decides for himself what is right and what is wrong, then no one has the ability to judge someone else. That's the beauty of having no standard. Each person's standard is good for himself and no one else, so he can't judge another person's standards. Everyone is right in their own eyes, and as long as they're not hurting other people, then they're free to do what they want.

"And besides, isn't that what love is all about? Not judging people? That's what Christianity was founded on, if I remember right. Love your neighbor as yourself. Treat others the way you want to be treated. Funny how these virtuous Christians tend to forget that."

"Wow," Sarah said. "You sound pretty opinionated on this topic."

Damon snorted. "You have no idea."

"How come?" Sarah asked. "Did you ever go to church?"

"Nope, I've never gone to church. And let's just say I have my reasons." Damon suddenly seemed mad. "Bible-thumping hypocrites being one of them."

"Oh." Sarah winced at his tone. "Well, I didn't mean they were *all* like that, but a lot of them seem that way. I met this one older lady at church...Mrs. Thompson, that was her name. She taught my Sunday School class, and she was really nice. She seemed genuine, just like Jesus in the stories—"

"Jesus?" Damon laughed. "You don't believe in that guy, do you? Santa Claus is more real than he is."

"Well, I dunno. I mean...." Sarah looked down at her plate. *He thinks I'm an idiot! What do I say—wait a sec.* She looked up at him.

"I believe in Santa Claus," she said proudly.

Damon furrowed his brow. "What?"

"I said I believe in Santa Claus."

"Um, okay. And?"

"And if I want to believe in Santa Claus, then you can't judge my beliefs because they're *my* beliefs." Sarah crossed her arms. "What's right for me doesn't have to be right for you, right? Isn't that what somebody just told me?"

"Okay, okay!" Damon threw up his hands. "Don't shoot!"

"I guess I won't." Sarah smirked triumphantly. "*This* time. But you see? Those who cry the loudest for tolerance are oftentimes the most intolerant people. So, I'm not sure that your whole 'don't judge' theory works, really. There's got to be an absolute standard…a way to know the difference between right and wrong and to stand up for what's right without holding yourself above everybody else." She made a face then. "I'm just not quite sure what that way is."

"Dang. Remind me never to get into an argument with you." Damon wiped his brow with his arm. "Phew. And you think I'm opinionated."

"Yes, you are. I'm glad you agree."

"I didn't say I—" Damon pursed his lips and glanced at the ceiling. "Maybe I should just stop talking now."

Sarah laughed. "That would probably be a good idea." She hopped off her stool and swung her purse over her shoulder.

"Where are you going?" Damon asked. "I didn't make you mad, did I?"

"Ladies' room," Sarah said. She smiled at him. "And no, I'm not mad. Can you watch my drink for me?"

"Sure, no prob." Damon pulled her drink closer to him. "But you're not mad, right? I'm sorry if I said the wrong thing."

I couldn't be mad at you if I tried. "I'm not mad. I promise," Sarah said. "I'll be right back."

She watched the worried expression on his face relax into a smile.

"Okay," Damon said. "Take your time."

She met his gaze just as she turned away from the table, but she could not hide the girlish grin that swept across her face before she managed to take two steps towards the bathroom.

Come on, Sarah! At least try to play a little hard to get! She could feel his eyes following her as she strolled across the room, but she dare not look back. If she met his gaze one more time, she knew she would be blushing all the way to the bathroom, and Damon would be sure to notice that too.

Sarah maneuvered between the tables, clutching her purse against her and smiling politely at people as she walked towards the entrance. The swinging kitchen door suddenly burst open, and a waitress dashed into the room, skillfully scooting around Sarah and stopping at a table behind her. Sarah craned her neck towards the door as it swayed shut.

There it is.

The bathroom door was just to the right of the kitchen door, along the wall by the entrance. She had assumed correctly.

Sarah quickened her pace a little and steered herself around the last few tables, angling towards the door with the feminine stick figure etched on its upper center. Without missing a step, she placed her hand on the metal plate along the edge of the door and pushed.

The boisterous music instantly became a muffled thumping as the door closed behind her, and the stale smell of cleaning chemicals overwhelmed her nose. The tiny bathroom was as dingy as the bar, and cramped and sullied too. Three shabby stalls crowded against the right wall, and one sink with leaky piping teetered against the left wall. The rectangular mirror above the sink was smudged and streaked with a dried film, and the gray tiling on the floor was dusted with hair and toilet paper.

Sarah wrinkled her nose. *Do I really have to go that bad?* Daintily she crept to the first stall, watching where she placed her feet and wishing she had not worn her open-toed heels. She brushed her fingertips against the stall's cockeyed door and gingerly flicked the door open.

A foul combination of wet toilet paper, graffitied walls, stained porcelain, and yellowed water greeted her with a stench too grossly human to abide.

Sarah recoiled in disgust, stepping back as the door slammed against its metal latch.

Nope. I can wait 'til I get home.

The floor seemed to move beneath her feet just then, and she double-stepped to the side to catch her balance. She walked to the sink, feeling a shade of grogginess drifting over her, and peered into the filthy mirror.

Her eyes looked tired, and her cheeks were flushed. The faint headache deep within her head explained everything.

"What are you doing, Sarah?" she asked the girl in the mirror. "You never drink this much. You've got to stop, or...you can't...."

She looked at the girl and exhaled. *Damon is a nice guy. He would never take advantage of me.* She was good at reading people and knew he was not that kind of man. *Yes, he brought me to a bar. Yes, he told me to order a margarita. But that doesn't mean he's trying to get me drunk. I chose to drink. He didn't force me.*

But the evening was almost over. What Damon wanted, what he expected, Sarah did not know for sure. She may not have been a religious person, but she did have morals, standards. Standards which had earned her many cruel jokes and much ridicule over the years, but standards from which she would not budge, no matter what man asked her to do so.

And she had no intent of swaying from those stubborn rules tonight, even for Damon, but the alcohol dulled her intent and weakened her stubbornness. Mixing this impairing effect with her own feelings for Damon—her own desires—would take her down a road from which she could never return.

Sarah tucked a strand of hair behind her ear and tore her gaze away from the mirror. She bent over the sink, lightly touching the faucet and pulling the handle towards her, and washed her hands in the warm water. She pushed the handle back with her wrist and flicked her hands in the sink, looking around for a hand-dryer or a paper towel dispenser.

She saw the hand-dryer lying broken and cracked on the floor near a trashcan, and there was no paper towel dispenser anywhere. Sarah flapped her hands and wiped them on her pants. She walked to the bathroom door but hesitated when she reached for the grimy handle.

I just washed my hands.

The handle flew towards her unexpectedly, and a heavily made-up woman strutted into the room and glanced at her indifferently. Relieved that she did not have to touch the door, Sarah smiled back and quickly exited the bathroom before the door could shut.

She retraced her footsteps through the restaurant, weaving through tables and shuffling between scooched-out chairs. When she finally glimpsed Damon's red, collared shirt stretching across his broad shoulders, all of her troubling thoughts fled from her mind. She rounded their table and glanced out the windowed wall.

"Oh, it's raining outside," Sarah said. "I didn't think it was supposed to storm today."

Damon looked up. "Hey, you're back! Did you find the bathroom okay?"

"Yeah. It's pretty dirty though." Sarah set her purse on the table and climbed onto the stool. "It always amazes me how nasty women can be."

Damon laughed. "True, but I'm sure the men's room is just as dirty." He nodded toward the window. "And it started raining not long after you left. It's lightning pretty good."

Sarah looked over the river. "I see that! Looks like a big—" *Wait a minute.* She made a face. "Actually, where is the men's bathroom? I didn't see it when I walked over there."

"Uh, I think it's right next to the women's," Damon said, grinning. "At least, last time I looked it was still there. That's a random question."

"No, I meant—" Sarah looked at him. He was watching her. "I mean, I just didn't see it when I walked over there. I guess that was kinda random, wasn't it?"

Damon nodded. "Just a little."

Sarah smiled sheepishly. "Sorry, I'm random sometimes. A lot of the time. Yeah."

"That's okay. You look cute when you're random." Damon smiled. "Hey, here's your drink. I went ahead and ordered myself another beer. I thought we could finish these and talk if you wanted."

"Sure, that'd be great." Sarah slid the bowled glass towards her and sipped the red slush. "Mmm, tastes even better than before...like sweeter or something."

"Must be 'cause it's melting," Damon said. He took a swig of his beer. "The alcohol gets watered down and you can taste the fruity flavoring better."

"Could be. I like it. Tastes like a melted cherry popsicle." Sarah swirled the straw in the icy mixture and took another slurp.

"You look like a happy little kid right now," Damon said. "A happy little kid with her popsicle."

"I am a kid," Sarah said. "A twenty-six year-old kid."

"Really now?"

"Yes, really."

"Well, I'm a twenty-nine year-old kid then," Damon said. "So if you're twenty-six, how long have you worked at Leon's Grille?"

Sarah bobbed her head from side to side in thought. "Um, ten years?" She took another long slurp. "Yes. Ten years this past July. Since I was sixteen."

"Wow. How have you worked there that long?" Damon asked. "I mean, I don't think I could work fast food. It's so, so—"

"Hectic? Greasy? Stressful?"

"Yeah, exactly. Do you like working there? Or not so much?"

Sarah frowned and looked over her glass at Damon.

"Okay, I'll take that as a no," Damon laughed. "Why do you still work there then? Aren't you a supervisor or something?"

"Yeah, I'm the first assistant. That means I'm directly beneath the store manager," Sarah said when she saw the confused look on his face. "I never went to college, and there's not a lot of good jobs in this area if you don't have a degree. Not that college is the answer these days. I work with people who have college degrees but can't find a job in their field. So, I guess I'm there for now until something else comes along." She shrugged. "It's a job, and it pays the bills. And I like most of the people I work with too, so that helps."

Damon nodded. "Yeah, that does help. If I didn't like the people I work with, I'm not sure what I'd do for a living."

"I never asked you," Sarah said between slurps, "where do you work? Did you go to college?"

"No, I'm kinda like you when it comes to college," Damon said. "I decided I didn't want all the debt that comes with school, so I hopped from job to job until I found one I liked. I've worked in retail, construction, and landscaping, but right now I'm a recruiter. I love it. And it pays well too."

"A recruiter?" Sarah asked. "Like for the Army or something?"

"Sorta," Damon said, sliding his finger along the moisture on his glass. "I work for a recruitment agency that specializes in finding workers for the right jobs. Basically, I help people find work. We find workers for factories, telephone companies, government jobs, and lots of other businesses too. I interview people and test them and see if they'd be a good fit for a certain job. It's cool."

"That does sound interesting," Sarah said. She sipped the last few drops of the margarita. "Hey, maybe you could find me a job."

"Maybe! What would you like to do?"

Sarah played with her straw distractedly. "Hmm...let's see. Maybe a flight attendant so I can travel. I *love* to travel. What do you think?"

"A flight attendant it is!" Damon said. "Your airplane awaits you, my lady."

Sarah giggled. "Sounds good to me."

"Wow, I can't believe you actually drank all that," Damon said. He nodded toward her empty glass. "It must have been good."

"It was...it was," Sarah said, nodding slowly. "So, are you from Richmond? Does your family live here?"

"No, I don't have a family." Damon suddenly scowled. "They died a long time ago, and I moved to Richmond alone."

"Oh goodness, I'm so sorry!" Sarah flinched at the chill in his voice. "I should never have asked."

"Oh no, it's alright." Damon became friendly again. "I just don't like to talk about it, that's all. What about your family? Do they live in Richmond?"

"Uh yeah, my family...." Sarah tried to remember. "I mean, my family...no. No, they live in Richmond."

"Uh, yeah." Damon chuckled. "That's what I asked. If they lived in Richmond."

Sarah leaned her elbow on the table and rubbed her forehead. "Oh right, I'm sorry. Yes, they live...um, on the east side of Richmond. My younger brother Andrew...and my dom and mad. I mean mom and dad!" She forced an uneasy laugh. "Wow, I'm losing it."

"Dom and mad, huh? Never heard of 'em," Damon said.

The room started to spin, and her stomach churned. She wrapped one arm delicately around her waist and kept her other arm on the table.

"Mom and dad...you know what I mean," Sarah said lightheartedly. She rested her head against her hand. "Mom and Dad Ryans. Your last name was Jefferies, right?"

"Yup, Damon Jefferies."

"That's good." Sarah closed her eyes. "Damon...Jeff...yeah. And you drive the, um...what kind of car was it? I forget. It's really nice."

"It's a black Ford Mustang. Eight cylinder engine, manual transmission, turbo-charged...."

His voice faded into the confusion of noises and sounds swirling around the room. Her head swam and her whole body tingled. The light stung her eyes when she opened them. *When did it get so bright in here?* It was all she could do not to vomit right then and there.

"Sarah? Are you alright?"

The faint words echoed in her dazed world, and she heard herself replying. "Yeah...I'm fine. I'm...what time is it?" She raised her head and looked at Damon, now a red blur that seemed to be moving toward her.

She felt his arm slide around her waist.

"It's about ten o'clock," he said. "Do you work tomorrow? We can go now if you want."

Sarah leaned into his chest and closed her eyes again. The sickening colors of the room were too much.

"No, I don't. Well, I work tomorrow night...I think." She swallowed. "Tomorrow night. But yeah...can we go? I don't feel good."

"Sure thing, honey," Damon said. "Here, let me help you down."

She floated from the stool, but her heels suddenly crashed against the hardwood floor, and she reeled from the impact. Everything around her was one horrible spinning haze.

"Easy there!" Damon said. "Do you think you can stand up?"

"I think...I can fall. If you help me," Sarah said. "I'm okay."

Damon chuckled. "I think somebody drank too much."

Why is he laughing at me? Sarah staggered forward while she held her stomach.

"Wait a sec, Sarah," Damon said. He pulled her back. "Don't forget your purse. And I'll carry your jacket."

She felt a heavy weight being strapped around her shoulder. She swayed groggily.

"Damon, what's wrong...with me? I've never felt...so sick." She could barely hear herself talking.

"You're fine," said Damon. His voice was void of sympathy. "I'll take you to my place and you can rest. I only live ten minutes away, so it's closer than your house."

Your place? I'm not going to your place! A subconscious rush of fear made her dizzier.

"Okay?" Damon asked. "Does that sound okay with you?"

"Yes," she said numbly. "Okay."

Damon muttered something, but Sarah could not understand him. She felt herself moving, tripping, falling around the tables as he led her to the entrance. The music shrieked in her ears and the colors blurred in a mesmerizing circle, as if she was stranded in a nauseating optical illusion.

Damon stopped at the counter and pulled something from his back pocket. He handed it to a girl behind the counter, but she gave it back to him. The girl looked at her and asked a question. Damon laughed and pulled her close as he said something, and the girl smiled and nodded.

Sarah did not understand.

Everything started spinning again as Damon gently pushed against her back and led her outside. A steady, wet dripping streamed down her face and soaked her blue blouse. She sensed a splashing upon her feet as Damon silently guided her across the street, his arm always wrapped securely around her back.

"Where are...you taking me?" She raised her head to try to see his face.

He smiled. "My place, remember?"

No, she did not remember. But then, maybe she did.

"Oh...yeah."

Damon looked at her but said nothing and kept moving. Sarah buried her face in his side, suddenly too weak to hold her head up.

A loud *thunk* popped in front of her, and she felt herself falling onto a dry, leathery seat. Something clicked into place as her head drooped against her shoulder, and a second *thunk* shuddered within her. The same sound repeated itself twice to her left, and the seat vibrated as a distant hum roared.

Varying shades of light and darkness dimmed and brightened behind her closed eyelids, and Sarah could vaguely sense the movement of the world around her. She slid to her right. She leaned forward and lurched back. She slid to her right again. A sweet smell constantly filled her nose, something like apple cinnamon. Everything hummed. She slid to her left.

Then everything stopped.

A muffled *thunk*. A loud boom. Silence. A second muffled *thunk*. Unclicking. Hands and arms all around her. She was weightless. A second boom.

Everything moved. A steady, rhythmic stomping beneath her. Her head flopped against something warm and soft, but firm. She bounced while her legs dangled and her hands lay limply in her lap. The wet droplets pelted her again.

The movement stopped. A metallic jingling. Something scraped open and squeaked shut. The air warmed. No more dripping.

Up they ascended. Marching. Slowly and deliberately. She groaned.

Hinges creaking. A faint glow. Footsteps. Her body floated in the air.

She sank into something soft, with her head cushioned against a fluffy cloud. Darkness surrounded her. Debilitating numbness.

All her remaining strength surged to her eyes, and Sarah forced them open. Two dim slits appeared in the darkness.

Damon?

He hovered over her, close.

Much too close.

She could feel his breath on her face.

No!

With all her might she screamed, but only silence echoed in the darkness. With all her might she thrashed, but her paralyzed limbs did not move.

He brushed her hair away from her face. Loving, delicate was the touch. A finger caressed her cheek.

She could see the outline of his face. The blurry shadow was looking at her.

Watching her with his sapphire eyes, radiant and focused. But they were no longer blue like she remembered.

They were red. Bright, fiery, wickedly red. Two crimson pinpricks searing into her soul.

She thought she heard herself scream.

And all was darkness.

CHAPTER 7

Soaring across the tranquil waters of the James River, the CSX A-Line Bridge was originally built in 1919 to provide a direct route through Richmond, Virginia for passenger and freight trains traveling in and out of the city. One of the earliest examples of a railroad bridge to be made from poured concrete instead of timber or iron, the double track bridge stretched for nearly a half of a mile, a series of majestic stone arches leapfrogging over the river one after the other. The busy Powhite Parkway zipped to the northwest while the serene landscape of trees and wildlife lay to the southeast, and the two opposing worlds met in a setting of peaceful solitude, where the magnificent bridge both separated and joined simultaneously.

Because of this unique collision of realms, the view from the top of the bridge was equal parts calming and thrilling, and alluring but threatening. Birds sang as they flew through the clouds, while cars droned on the nearby highway. Trees swayed in the breeze as animals scampered on the riverbank, but skyscrapers and rooftops cluttered the sky in the far distance. The teal waters flowed beneath the stone arches and lazily meandered southeast to the ocean, while clusters of rocks and boulders jutted out from the peaceful river as a warning to all who looked down upon them.

The one hundred foot plunge would be swift and sudden, concluded before the realization of what was happening could sink in. One precarious step over the railroad tracks, and then another, while a few pebbles would skitter over the bridge's edge, *plooping* into the water below. Another inch would be shuffled, followed by an uncertain centimeter, until the toes would peek over the water and the smell of the river would waft into the nose. A lean forward would tilt the body at the proper angle, and the deadly rocks would come into view but remain unseen. Relaxing the muscles and inhaling one deep and final time, the eyes would close and the body would tumble through the air like a rag doll, falling for an eternal second in peace.

Until the wrenching impact when bones would snap, the skull would explode, and organs would rupture as an excruciating pain seared into the brain, and everything would turn shockingly white.

Then the darkness would ensue, and all would finally be at rest.

He had always imagined it would feel that way when he jumped, ultimately ending his life upon the rocks beneath the CSX A-Line Bridge. But now, reeling away from his voluntary death, Luke would never know for sure.

The scarred hand released its hold on his shoulder, and Luke staggered backwards from the momentum, tripping over the railroad tracks and falling on his backside in the gravel. The abrupt *thud* knocked the wind out of him and sent jolts up and down his spine. He coughed and grimaced.

"Wow, that *is* a long way down."

Luke looked up and squinted towards the shadowed figure as it peered over the bridge's edge. The rain had stopped and the storm had passed, but the night remained moonless and starless. Everything was dark and foggy atop the bridge.

"Who...why did—" Luke squeezed his eyes shut and sucked his breath through his teeth. His head throbbed in confusion.

The gravel crunched beneath a pair of boots. Something touched his shoulder.

"Luke, are you alright?" a man asked gently. "I saw you out here joggin' when I was walkin' home, so I followed. Thought I'd say hi. But when you tripped and almost fell...well, I'm just glad I was close enough to grab you. Sure did give me a fright."

Luke furrowed his brow and looked up. "Tripped? I didn't...who are you?"

"It's me! Chris, Chris Scarlett. I found your dagger earlier today and brought it back to you." Chris stepped back and looked at Luke's face. "Are you okay? I can't imagine what a shock that musta been when you 'bout tripped over the edge."

What shaded light there was caught Chris's face just right, and Luke recognized the patchwork of scars burned into the skin around the beard and forehead. Chris was still wearing the same brown hooded sweatshirt and blue jeans as before. He stood with his legs spread slightly and his hands in his pockets.

Does he really think I tripped? "Uh...yeah," said Luke. He stretched forward and wobbled to his feet. "I can't believe I tripped like that. I think it was the tracks or something. I hopped over 'em, and that's the last thing I remember."

Chris nodded. "Yup, that'll do it. Must be them big feet o' yours."

"Oh." Luke glanced down at his boots. "Uh, yeah. Must be."

"Well, people with big feet shouldn't jog on bridges, ya know," said Chris. "Especially at night. This bridge is wide enough for two trains to pass each other, but with no railings it's pretty dangerous for people to walk on."

"Yeah, I know. But I just needed to...." Luke exhaled. "I was just in the mood, I guess."

"In the mood for what exactly?" Chris asked.

"Oh, um...a run, man! I mean a jog, yeah." Luke could hear the lie straining his voice. "Like you said. Just wanted to go for a run tonight."

Chris glanced at the ground and seemed to smile. "So you always jog in your boots?"

Crap. Luke bit his lower lip. "Uh, sometimes? I mean, sometimes. Yeah. These boots are more comfortable than you think."

Chris quietly turned away and walked to the same spot where Luke had teetered only minutes earlier. Chris stood with his left boot out a little farther than his right and casually looped his thumbs through his belt loops.

"I knew a man once," Chris said as he gazed over the river, "who liked to run, just like you. He ran from his family, away from the people who loved him, and ran into the arms of those who really could care less about him. He ran into trouble. Went to jail for a little bit, if I remember right. After he got out, he ran back to it all—to the drugs, the alcohol, the women—you name it, he did it. All his life, he ran and ran and ran. Always runnin', and in the wrong direction too, with no rest or peace whatsoever in his life. And ya know what happened to him?"

I don't want to know, but I'm pretty sure I already do. Luke shook his head silently.

"He ran to his death," Chris said. "He ran 'til he could run no more. 'Til the fatigue became unbearable and the weariness over-whelmed him. He ran home one night after work and ran straight to his gun cabinet." He turned around then, boots dangerously close to the concrete cliff, and looked Luke in the eye. "Do you ever wonder what happens when you stop runnin'?"

"Wha...what?" Luke winced as some gravel disappeared over the precipice. "H-hey man, watch what you're—"

"What? What's wrong?" Chris asked. He scooted his heels back until they were flush with the edge. "You look scared."

"Dude, that's not funny," Luke said. "You're gonna fall right off there. Don't—"

"What's not funny? I'm not laughin'. Are you?" Chris swayed backwards a little. "I'm done with this life. It's not worth it."

Luke lurched. "Whoa! What're—are you serious?"

"Yup. I'm not doin' this anymore." Chris looked at Luke and tipped farther. "There's no point."

"No!" Luke leaped to the edge and grabbed Chris's scarred hand. "Are you crazy! What the—you idiot! Your life's worth more than this."

Chris moved away from the edge, and Luke followed him.

"You think so?" Chris asked. "You really think my life is worth something?"

"Yeah! Sure!" Luke said. "Whatever's goin' on in your life isn't so bad that you haveta kill yourself. There's gotta be hope somewhere."

Chris looked at him. "Why?"

"Why what?"

"Why does there have to be hope out there?"

"Because there just has—" Luke suddenly understood what was happening. He jabbed his finger into Chris's chest. "Do you think I'm stupid or somethin'?" He jabbed again. "That you can trick me into agreein' with you?"

"No, I don't think you're stupid." Chris calmly stood his ground. "I think you're hurting."

Luke snorted. "Hurting? Who are you, my therapist? I don't need your sympathy."

"You didn't answer my question."

"What question?" Luke glared at Chris. "Ya know, you're really startin' to get on my—"

"What happens when you stop runnin'?"

"How should I know!" Luke said. He stomped a few steps away, then turned around and gestured angrily with his hands. "You make no sense at all! First, you pull me back from the edge. Then you pretend you're gonna jump, which not only is flat out stupid but ticks me off too. And now you're gonna try to lecture me? Yeah, thanks for nothin', man. You shoulda just let me fall. I'd probably be in a better mood right about now."

"You think so?" Chris asked. "If you were dead now, you think you'd be happy?"

"Well yeah, that's what I said!" Luke replied. "Do those scars make you deaf as well as ugly?"

Chris smiled a little. "No, no. They don't make me deaf. They help me listen and see more clearly. I see you."

Luke raised an eyebrow. "Oh? And what do you see?"

"You have scars too," said Chris. "Invisible scars upon your heart...your very soul. Scars that blind you and prevent you from seein' the truth. Scars that'll never heal on their own. That's why you were goin' to jump. And why you can't answer my question now."

"You know *nothing* about my life," Luke said scornfully. "There's no scars on me. You'd haveta be crazy to think there was."

"Ya know," Chris mused, "for a man who nearly took his own life, you seem pretty sure of yourself."

"I didn't—" Luke ground his teeth together. "What do you want?"

"I want you to answer my question."

"Then you'll leave me alone?"

"Yes," Chris said. "Then I'll leave you alone."

"Fine." Luke crossed his arms and spread his feet apart. "Ask away."

"What happens when you stop runnin'?"

"And by *stop running*, you mean *dead*, right?"

"Right."

"Yeah, I thought so," Luke muttered. *I can't believe I'm talkin' to this guy.* He considered a moment. "Well, when you're dead...you're dead."

Chris chuckled. "Are ya sure about that now?"

"I'm still thinkin'," Luke said harshly. "Give me a sec."

Luke glanced down at the railroad tracks and twisted his foot in the gravel. He could hear the frogs chirping in the river and smell the cool mist leftover from the rain. Night shrouded the landscape, but his eyes had grown accustomed to the darkness, and he could make out the shadowed countryside. A few stars tried to peek through the clouds overhead.

He looked at the river far below him and exhaled.

"I don't know," he mumbled.

"What?"

"I said," Luke raised his voice, "I don't know. When you're dead, you're dead. That's it. Maybe you go to heaven if you're good, maybe you don't. But that's it. I never really put much thought into it."

"Considerin' you welcome death so eagerly," said Chris, "I'd think you would've put a lot of thought into it."

"True," Luke said, "but I didn't. Just wanted it to be over...the pain, this life. That's all I thought about."

"I see." Chris nodded slowly. "This life's a real struggle at times. I understand where you're comin' from. Did you ever try to get rid of the pain? Without takin' your own life, I mean."

"Yeah, sure. I guess." Luke shrugged. "I drink sometimes...and other things. But who doesn't? Not that it matters. Nothin' works."

"Drugs?"

"Not really your business."

"Fair enough," Chris said, tipping his head respectfully. "But let me tell you somethin', Luke. Drugs, alcohol, things like that—they're more than just substances to numb the pain. By puttin' those things in your body, you invite even more pain into your life, though you don't know it at the time. They can relieve your hurt temporarily, and they might even make you feel like you're havin' a good time, but they control you and take hold of you and never let go. Those kinds of poisons let you tap into a world you can't see—a world of emptiness, suffering, agony.

"And the thing is, that world looks real nice at first, when you do that first hit or take that first swallow, and then the fog creeps into your mind and you feel nothin'. But in the end, when the veil is torn away, that's all you're left with. Nothin'. Nothin' but death and hopelessness."

Luke grimaced as forgotten images raced to the forefront of his memory. The demonic beast devoured Eddie's headless body, while the blood dripped from the beast's jaws. Invisible flames blazed through his body and seared into his heart. A pair of red eyes flashed in the darkness. The ghostly voice whispered in his head.

You're mine. Forever.

He looked at the ground as he tried to hide his painful thoughts, seemingly unaware that he was rubbing his chest.

"So, what's the point then?" Luke asked.

Chris laid his hand on Luke's shoulder. "Walk with me?"

Luke looked up. "Walk where?"

"Just walk with me."

"Alright," Luke exhaled. He looked over the river. "I don't have anywhere else to be."

Chris squeezed Luke's shoulder and walked along the bridge. Luke followed him reluctantly. The gravel crunched beneath their boots as they walked between the two sets of railroad tracks, while the river purled through the stone arches and around the boulders a hundred feet below. The sky was cloudless now, and the dim starlight painted the concrete bridge in a pastel glow.

Maybe he'll leave me alone if I tag along for awhile. "So...where you takin' me?" Luke asked. "I live a few blocks north of here if you want to head that way."

"Well, I figured I'd walk you to the street and get you off the railroad tracks." Chris nodded toward the security lights at the end of the bridge. "That way you can make your way home. I live the other way, back across the river, so I'll head home once I see you to the other side."

Luke made a face. "What, are you escorting me or somethin'?"

"Yup."

"You don't haveta—"

"Yes. I do."

"Fine," Luke said. He was annoyed but felt a little ashamed too. "So what'd you wanna talk about?"

Chris smiled. "Hope."

"You hope what?"

"No. I want to talk to you about hope."

Luke looked at Chris mistrustfully. "What hope? You just said everything is hopeless."

"You're right. I did say that," Chris replied. "But," he held up his hand, "I meant everything is hopeless if you give your life to the wrong things, like drugs and alcohol. There is no hope in those things."

"Ookay," Luke said. "So I take it there's right things and wrong things to give your life to?"

"Yup."

"And the right things are?"

"Not things," said Chris. "Thing."

Luke chuckled. "Alright...*thing*. My bad. So what's this *thing*?"

"Jesus Christ."

"For real?" Luke stopped walking. "Did you really just say—"

"Yes." Chris stood steady, shoulders squared and voice confident. "Jesus Christ."

Luke lost it. "Of *course* it is," he laughed. "Why didn't I think of that? Jesus Christ who died and rose again and loves everyone, right? I've heard this story before."

"It's no story," Chris said calmly. "It's the truth. He is the only hope for this world."

"Right. Now you sound just like my parents," Luke said. "They got all churchy and religious when I was eighteen—tried to get me to go with them. Nope! I wasn't goin' to no church and prayin' and readin' the Bible and all that stuff. You know what I did? I moved the heck out and got my own place. Been on my own ever since. Oh sure, they still talk to me and try to...to uh, what do you guys call it? Witness! Yeah, they try to witness to me, but I don't go for it. How could you give your life to somethin' that you can't see or aren't even sure exists? No thanks, I'm good."

"You're good?" Chris asked.

Luke nodded once. "Yup. Fine and dandy. I'm a grown man. I don't need an invisible god to lead me around this life."

"Interesting." Chris glanced at the sky and walked again.

Luke followed. "What? What's so dang interesting all of a sudden?"

"Only that for a grown man who claims to be completely okay," said Chris, "it's kinda odd that he would jump from a bridge to end his own life. A life that he's supposedly fine and dandy with."

"Now wait just a sec," Luke said, glaring at Chris. "Listen man. I like you. I really do. You seem like a down-to-earth kinda guy. But don't you dare act like you know what's goin' on inside my head. Or what I'm thinkin' or how I feel. You—"

"So why'd you do it then?"

"Do what?"

"Jump," Chris said. He paused mid-step and looked Luke in the eye. "Why were you goin' to jump? What was runnin' through your mind just before I grabbed you?"

No one cares. I can't do this anymore. The world would be better off without me. It's not worth it....

"I don't remember," Luke said quickly.

"You don't remember?"

"Nope."

"Alrighty then, I'll tell you why." Chris thrust his finger into

Luke's chest. "Because your life's *missin'* somethin'.'"

Luke shoved the burned finger away. "What do you mean my life's—"

"Just listen to me, Luke," said Chris. "Don't get mad...think about it. If you were really satisfied with your life—happy, hopeful, at peace—why would you want it to end? You wouldn't! That's just common sense. You'd want to live."

"So?"

"So, my point is, you yourself know that you're not happy, whether you'll admit it to me or not. You want more—more than this wretched existence you're sufferin' through. And somethin' inside you knows that you'll never find it here, in this world. So you've given up. Because why try anymore? There's no hope. Everything's pointless."

More than this wretched existence.

Luke narrowed his eyes. "How did you—"

"And you're right!" Chris said, extending his hand toward Luke. "This world *is* hopeless. And I think you know that all too well. But there is hope—a hope not of this world that is greater than all the pain and sorrow and emptiness. Jesus Christ is that hope. He's the only way to find true peace and rest. Believe in Him—"

"So that when I die, I'll go to heaven." Luke rolled his eyes. "Either way, I die. So what's the point? Whether here on this bridge or fifty years from now in my bed, I will die eventually."

"Yup, that's very true," Chris said. He started walking again. "Someday you will die. But death is not the end. Your body will die, but you...*you* will live on forever. Heaven and Hell are very real places. Places that we can't see with our human eyes, but places that exist nonetheless. The Lord created you and gave you a soul. And that soul is what yearns for somethin' more, somethin' beyond this life and this world. Your soul—*you*—will spend eternity in Heaven with Christ or be tormented forever in Hell, dependin' on whether you give your life to Christ or give your life to the things of this world."

"Right," Luke said scornfully. "And why should I believe any of this? It might be good for you, and that's fine. It's a free country. You're entitled to your opinion. But what if I wanna believe in, say...Buddha?" He cocked his chin and looked over at Chris. "Yeah, Buddha. Or maybe that Muhammad guy. What makes Jesus so much better than them?"

"Resurrection."

"Uh, what?" Luke chortled as he looked at him. "Are we in a rebellion now?"

"Not insurrection." Chris didn't seem to miss a step. "Resurrection." He looked straight ahead, his gaze as confident as his voice. "Buddha and Muhammad were both men who died. Buddha's corpse was cremated and Muhammad's corpse was buried. If they couldn't save themselves, what makes you think they can save you?"

"Hey, I didn't say—"

"Jesus Christ is a man but also is the Son of God, and He proved His divinity by dyin' and comin' back to life. Even death couldn't hold Him. Because of His resurrection, I have life. Eternal life. My faith isn't in a fourteen-hundred-year-old skeleton or a jar of cremated remains. My faith isn't in the grave. My faith's in the living Savior. My Hope is alive."

"Prove it," Luke said. "Prove that Jesus actually rose from the dead."

"Prove that He didn't. He isn't buried anywhere, and His body never saw decay. And I have eyewitness accounts from lots of people who spent time with Him after His death." Chris seemed to grin a little. "But I s'pose we could take a broom and go to Asia and sweep up Buddha's ashes. Or maybe go to Saudi Arabia with a shovel and dig up what's left of Muhammad."

Open mouth, insert foot. Luke exhaled. "You have an answer for everything." He shook his head but decided to go with it. "Okay. Why should I believe you then?"

Chris shuffled down the concrete slope where the bridge ended and the railroad tracks sloped to the ground. Luke did the same. He could see a few houses behind the line of trees which separated the tracks from the street. The sound of a car's engine came and went. He moved alongside Chris.

"Well?" Luke asked. "Did I stump you?"

Chris smiled. "No, no. I was just thinkin'. That's a good question."

"Mm hmm. Yup," Luke said. "So what's your answer?"

Chris stopped walking and looked at him. "You shouldn't believe me."

"What?"

"You shouldn't believe me."

Luke stared incredulously. "What do you mean I shouldn't believe you? You just said—"

"It's not up to me to persuade you, Luke," Chris said carefully. "I can tell you about Christ and reflect Him through my actions, through my life, and I can pray that He will work in your heart, but you must believe on your own. You must choose to follow Christ. Don't take my word for it. Find out for yourself. Would you be willin' to do me a favor?"

Luke looked at Chris suspiciously. "What kind of favor?"

"Go home and think about what I said. Think about what happened tonight, and ask yourself what you believe. If not in Christ, then in who? Or what? And why? Then I want you to do somethin' else, if you're willin'."

"Yeah?"

"Meet me for supper tomorrow night. Say, around five o'clock at Leon's Grille. Do you know the place?"

"Yeah."

"I'll pay for your food," Chris said. "And then we can talk some more and just hang out. Sound good?"

Don't know about talking and hanging out, but if he's payin'.... "Sure. Okay," Luke said. "I'll meet you there at five."

"Good." Chris smiled. "I'll see ya then. Do you think you can make it home from here? Or do you want me to—"

"No," Luke said gruffly. "It's cool. I can walk home."

"Oh, okay. I'm gonna head back then," said Chris. "See you tomorrow?"

"Yeah."

"Alrighty."

Luke jogged down the embankment, eager to go home. Just as he reached the tree line, a thought struck him.

"Hey!" he shouted as he turned around. "How did you find me—"

Chris was gone.

Luke scanned the railroad tracks and jogged back up the embankment. He looked across the bridge.

Nothing seemed to move in the darkness.

That's weird. He was just—

"I told ya I was walkin' home," a voice said from across the chasm, "and I saw you wanderin' in the wrong direction. You looked lost, so I went after you."

"Oh right," Luke said to himself. He cupped his hands around his mouth. "Yeah, thanks!"

Silence drifted across the bridge as he waited for a reply, but the only response was the rustling of some leaves and the rushing of the river below. *Whatever.* He shrugged.

Running down the embankment, Luke left the bridge behind and walked home.

CHAPTER 8

The faint ringing grew into a bird's chirping, and the imperceptible shadows morphed into distinct shapes.

A pleasant coolness brushed against her cheek, followed by a faint stirring of leaves shaking themselves awake. She felt warm and comfortable. The warm blankets hugged her body like a cozy cocoon, and she gently rolled onto her side and stretched her legs beneath the soft wool. She slid her hand under the pillow until it rested in the crook of her arm. A sleepy sigh escaped from her lips.

Awareness drifted to her eyelids as the drowsy tingle faded. She blinked dreamily.

Two glowing embers ignited in the dimness, as if two matches had been struck simultaneously. They flickered, flames dancing in an unseen breeze, and waned. The embers died, dwindling into gray wisps of smoke. She watched the smoke curl into two tiny circles, each a small dot of floating mist. The smoke swirled within the little balls and flowed in dizzying contortions. She felt ill and oddly afraid.

The two gray puffs darkened and smoldered, but a faint orange gleam flared around the smoky pupils. She cringed and tried to look away, but she could not stop staring. The orange gleam intensified to a crimson blaze, while her fear escalated to terror.

Two red eyes glared at her from within the dark haze as the panic surged through her. She shuddered and rolled over. Then she rolled back, but the eyes did not sway from their fixed gaze. She fought to awaken. The eyes grew redder, hotter, deadlier. A spasm of consciousness tore through her.

Sarah opened her eyes and flew forward, flinging the covers from her body. She managed to hold back the scream that shot into her throat as the room whirled around her. It was small and unfamiliar, with a doorway on a different wall than she was used to. And the blankets. *Where did I get these blankets?* She looked up when she felt the bed move.

Him. I know him.

"Finally awake?" Damon asked. He watched her from the foot of the bed, where he reclined against his elbow while his legs hung over the side of the bed.

How long has he been there? Sarah gazed confusedly at him. "How did...did we—*oh.*" She winced and cupped her forehead in her hand.

"Did we what?" Damon tilted his head to the side. "I'm afraid I didn't understand you. Does your head hurt?"

Sarah groaned. "Aye, it does. And it never hurts—" She sucked her breath through her teeth. "Like this."

Damon chuckled. "Surely it's not so bad."

Sarah stiffened at his tone. "It *is* bad and it *does* hurt."

"So you say." Damon rolled his eyes. "Perhaps if you hadn't drunk so much, you wouldn't be feeling so ill."

"I did not—" Sarah saw the smirk on his face and narrowed her eyes. *Did I?* She looked at the floor. *But I only drank the one glass.* "Why did I become—"

"So drunk?"

Sarah looked up at him. "What happened last night?"

"What do you mean?"

"Did we...did you—"

"Did I what? Rape you?" Damon asked. "Is that what you're trying so hard not to ask?"

Sarah dug her fingers into the blankets and tensed the muscles in her legs. *He says it so carelessly.* She watched him while she focused her senses inward. *Nothing feels different. But then, would it?*

Damon laughed. "Can you remember nothing from last night?"

"No, I can't." Sarah pursed her lips as her head pounded harder. *Why he is enjoying this so?* "Tell me, now. What did you—"

"Calm yourself, Sarah. I did no such thing to you." Damon shook his head and exhaled. "You could barely walk when we left the tavern. We went to the Night's River, in case you forgot that as—"

"I remember the tavern, Damon." Sarah glared at him. "What happened afterward?"

Damon shrugged. "I brought you here, to my shanty, but you swooned soon after. A disappointing evening, really."

"But why do I feel so ill?" Sarah wrapped her arm around her stomach as it gurgled. "I never feel like this. Did you intend to...."

Damon grinned lewdly. "I had hopes that you and I might come together after I brought you here, but you fell asleep before those desires could be realized. As to your sickness, I warned you last night of the potency of the tavern's ale."

Sarah grimaced and swung her legs over the side of the bed. She needed to retch, wanted to retch, but swallowed instead. "What are you saying? Did you do this to—"

"Sarah, look at me."

Sarah did as he bid. *Why does he stare at me so?*

"Do you know where you are?" Damon asked.

"What?" Sarah asked. "I don't understand."

Damon flippantly waved his hand. "Yes, so I assumed. I'll ask again," he said deliberately. "Do you know where you are?"

Sarah felt lost. "In your shanty? You told me as much awhile ago."

"Yes," Damon said slowly. "And where is that?"

"What do you mean? I don't—"

"What kingdom?"

Sarah narrowed her eyes. "I'm in Rich...Rich—"

"Rich?"

"No, not Rich. I mean...Virginia?"

Damon chuckled. "Are you certain?"

Sarah lowered her gaze back to floor, suddenly wanting to cry. Her mind was clouded in fog, and the blurry memories faded until she could no longer see them at all. The word *Virginia* was empty and meaningless, more an unfamiliar sound than an actual word. *Maybe I truly am lost. Utterly lost and terribly sick.*

"I...I don't know," she said glumly. "Why did I say Virginia? I don't know what that is."

"Consider carefully and it will come to you," Damon said. "One more time. Where are you?"

As if shaken by the finality of the question, her memories shifted and fell into place, and understanding assimilated within her. The fog vanished as quickly as it had come, leaving behind the awareness she'd been searching for. She remembered exactly where she was.

"Terra Caligines," Sarah said confidently.

Damon smiled. "Now you are awake." He pushed himself from the bed and stood.

Sarah made a face as she looked at him. "I've been awake for some time now."

"Have you truly?"

"Aye, I have," Sarah said. "Why must you keep asking so many—*oh!*"

The fierce sting stabbed into her chest, just above her left breast, and radiated into her back. She dug her fingers into the flesh above her heart, desperately squeezing to numb the pain. She yanked her tunic away from her chest and looked down.

The skin was pink and tender, as if a rash had infected the flesh while she slept. Two reddened slashes crisscrossed over her heart and burned warmed to the touch.

"What have you done to me!" Sarah shrieked. "This wasn't here last—"

"I did nothing to you," Damon said. "You did it to yourself."

"No!" Sarah stood from the bed, suddenly forgetting how sick she felt. "It was you! You did this—"

"*You* drank too much," Damon said as he grabbed her arm. "I didn't force the ale down your throat. And as for that mark," he wrenched her closer, "you've had that your entire life. But it's only now that it's seeped through."

Sarah tried to pull away, but his grip was too strong. "What are you saying?"

"Sarah, Sarah. My feisty lady." Damon smiled as he let go of her. "Everyone in Terra Caligines has a mark, a wound over their heart, and that mark is what proves their citizenship. But I think you know this already, don't you?"

Sarah narrowed her eyes. She did not know, but then...yes. *I remember.* "Other people have them, aye. I know this. Every person is born with a mark upon their heart." *A mark which proves they are citizens of Terra Caligines.* She laid her hand over her heart. "But how did...why can I see it only now?"

"An exceptionally difficult question to answer," Damon said. He sighed as he looked at her. "Simply put, a person's mark becomes visible when he reaches a crossroads in his life and is faced with a choice." He held up his hand. "But, bear in mind that this choice is not just any choice. It is a decision that will ultimately determine the course of that person's life. A point of no return, if you will.

"For you, that moment came last night when you went to the tavern with me. That one decision served as a catalyst, launching a series of decisions in your life that, if left unimpeded, will solidify your citizenship in Terra Caligines for eternity. That is why the wound over your heart is enflamed and sore, because his hold over you is strengthening with each decision you make."

"*His* hold?" Sarah asked.

"Leone Mortuo, the Prince of this world," Damon replied. He pointed his finger at her. "*You* are his subject. And in a way, you belong to him. As do I. I serve him and persuade others to do the same. This is why I asked you to come to the Night's River with me. It was all part of Prince Leone's plan, only you couldn't see what was taking place in this world."

Sarah smirked. "What world? You said this was my choice. I've lived in Terra Caligines for as long as I can remember and never heard any of this before."

"And precisely how far back do you remember?" Damon asked.

"I remember everything," Sarah said, crossing her arms. "I live on the southwest side of the village, close to the James...no, the Dedanima River, rather. My mother and father and brother live here too. I serve in Leone's Inn as a hostess. I've lived here since I was a child...well, maybe fourteen years old." She glanced at the ceiling as she thought. "Thirteen years old? Everything is hazy before then."

"Yes, I suppose it would be, wouldn't it?"

Sarah looked at Damon. "And why is that so?"

"Children are," Damon rubbed his bearded chin thoughtfully, "very unique individuals, you might say. Their citizenship in Terra Caligines is not, ah, official until they are of an age to realize...to *understand* the consequences of their actions. That age varies from child to child, but until that time, they belong to...."

"To who?"

Damon suddenly scowled. "Never mind. I've said too much. Get your things. I'm taking you to meet Prince Leone."

"Prince Leone?" Sarah asked. "But I'm the serving hostess tonight at Leone's Inn. I can't...why are we going to—"

"Prince Leone is eager to meet you," Damon said. "I am to bring you to him later today. On our way there, we can pick up your hostess's garb, if you wish."

"Why would Prince Leone want to meet me?" Sarah asked. She felt flattered but nervous too. "I'm no one of importance."

"*That* is where you are wrong, Sarah." Damon walked away from her but turned around near the doorway. "The Prince desires everyone to be his loyal subjects, no matter how prominent or ordinary they may be. You see, one more subject for Prince Leone is one less for King Omnideus. Every person is vitally important to the Prince for that reason. You do remember King Omnideus? And the War of—"

"The War of Citizenship. Aye, I remember," Sarah said. *King Omnideus defeated the Prince and provided a way for the villagers to cross the Abyss into Rovenia, but the crossing of the Abyss requires a leap of faith. I know what the histories say.* She chewed her lip in thought. "Rovenia doesn't seem so terrible, Damon. Have you ever considered—"

"Enough!" Damon cut the air with his hand. "*Don't* mention that place again, especially in front of His Majesty. That would be extremely foolish."

Sarah caught her breath. "Oh, I would never...forgive me, I was simply saying—"

"Then don't." Damon glowered from within the doorway. "I'll be waiting outside."

He vanished before she could reply, but she heard his boots stomping down the staircase. A door creaked opened and slammed shut, leaving her all alone in the small shanty.

I didn't mean to anger you. Sarah plopped down on the bed. She noticed her sandals lying on the floor then and slid her feet into them. She wove the sandals' elongated straps around each shin and tied them off just below her knees, crisscrossing the leather laces around her legs until they were snug against her black tights. Pushing herself from the bed, she smoothed the wrinkles from her blue tunic and ran her fingers through her hair. A bath would have served to wash the night from her body, but it would have to wait. Damon had given his orders.

Who gave him authority over me? I don't take orders. Sarah looked around the room for the first time. The small space resembled a loft, just big enough to hold a bed, a dresser, and a tiny wooden stool. Slanting to the outside of the shanty, the ceiling dropped two or three feet by the time it reached the wall, where a square hole served as the only window in the room. The shutters were open, and the sunlight streamed onto the unmade bed. She walked beside the wall, stooping beneath the ceiling as she went, and moved around the bed to the dresser. She picked up her cloak and satchel from the floor and stood tall.

A mirror. Sarah saw it hanging above the stool by the doorway. She walked over to it and bent down, turning her face this way and that as she tried to straighten her hair. She cupped her hand around her mouth and nose and let out a short puff of air. Her breath was stale. *I need some mint. Or an apple.* She exhaled. *That will have to wait as well.*

Wrapping the black cloak about her shoulders, Sarah hurried down the steps and walked through the shanty's living quarters. An old table and a stone fireplace were the only furnishings in the room. The dirt floor was bumpy and uneven, and the paneled walls were windowless. A breeze whispered through the walls as the rickety front door flapped against its frame. She pushed it open and stepped outside.

Sunlight washed over Sarah, forcing her to squint and reminding her of the persistent pounding within her head. She arched her hand over her eyes.

The narrow street was crowded and dusty, but Damon was nowhere to be seen.

Maybe he left without me. Part of her was saddened by the thought, but the other part was relieved. *I am fond of Damon, mostly.* "But he's acting so cruel towards me today," Sarah said to herself. She looked up and down the street indecisively. "Perhaps I should go. Simply walk home and forget—"

A moist nudge against her elbow bumped the words back into her throat. She turned and squinted into the light.

"Forget what?" Damon asked.

He was high above her, mounted in the saddle atop a magnificent black stallion, and he smiled down at her as the sunlight streamed around his shoulders and face. A dark cape framed his broad shoulders, while a red tunic and black belt hugged his strapping body. His charcoal breeches and black knee-high boots straddled either side of the stallion, and his brawny arms angled towards the reins, which he gripped with his bare hands.

Sarah forgot what she'd been saying. What sickness she'd felt earlier suddenly left her as well. "Oh, I was...well, I thought—" She tucked a strand of hair behind her ear. "Where did you go?"

"I left to saddle my horse," Damon said. He nodded across the street. "I keep him in the stables over there. Are you ready to go?"

His blue eyes seemed to sparkle in the sunlight, while his blonde hair and chin beard enhanced his knightly appearance.

Sarah nodded.

"Alright then." Damon chuckled. "Come on up."

He leaned forward and extended his hand to her. She held her breath and slid her hand into his.

"I've never ridden a stallion before," Sarah said. She gazed at his hand, distracted by the gentleness of its grip.

"Don't worry," Damon said. "He won't bite. I promise. Now put your foot in the stirrup and swing your other leg over. I'll pull you up."

Sarah swung her satchel over her shoulder and raised her foot to the stirrup. She braced her free hand against the horse, squeezed Damon's hand, and launched upwards.

The world blurred by as she vaulted over the horse and landed right behind the saddle, with the horse solidly between her legs.

"There ya go!" Damon said, letting go of her hand. He took the reins in both hands and looked over his shoulder at her. "You may want to hold on."

Sarah saw the glint in his eye and could not hide her girlish excitement. She leaned forward and wrapped her arms snugly around his chest. As she pressed herself against him, she laid her cheek against his shoulder and breathed in the virile smell of his cape.

"Ready?" Damon asked.

Sarah felt the muffled rumble of the word within his chest. "Ready," she said.

Damon thrust his heels into the horse's flanks, and the horse bolted forward. Sarah held on tightly as the horse leaped over a vegetable cart and ran through the narrow streets. Its hooves pounded rhythmically against the cobblestone street, kicking up a light cloud of dust around them.

She peeked over Damon's shoulder then and caught sight of the river just beyond the village's edge. But no sooner did she look than Damon leaned to the right. The river disappeared from view as the horse turned west.

I know this street. The more Sarah looked, the more she remembered. The sights, the smells, and the sounds of the village all were familiar and memorable, like a dream she had forgotten but was now reminded of. She knew Lake Solardens lay to the north, the Dedanima River to the south, and the Lumbrai Forest to the south where it eventually circled east and west. She recognized many of the faces in the crowd as people she worked with and patrons she served and friends she mingled with. The ale-induced haze left her completely, and she remembered.

"Whoa!" Damon said. His voice was deeper than usual. "Whoa, boy. Whoa." He pulled back on the reins, and the horse trotted to a halt.

Sarah craned her neck to see where they were. The top of the door to her shanty stood even with her left knee. "That was fast," she said breathlessly. She slid her arms from around his chest and sat straight up. "I'll go get my things."

"Be careful gettin' down," Damon said. He held out his hand as she swung her leg over.

Sarah gripped his hand and hopped to the ground. She turned around and looked up at him. "I'll only be a moment."

Damon smiled. "Take your time. I'll wait for you."

Sarah melted at the velvety smoothness of his voice, and her once queasy stomach now fluttered with delight. *Why can't you always be like this?* She turned from his entrancing gaze and walked into the shanty.

Sarah practically danced up the stairs into her bedroom. She threw open the closet doors and tugged a red tunic from its peg and pulled a pair of black tights from the wooden crate on the floor. She stuffed both the tunic and the tights into her satchel, and she scurried out of the room and down the staircase. She tossed a pair of boots in an old knapsack and threw the sack over her shoulder, along with her satchel as well.

Sarah reached for the door and pulled it open. She stepped outside, making sure to bolt the door securely, and walked to Damon.

"Got everything?" Damon asked from the saddle.

Sarah adjusted the leather straps around her shoulder. "Yep, I think so! Let's go." She took his hand and swung herself onto the horse.

This is my favorite part. She slid her arms around his chest and pulled herself against him. His muscles tightened beneath her hands.

"*Hyah!*" Damon snapped the reins. "*Hyah, boy!*"

The horse raced into the street, galloping around the western border of the village. Sarah tightened her legs around the horse's back and leaned into Damon as the horse stampeded northwards.

The horse veered onto the main road leading to the castle gate just as Lake Solardens came into view. Up the slope Sarah soared, closer and closer to the bluffs, while the shimmering lake grew and consumed the northern horizon. Frothy waves beat the rocks along the beach, while the mad waters dashed themselves against the cliffs beneath the castle. The sound of the sea boomed steadily in her ears, matching the thunderous tempo of the horse's hooves upon the cobblestones.

Damon hunched in the saddle, anchored and unmoving like solid rock. Sarah embraced him so tightly that she wondered if he could breathe, but he did not seem to be bothered. When a dark shadow suddenly loomed above her, she felt the horse slow. It trotted upon a new kind of stone, which echoed deep and hollow, and finally halted.

"You there!" Damon yelled. "Upon the gate!"

Sarah eased her grip around him and sat tall. She gasped.

The black castle towered above her and vanished into the low-lying clouds, while its wooden gate yawned like a mouth ready to devour its prey.

An armored man appeared between the wall's crenellations. He looked down at them but said nothing.

Damon cupped his hand beside his mouth. "I've brought a loyal subject to meet His Highness! Let us pass!"

"Good heavens! Is that you, Damon?" The armored man laughed. "I should've known! You're quite the finder of these people, aren't you? His Majesty will certainly be pleased. He's in the courtyard now. You may approach him there."

Damon swung his leg over the horse and jumped down. "Sarah, we walk from here."

He reached up and placed his hands on either side of her waist, guiding her to the ground. When her feet touched the cobblestones, she looked up at him.

"Thank you," Sarah said. She laid her hands on his, which yet rested upon her hips.

Damon smiled at her.

The wooden gate suddenly groaned as it split in half, and a tiny slit of light appeared between the two gigantic doors.

Sarah grabbed his hand as it left her side. "Damon...."

"I'm here, Sarah," Damon said softly. "This won't take long. I'll introduce you, and the Prince will greet you. Then we'll go."

Sarah nodded quickly while she watched the doors creep inward and listened to their hinges moan in protest. Finally, the doors boomed against the walls. The ensuing tremor quaked in the stones beneath her feet.

Damon let go of her hand and slipped his fingers beneath the horse's bridle. He looked at her. "Ready?"

No. This time I'm not ready. Sarah pursed her lips. "I think so."

"Good," Damon said. "Follow me."

Sarah watched him guide his horse towards the gaping doorway, and she forced herself to move, trailing a few steps behind him. She moved beneath the giant granite stones, which gleamed like marble above her. *They look wet.* She reached out her hand and flattened it against the cold stones. They felt like glass, but seemed much thicker, and were completely dry. *I've never seen stones so glossy as these.*

Row upon row of black stones soared up and up and higher still until they curved dangerously over her head and descended row upon row down the other side of the massive doorway. The threatening archway towered above her head, and she gazed at its structure. The sky was completely gone now, replaced by a dome of menacing blackness.

The horse's hooves *clip-clop-clopped* steadily on the stone walkway, while Damon marched like a soldier through the tunnel, his dark cape billowing gently behind him. Sarah watched his long strides and traced the lines of his manly figure. She saw the horse swish its tail from side to side.

A shaft of light unexpectedly washed over Damon and his horse, and Sarah looked up just as the blue sky returned above her. She emerged from under the archway into a whole new world.

She saw the garden first. Flowers, trees, vines, and a bubbling spring lay to her left just inside the outer wall. No structures of any kind stood in the garden except for a single fountain erected in the garden's center.

Made from the largest obsidian boulder Sarah had yet seen, the black fountain was carved in the likeness of a monstrous lion rearing on its hind legs in frozen attack. The water gushed from its roaring mouth, where its lips curled over its gums and exposed its dagger-like teeth. From the tip of its curving tail to the peak of its bushy mane, the statue stood as tall as a small tree.

The statue's eyes gleamed as Sarah walked by and seemed to move with her, like a prism rotating in the sunlight. The eyes were black at first but then burgundy. And from burgundy they flared a deep maroon. Shimmering to a vivid crimson, they finally dazzled a blood red—

"—pleased you have come!"

Sarah turned her head in the direction of the distinguished voice.

A crowd of people gathered several yards ahead of her, beyond Damon and his horse, at the very edge of a stone courtyard. A pillared wall to the right of the courtyard separated the castle from the grounds outside, where a mosaic of colorfully shaded bricks served as the courtyard's floor. Towers and turrets soared behind the pillared wall, and she could only imagine the grandness of the throne room hidden within those walls.

Exuberant applause suddenly resonated from the crowd. Damon walked to the left end of the gathering and stood. Sarah quickened her pace and squeezed in front of him so she could see what was happening.

Two men kneeled before the Prince. Both men were young and handsome, but each was distinctly different from the other. One was muscular and well-built, while the other was slender and graceful. The strong man's hair was dark and shaved, but the elegant man's hair was fair and long. Neither man had a beard, but the first man's complexion was much rougher than his friend's. Both were dressed in black breeches and boots, and each was wearing a tunic, one a dark green and the other a light blue.

Sarah looked closer.

The men were holding hands.

"Love knows no bounds, my friends!" the Prince shouted to the crowd. He laid his hand on the shoulder of the burly man. "What right have we to judge...to *condemn* the feelings that this man has for the other? Against all odds they have fought to be together. In the face of ridicule, intolerance, and outright hatred, they have persevered and remained faithful to each other, even unto the threat of death. I ask you, what greater love is there than this?"

The crowd cheered and clapped enthusiastically, and shouts of *'here here!'* echoed from the castle walls. Damon raised a fist and punched the air. Sarah watched the scene quietly.

"Arise, my dear brothers!" the Prince said, helping the two men to their feet. "I bless your union and urge you to stay in my kingdom. Here, you are free to love whom you choose. Go now. Be true to yourselves and live your lives together, as you were destined to do."

Cheering erupted from the crowd as the two men triumphantly raised their clasped hands into the air. They smiled and waved. Then they turned to each other and embraced.

Sarah looked at the ground just as the men kissed passionately. The excited roar from the crowd seemed to celebrate the men's tender caresses, but something about the affectionate scene felt wrong. Unnatural.

"Is this her, Damon?"

Sarah jumped when she heard the deep voice boom right next to her ear.

"Yes, Your Highness," Damon replied. He bowed his head respectfully. "Her name is—"

"Sarah, my beloved girl," the Prince said. "What a pleasure to finally meet you. I am Prince Leone Mortuo, as I'm sure you are already aware. I know you've lived here for many years now, but I am always pleased to meet one of my subjects, whether young or old."

He was tall and broad, a giant to Sarah, but thin and gaunt. Shrouded in a black cloak, his entire body was hidden from view, except for his hands and his face. His hair was jet black and brittle, hanging just above his shoulders, while his eyes were dark and seemingly pupilless. His skin was an odd mottle of tan and pale, healthy and sickly.

He wears no crown. "Thank you...Your Majesty," Sarah said. "I'm...I'm pleased to meet you as well."

Prince Leone smiled. Or sneered. She could not tell which.

"And Damon tells me that you work at one of my taverns, yes?" Prince Leone asked.

He's watching me! Sarah swallowed. "Um, aye...that is, yes! I do, Your Majesty. I serve as a hostess at Leone's Inn. I've been there for ten years now."

"Excellent," Prince Leone said. "I am pleased that you work for me. Do you like it there?"

"I...I—" Sarah nervously scanned the ground for an answer. "Forgive me, Your Highness, but—"

Damon laughed. "No, my Prince. She does not like it."

"Da*mon*," Sarah said through clenched teeth.

The Prince chuckled and gently held up his hand. "Sarah, do not fear. I wouldn't want to work at a tavern either. Perhaps I can find you another trade. Something you might enjoy? I control much of the commerce in the kingdom. What would you like to—"

"Your Majesty!" a man said behind her. "He is here again."

Without moving his head, Prince Leone flicked his gaze in the direction of the voice.

"He?" the Prince asked. "*He?* Tell him—"

"I don't believe you possess the authority to give me orders, Leone."

The tone of the new voice was strong and resolute but not unkind. Sarah turned.

A knight stood guard off to the side. No doubt he had been the first man to speak. But the second man, the one who now stood in front of her, was clearly a commoner. His boots were worn and dusty, and his brown breeches and cream-colored tunic were old and faded. He was not tall but not short, not robust but clearly strong. His face was friendly and stern at the same time.

Sarah winced sympathetically. The man's face was pocked with leathery, pink scars. And so were the man's hands.

"You," Prince Leone said lowly. "What are *you* doing here?"

"I think you know."

The Prince immediately looked at Sarah, and she saw an infuriated look of understanding wash over his haggard features.

"Damon," Prince Leone said. He never took his eyes from her. "Take her and go."

CHAPTER 9

As he heaved the third garbage bag over his shoulder, Luke was shocked at how much trash there was in his life.

He dropped the bulky bag onto the floor next to the front door, carefully scooting the bag against the wall so it would not spill its contents. The bag shifted a little but stood tall in line with its two black brothers, which were also waiting by the door to be taken outside.

"Phew," Luke said. He rested his hands on his hips. "Dang."

It was the only word he could think of, but it summed up his entire Saturday morning and afternoon in one syllable. He ran his hand over his mouth and cheeks, feeling the rough stubble scratch against his palm, and turned around to face his apartment.

Dang.

He could not explain why or how or when it had happened, but at some point last night, Luke had been bitten by the cleaning bug.

Everything had started when he'd woken up this morning around ten, which was early for him considering he usually did not rise before noon. Today he'd sat up in bed and felt different. He had not wanted to roll over and go back to sleep, which was his normal morning routine. He'd wanted to get up. And not only get up, but *do* something. For the first time in months, he'd felt motivated.

And he'd wondered if this mysterious feeling of inspiration had something to do with last night. Despite his efforts not to think about what he'd nearly done, Luke had brooded over his attempted suicide all morning and could not stop thinking about it. Hours later, looking back on his crazed desperation, he could not believe he'd actually tried to kill himself. What if he had succeeded? He would be dead. End of story. That grim realization was enough motivation in itself.

So from the moment he'd hopped out of bed, thrown on his old Dallas Cowboys jersey, and put on his favorite pair of holey jeans, Luke had found himself considering the question that he'd intentionally ignored his entire life.

What do you believe?

Chris had posed the question to him last night before they went their separate ways and had asked Luke to think about it. Whether Luke intended to ponder the question was doubtful, and honestly he did not buy into Chris's lecture on Jesus and life. But for whatever reason, the scarred man's words had repeated themselves over and over again in his mind.

Think about what happened tonight, and ask yourself what you believe. If not in Christ, then in who? Or what? And why?

So now, as he looked around the semi-organized, partially tidied room, Luke shook his head.

"I just don't know," he said.

He had not known last night when he teetered high above the river gorge, and he did not know now after hours of debating the question.

I have no idea what I believe.

Earlier in the morning, while separating his laundry into piles of dirty and clean clothes, Luke had considered the possible answers to the question. He'd decided that a god did indeed exist and might be in control of things. Perhaps his name was Allah, or Jesus, or All-Powerful, or The Man Upstairs. Or maybe god was no *he* at all. Maybe god was a *she*. That had been an interesting thought, but one which he'd ultimately decided was not possible. If god was a *she*, then she would be a goddess and not a god, and that would just lead to more confusion. Not to mention having a woman in charge of everything would just be plain scary.

After he'd sorted his laundry, Luke had folded the clean clothes and laid them neatly in two oblong cardboard boxes that narrowly fit beneath his bed. The dirty clothes he'd piled in the newly discovered hamper, which had been buried beneath a mountain of clothing for the past several months. Next he'd smoothed the wrinkles from the sheets and tucked the ends of the comforter beneath the mattress, officially making his bed for the first time this year.

He'd looked up and glanced towards the kitchen then, but quickly realized he'd made a mistake by peeking in that direction. Filthy dishes, moldy food, and scurrying gnats filled the sink, but Luke had reluctantly conceded that he'd found his next task.

As he'd walked to the kitchen, he'd accidentally kicked something and sent the cold object rolling across the carpet. A hollow *tink* clinked beneath the table, like glass hitting glass. He'd recognized the familiar sound and saw the amber-stained bottle reeling from the impact with its friend.

Now distracted, he'd decided to clean up a different mess first.

Tearing a garbage bag from the roll beneath the kitchen counter, Luke had moved to the lonely table and gathered the dozens of beer bottles from the floor. One after the other, he'd tossed them into the deep bag and listened to them clink into place. To him, each *tink* represented a depressed thought, or a comfortless hour, or a hopeless day. He'd reached for the last bottle then, which hid behind the leg of the little wooden table.

Everything is hopeless if you give your life to the wrong things, like drugs and alcohol.

Chris's words had echoed within his mind just as he'd taken the glass bottle in his hand.

Everything is hopeless. The miserable phrase had struck again, this time piercing not only his mind but also his heart. He'd winced and risen from his crouched stance, still holding the bottle but distracted from throwing it away.

He'd wrapped his fingers around the bottle's colorful label and gazed at the yellow-browned glass. Nothing about the bottle had been special or unique. It was an ordinary beer bottle with an elongated neck and a cylinder base. A ridged collar ran around the mouth of the bottle, while a feathery, chinked circle was embossed upon the bottom of its base. A crack in the bottle's side was evidence of a collision with the table's leg.

Despite its common qualities, the bottle had possessed one noticeable feature, which had absolutely nothing to do with its glass figure.

The bottle had been empty.

On any other day and in any other circumstance, Luke would have paid no attention to this detail. But the longer he'd looked at the bottle, the deeper Chris's words sank into his heart, and an unexpected comparison had crept into him.

Luke was just like the bottle.

Nothing about him was special or unique. He was an ordinary man with black hair and gray eyes, a scruffy complexion, and an averagely built body. He had one tattoo on his upper left shoulder, which he now regretted getting as a rebellious eighteen year-old, but he possessed no other features or traits which set him apart. He was broken and damaged—cracked in a variety of ways and for a variety of reasons.

And empty. Empty just like the bottle.

Hopeless.

Luke had sighed then and tossed the bottle into the garbage bag, ridding himself of his pensive thoughts as well. He'd grabbed either side of the garbage bag and struck it against the ground to shift the bag's contents. Tugging the yellow plastic drawstrings from the bag, he'd yanked them taut and knotted them twice for good measure.

The garbage bag had been heavier than he'd thought it would be, but with one arm he'd lugged it to the door and propped it against the wall. He'd gotten another bag from the kitchen then and snapped the crinkly plastic sheet open by the table.

Without hesitating, he'd held the mouth of the bag even with the edge of the table and placed his other hand in the table's center. He'd cupped his hand into a scoop and turned it on its side, then swooped his hand towards the edge of the table.

An explosion of chalky, white dust puffed from the table and fell into the waiting garbage bag. Luke had repeated the motion a few more times, brushing his hand along the table until the last flakes of the powdery drug had been swept into the bag.

"Never again," he'd told himself as he carried the dusty bag into the kitchen. He'd hated to admit it, but Chris had been right about one thing: drugs and alcohol were not the answer. Luke had already known this deep down, but he'd always ignored the knowledge. Until now, anyway.

For the next three hours, Luke had conquered the rotten disaster in his kitchen. The nearly empty garbage bag had quickly filled with spoiled eggs and milk, four-month-old Chinese take-out, moldy bread and crispy cheese, leftover food from greasy plates, and a pile of mush that may have been a sandwich. He'd thrown everything into the trash, including some plates which had been too disgusting to salvage. After washing the dishes, cleaning out the sink, and wiping both the counter and table down, he'd scrubbed the fridge and mopped the kitchen floor.

He'd tossed the second garbage bag next to the first and looked at his living room. He'd needed to sweep, but he did not own a vacuum cleaner, and he'd already picked up what trash was on the carpet. There had been only one thing left to do, and it had been bugging him for weeks now.

Grabbing a roll of duct tape from under his bed, he'd gone to the couch and jerked the torn cushion from its snug niche. He'd crammed the stuffing back inside the cushion and peeled the black tape from the roll. Sticking the tape over the leather rip, he'd wrapped the duct tape around and around and around. He'd slid the cushion back into place, nudged it a little with his knees, and set the duct tape on the kitchen counter.

The trashcan in the kitchen looked like a volcano of litter, so he'd tidied that corner up as well and pulled the swollen bag from the canister. After putting a new garbage bag in the trashcan, he'd heaved the full bag over his shoulder and dropped it by the other two next to the front door.

Dang.

Luke looked around the room. The unanswered questions continued to play over and over in his mind like a broken record.

Think about what happened tonight, and ask yourself what you believe. If not in Christ, then in who? Or what? And why?

Luke sighed. "Chris, why did you have to—"

Pound! Pound! Pound!

"Dude, it's me!" a voice said from the other side of the door. "Let me in, man! I got somethin' for you."

"Eddie?" Luke pulled the door open. "Hey man, what's—"

"What the—" Eddie pushed past Luke and barged into the room. "Your apartment's actually clean! I mean, still kinda run-down and all, but it's actually decent. So where's your maid? Or better yet, where's your woman?"

Luke closed the door. "I cleaned it, thanks. Glad you noticed."

"You? Clean?" Eddie guffawed. "Now that I find hard to believe. Come on, man! Stop jerkin' me around. Where's the slut you paid to—"

"Don't," Luke said sharply. He walked to within arm's reach of Eddie. "Just don't."

Eddie raised his eyebrows. "Well, *excuse* me. Aren't we testy today?"

Luke glared at Eddie.

"Chill out, man!" Eddie smacked Luke's upper arm. "This'll put you in a better mood."

Eddie reached into his pocket and pulled out a thumb-sized plastic bag. It reminded Luke of a baggy that would hold an extra button for a shirt, but there was no button in the tiny, white pouch.

Luke balled his hand into a fist. "No, I don't want—"

"And all I need is fifty bucks," Eddie said merrily, "and happiness is yours!"

"I said no, Eddie. Get that stuff outta here."

Eddie instantly stopped smiling. "What?"

"I'm not doin' that stuff anymore," Luke said. "It messes with my head and I don't like—"

"Aw, come on!" Eddie whined. "I owe this guy like fifty bucks, and I don't got any cash. Just buy it from me. It's a better batch then the last one, I swear! You can smoke it tonight and then you'll see."

"No. I've got plans tonight," Luke said. He was losing his patience. "And even if I didn't—"

"Plans with who?" Eddie narrowed his eyes, then smiled slyly. "Oh, in that case, just bring her here and she can smoke it with you."

I could punch him. It wouldn't hurt his face. Might even make it look better. Luke gritted his teeth. "It's not a girl. I'm hangin' out with Chris and gettin' something to eat."

"You mean the scarred dude? As in Quasimodo the Amish man?" Eddie made a face. "What the heck? Why would you—"

"He's not Quasimodo. Don't call him that," Luke said. "You don't know him. He's a good guy...and I sorta owe him one."

Eddie snorted. "Owe him how? 'Cause he brought your blade back? It's just a knife, for cryin' out loud. Stay here and chill with me...don't go with Chris. We can get high—"

"No. I told Chris I'd be there at five, and I'm not goin' back on my word. He deserves better than that."

"Luke, all he did was save your knife. Why do you gotta be all loyal now? Just ditch him!"

He saved much more than just that. Luke turned away from Eddie and opened the door. "You wouldn't understand," he said quietly. "You need to go."

"For real? But Luke! I'm tellin' ya, I'm in a hole...like real deep!" Eddie tugged nervously at the collar of his AC/DC T-shirt. "I gotta go meet our dealer tonight, and I'm s'posed to bring fifty bucks with me. If I don't...come on, man! Can't you help me out?"

"I can't," Luke said. "I'm sorry."

"Worthless piece of—oh, forget you!" Eddie stomped to the door. "I hope you and your scarred Quasi have a wonderful evening together. Just don't come whinin' to me when he starts preachin' at you. Sounds like he's already got you brainwashed."

Eddie pushed past Luke into the hallway, but Luke gripped Eddie's arm.

"I'm *not* brainwashed." Luke glared into Eddie's bloodshot eyes. "And what do you mean, when he starts preaching to me? What makes you think he preaches at all?"

Eddie sneered. "I know a churchy Christian when I see one. You can just smell religion on people by the way they carry themselves. And that Chris dude...well, he reeks of Jesus. Take my advice. Don't get too close to him, or you'll start smellin' too."

"Chris isn't like that," Luke said. "You don't know what you're talkin' about."

"Don't I?" Eddie wrenched his arm from Luke's grasp.

Luke watched him walk away, moving farther down the hall, and started to close the door.

"And when you give up on this Chris fellow," Eddie suddenly called over his shoulder, "and you're ready for some more drugs, you let me know! I'll be waiting for you. You'll come back! Everyone always—"

Luke slammed the door.

But he could not shut out the doubt. Eddie's spiteful jabs had hit their mark.

What if he's right? What if Chris is just trying to brainwash me? To turn me into some goody-goody religious person? Maybe I oughta stay home.

Luke trudged into the bathroom and looked in the mirror. The scruffy, sad-eyed man looked back at him.

"No," he said to the man in the mirror, "Chris saved your life. You're gonna go. No matter what Eddie thinks."

So Luke shaved the thick stubble from his cheeks and showered the grime from his body. He decided to wear a pair of blue jeans that did not have any holes in them and a black and blue, short-sleeved plaid shirt, which he left casually untucked over his belt. After his hair dried, he pulled the black strands into his usual ponytail.

With the stubble gone from his face and his hair gathered neatly behind his head, Luke could almost pass for a clean-cut young man. He had shaved his stubbly beard into two thin lines which traced his jawline and framed his mouth but left his cheeks bare and smooth. With almost no facial hair, Luke reminded himself of what he once looked like in his late teens.

He double-checked that his knife was at his side, and it was, right where he had put it. The curved hilt peeked out from the black sheath attached to his belt.

Luke glanced at the clock above the towel rack. It was just after 4:30.

Time to hit the road. He flipped the bathroom light off and walked into the living room, where he sat on the couch and tugged his boots over his feet. He would walk to Leon's like he always did, since his car did not run, and he should get there a little before five.

Luke grabbed his keys and slid his wallet into his back pocket. He walked to the door and opened it, and stepped out into the dimly lit hallway. He had nearly pulled the door closed when a faint voice seemed to echo from inside the room.

What do you believe, Luke?

He could feel the tug within his heart as he heard the question within his mind.

"I don't know," he whispered. *But I've got to figure it out.*

Luke closed the door and went to find Chris.

CHAPTER 10

Damon slipped his arm around her back and leaned into her. "Let's go," he said lowly. "I didn't know Mr. Morten had a meeting scheduled. We'll come back another time."

"As a matter of fact, I also was unaware that Mr. Morten had a meeting scheduled," Leon Morten said. He glared at the scarred man from across the room. "But yes, Damon, please bring Miss Ryans back any time. I would be glad to help her find a job she would enjoy. Perhaps we can discuss a particular vocation next week?"

Sarah looked from the scarred man to Mr. Morten. She hesitated. "Uh sure...I mean, yes. Yes! That'd be great."

Mr. Morten smiled. "Very good." He walked to his desk and sat down behind it. "Now if you'll excuse me, Damon, it seems I have important business to attend to."

"Yes, sir." Damon guided Sarah towards the door. "Have a good day, Mr. Morten."

Sarah walked past the scarred man as she neared the doorway, but Damon stayed between her and the man at all times. She did not understand how such an ordinary yet disfigured person could march into the office and command a private conference with the head executive of the company.

"Oh, and Sarah...."

Damon and Sarah stopped and looked back simultaneously. The tall businessman in his black suit, red tie, and glistening black shoes lounged in a cushioned leather chair behind the antique desk.

"It was so nice to finally meet you," Mr. Morten said. "Please don't let this," his eyes momentarily darted to the scarred man, "*interruption* ruin our first meeting. I look forward to our next get-together."

Sarah glanced at the scarred man, who silently slid his maimed hands into his pockets. In his worn yellow work boots, faded carpenter jeans, and off-white hoodie, the man was the complete opposite of Leon Morten. The ordinary man's hair was brown and cropped short, buzzed around his ears and neck, while Mr. Morten's hair was long and black, slicked with gel to keep it stylishly smoothed over his head. The scarred man's face was partially bearded where the raw splotches did not prevent the hair from growing, but his brown eyes seemed kind despite his rough complexion. Mr. Morten's face was completely hairless and fair, but his dark eyes and sharp features made him look ill and conniving.

A sudden jab from Damon's elbow brought Sarah back to the stately office.

"Oh! Mm hmm," she said, nodding excitedly. "I look forward to it too. And it was nice meeting you too. Thank you, Mr. Morten."

"No. Thank *you*, my dear," Mr. Morten said, extending his hand politely. "And on that note, Mr. Scarlett, I believe the floor is yours."

Mr. Morten leaned back in his chair leisurely, while a look of sheer arrogance came over his face. He drummed his fingers on his chair. In the strained silence, his smug expression and intimidating gaze were louder than anything he might have said.

But the man called Mr. Scarlett, to Sarah's astonishment, showed no sign of unease in Mr. Morten's presence and remained silent but undeniably confident. He did not flinch as he approached the desk, but he did turn his head and look directly at Sarah.

The fleeting glance was over before it began, but in that moment the man's penetrating gaze stunned her beyond comprehension. Startling shades of strength, gentleness, and wisdom radiated from the fierce brown eyes, and Sarah stared back blankly, unable to look away. She felt the eyes studying her, searching her, *looking right through her*, as if somehow they knew her better than she knew herself. And then she blinked, and the riveting second passed. Mr. Scarlett tipped his head courteously and turned his focus to Mr. Morten.

"Who is he?" Sarah whispered.

"*Go,*" Damon said. With his arm still clamped around her back, he steered her out of the office and closed the door behind them.

Sarah struggled against his shoving. "What're you...don't—" Her shoes squeaked on the waxy black tile. "Don't push me so hard! Stop—"

"Shut...*up*! You're acting like a child!"

Every muscle in her body tensed at his insolent tone. She shoved his arm from around her and locked her jaw in anger.

"Don't you *ever*...if you think you can—" Sarah pursed her lips. "I am not some girl that you can just push—"

Damon laughed at her.

Who do you think you are? Sarah felt like she might explode. "I do not appreciate—"

"Sarah!" Damon said between laughs. "Your face is as red as my shirt! I wish you could see it."

From the blazing warmth spreading across her cheeks, Sarah could only imagine how fiery red her face was. Her face always flushed when she was upset, but knowing that Damon noticed irritated her even more.

"I know my face is red!" she said. "Thank you, Captain Obvious. Why don't you just—go away!" She whirled on her heel and stomped past the receptionist's desk and into the hallway.

"Sarah, wait! I'm sorry! You look pretty when you're mad!"

Sarah looked over her shoulder and glared at him.

"Aw Sarah, come on." Damon shook his head and followed her. "I'm...could you stop walking...."

She jerked her head forward and stormed down the majestic hallway, heels rhythmically tapping the black marble floor as she went. It was veined with delicate white streaks, she noticed as she glared at it, and these same shiny tiles covered the floor of the waiting area and Mr. Morten's office too. Elegant strips of the same obsidian material trimmed the gray walls and edged the ceiling, framing the entire hallway in polished marble. Several mahogany doors lined either side of the corridor, which ended at the brass-colored doors of an elevator.

She stopped when she got there, pressed the round white button on the wall, and crossed her arms. Silently she perused the wall and waited for the doors to open, ignoring the sound of footsteps behind her.

"Um, so look," Damon said over her shoulder. "I didn't mean to...well, I shouldn't have—"

"Been such a jerk?" Sarah said, not moving her gaze from the wall. She heard him exhale.

"Sure...yes, I mean," Damon replied steadily. "I shouldn't have been such a jerk. There, I said it. Now will you please look at me?"

She ignored him and continued to busy herself with her silent surveying of the wall. A gleaming wooden plaque with a golden plate screwed onto its front hung on the wall at eye level. Engraved upon the plate were the words *Morten, Inc Headquarters, Richmond, Virginia.* A black, roaring lion reared beside the fancy lettering.

"Sar*ah*." She heard him groan. "Come on. I said I'm sorry."

The elevator dinged abruptly, and the glistening doors glided open. She moved quickly into the carpeted compartment and pushed a button on the inside panel. Re-crossing her arms, she eyed Damon contemptuously.

"Well?" Sarah asked. "Are you coming?"

Damon opened his mouth to respond, but the elevator's high-pitched chime interrupted him. The doors rattled and started to slide together. Sarah watched him leap clumsily through the closing gap and stumble into the little room. She almost laughed. *Serves you right.*

The elevator lurched and hummed downward. Damon moved to the opposite side of the elevator and crossed his arms too.

"Look Sarah, there's no need to—"

"All I did was ask you a simple question," Sarah said, "and you treated me like some child not doing what she was told to do. Nobody treats me—"

"What question?" Damon asked sharply. He made a face. "I have no idea what you're talking about."

Sarah met his gaze. "*Him*, Damon. I asked you who *he* was. And then you shoved me out of the office and told me to shut up."

"Chris Scarlett?" Damon raised his eyebrows. "That's what this is all about?"

"Yes, Chris Scarlett. Him and the way you treated me." Sarah looked at the ground. "That's why I'm mad."

Damon exhaled again. "Alright. So what do you want to know?"

"Who is he?" Sarah looked up at him. "That's what I want to know.

Damon rubbed his eyes with his thumb and forefinger and then shook his head. "Not that it really matters, but Chris Scarlett is the son of Mr. Morten's competitor, an old man who's the head of a major rival organization overseas. Mr. Morten's company and Scarlett's company have clashed with each other for decades over the ownership of certain," he glanced at the ceiling, "property. Sometimes the old man will send Chris to discuss those conflicts."

"Conflicts?" asked Sarah. "Is that why Mr. Morten had to drop what he was doing? So he could talk to Chris?"

Damon suddenly glowered. "No. Mr. Morten does not do what Chris wants, if that's what you mean. Chris has no power or authority over Mr. Morten. Mr. Morten used to work for Chris's father, but he branched out and founded his own independent company. Mr. Morten has successfully persuaded thousands of the old man's clients and employees to join his company. But as you can imagine, the old man doesn't like that very much. So the two companies are at war constantly."

"Oh, I had no idea," Sarah said. "With all those scars and by the way he dresses, I never would've guessed Chris was that important."

The elevator slowed to a stop, and its doors dinged and slid apart.

"Well, he's not *that* important," Damon said, stepping out of the elevator. "Technically, Chris is just a firefighter, but he works for his father as well. If you ask me, he's too humble and laidback. And ugly too."

"That's mean, Damon," Sarah said reproachfully. She followed him into the building's lobby. "You said Chris is a firefighter. What if he got those scars from a fire? Maybe he rescued someone."

"Whatever," Damon said. "Can we talk about something else now? Are you hungry or anything?"

"No, I'm not hungry." Sarah rolled her eyes and kept walking. "Why don't you wanna talk about Chris? I thought he seemed—"

"Seemed what?"

The tone of his voice made Sarah look at him. Damon was watching her. *What did I do now?* She shrugged and held out her hands. "Well, I don't know," she said spitefully. "Like, just the way he dressed—the way he *didn't* respond to Mr. Morten's comments—there's something about him. Chris seemed honest...genuine. Not shady or plotting."

"Not shady or plotting like Mr. Morten?" Damon asked harshly. "Is *that* what you mean?"

"No, that's not—" Sarah stopped at the exit door and took a deep breath. "Mr. Morten seems...nice. But the way Chris looked at me was different than the way Mr. Morten looked at me. Does that make sense? I think I could trust Chris, but Mr. Morten seemed...well, sneaky."

Damon laid his hand on the crossbar of the glass door but paused mid-push. He seemed to scan the sky for a moment before finally looking down at her.

"Mr. Morten is *not* sneaky," Damon said steadily. "He *is* clever, I'll give you that much. But that cleverness is what makes him a successful businessman. As of today, he owns stock in multiple companies around the world, and that influence enables him to help ordinary people find good jobs. He might even be able to get you a better job. So I wouldn't be so quick to judge, if I were you."

Great. Now I ticked him off. Sarah could see the anger in his eyes. She tried not to aggravate him further. "Well, I didn't say...I mean, Mr. Morten seems friendly too. It's just that—"

"I know what you meant."

Damon shoved the door open and walked outside. He did not look back.

"You've got to be kid—Damon!" Sarah caught the door just before it swayed shut. "Damon, please. Don't be—ooh." She pursed her lips and stomped after him.

The streets of downtown Richmond were jammed with traffic on the busy Saturday afternoon. Vehicles idled noisily at stoplights and revved as soon as the lights turned green. A truck turned in front of a car, and the car let out a shrill *beep*. Young maple trees lined the street and beautified the sidewalk, which was crowded with window shoppers and sightseers and business workers. The tall office buildings and skyscrapers overshadowed everything, but Sarah did not notice any of the city's scenery.

The only thing she saw was the broad-shouldered, lean figure in the red shirt and loose jeans stomping away from her.

"Damon!" Sarah yelled after him. "Damon, I'm sor—"

A rusty truck clamored past her, reverberating with sputters and drowning her words. Damon disappeared into a parking garage before she could yell again.

My feet are killing me. Sarah winced as she tried to walk faster. *Stupid heels. Stupid everything.* She finally made it into the garage but could not remember where they'd parked. *In that row? No, we pulled in over there, not here. So that means—*

A car door slammed to her right.

The red taillights of Damon's Mustang came to life and illuminated the concrete wall on the opposite side of the garage, while the deep purr of its engine reverberated from the low ceiling. Gray steam wisped from its exhaust pipes, and the black car growled lowly as the white reverse lights flared.

The glistening car rolled backwards.

"Damon! Damon, don't leave me!" Sarah dashed towards the car, partly hobbling and partly sprinting. Her heels *clickclickclicked* on the cement floor as the car backed up and turned towards the gaping exit.

She bounded the last few steps and lunged at the passenger door, slipping her fingers beneath the plastic handle and giving her wrist a quick jerk. The door popped open. She dove inside and plopped into the leather seat, yanking the door shut behind her.

"What are you doing!" Sarah shrieked. "Were you just going to leave me here?"

Damon smiled at her. "No. But I think I've made my point." He shifted the car into drive. "Now, are you sure you're not hungry?"

"What?" Sarah asked incredulously. "Why would you ask—"

"Do you want to get something to eat before I take you to work?" Damon asked. "Are you—"

"No! No, I am not hungry." Sarah crossed her arms and glared out her window. "I'll just get something at work. We probably don't have time to eat anyways."

Damon drove out of the parking garage and turned onto the busy street. "True. It's after four-thirty now. You have to be at work at five, right?"

"Yeah."

"Okay."

Sarah kept her head purposely turned towards the window. Buildings and cars and trees blurred by for several minutes, but she did not really see them. *Never again. I'm never going out with him again. I deserve better than this.* A familiarly sweet odor of apple cinnamon swirled around her, and she glanced at the air freshener clipped to the air vent above the radio. *I will never allow myself to be trapped in that situation again.*

A faint shudder quivered through her seat, and the car's engine fell silent. She sat up when she recognized the paved parking lot surrounding Leon's Grille, and she hurriedly unclicked her seatbelt and grabbed her purse and knapsack from the floor.

Damon opened his door. "I'm gonna get some food, if that's cool with you."

"Fine with me."

"Okay."

Sarah opened her door and stepped out just as Damon closed his. She swung her bags over her shoulder and slammed the door, glancing in his direction.

Damon was watching her, but he looked rather lost.

Let him sulk. I don't care.

Sarah took off from the car, heels *clip-clopping* snobbishly on the pavement, and strode to the sidewalk. She held her chin high and lightly whipped her head to shake her hair into place.

She reached for the door handle, but his hand got there first.

"Sarah, can we talk for a sec?"

"I have to get ready for work."

Damon opened the door and Sarah strode into the vestibule, jerking the second door open and walking into the lobby. She walked through the gap between the front counter and the wall, while Damon got his wallet out and approached the cashier.

"I'll be out here," he said.

"Okay."

Without uttering a word to any of the workers, Sarah strode around the prep table, past the vats, past the grills, around a refrigerator, and into the back of the store. The employee bathroom door was open, and she walked inside and slammed the door behind her.

The bathroom was big enough to hold a toilet and a sink, but nothing else. She always forgot how cramped it was until she tried to change her clothes in it. She shimmied out of her blue jeans and tugged her black work pants on, then wriggled out of her blouse and pulled the red manager's shirt over her head. Lastly, she reached into her purse for a pair of socks.

And realized she did not bring a pair of socks.

She groaned and slipped her bare feet into her greasy work shoes. *This is going to be a great night.*

She did find an extra hair clip in her purse, though. So after clipping her hair into something between a ponytail and a bun, she gathered her things and exited the bathroom.

The employee break room was a mess as usual, so Sarah hid her bags in the far corner where they would not be bothered. She glanced at the clock on the wall above her. It was 4:52.

She decided to go up front and tell Damon that she would call him. *A lie, yes. But sometimes a lie is better. I can avoid him that way. Then I won't have to see him ever again.* She left the break room feeling relieved and even a little cheerful.

So she strolled past the refrigerator, the grills, and the vats, finally rounding the prep table and—

"Hey Sarah!" Damon waved to her from across the counter. "What are you doin' tomorrow night?"

Sarah gawked at the unexpected sight. She stopped, as if her slippery shoes were suddenly glued to the floor, but her upper body kept moving forward and forced her to take another step. What momentary relief she had felt fled as the agitation rushed through her.

"Sarah, come over here!" Damon beamed from ear to ear. "There's someone I want you to meet."

She assumed the *someone* Damon was referring to was the man standing next to him.

She hoped she was wrong.

Sarah forced herself to smile and tucked a strand of hair behind her ear. She strolled over to the two men, hoping they did not notice how hard she was gritting her teeth.

"Sarah, you'll never guess who this is!" Damon motioned toward the man beside him. "Me and this guy used to work for the same construction company. I haven't seen him in...what's it been? Two years now? Sarah, meet—"

"Mr. Porter," said Sarah. She held her hand out to him. "Nice to meet you...again."

The man winced sheepishly but shook her hand. "Hi...Sarah."

"So," Damon said, "I take it you two know each other?"

Yes, unfortunately. Sarah shrugged. "We've met."

"Really?" Damon asked. "Where did you meet Luke?"

"I come in here, um, a lot," Luke said. He looked away from Sarah and glanced at the floor. "And I, uh...I mean, I brought back my sandwich yesterday," he looked at Damon, "and I kinda—"

"We've met," Sarah said, crossing her arms.

Luke winced again. "We've met."

"Well, that's awesome, man!" Damon slapped Luke on the back. "Now we can all hang out tomorrow! Sarah, what are you doin'—"

"*We?*" Sarah put her hand on her hip. "Who's—"

"Me, you, and Luke. All of us," Damon said. "Tomorrow night at the Summer's End Festival, they're havin' a motocross race. It's not a professional race...just a bunch of country hicks who ride dirtbikes. I already entered and I'm tryin' to get Luke to enter too. It's only ten bucks a person, and there's usually only like fifteen people that race, but they pool everyone's money together and that's the grand prize. I'm tellin' ya, Luke, it's easy money! You should come with us."

Luke grinned. "Easy money, huh? And what if you win?"

"Then it was easy money for me!" Damon laughed. "So what do you say?"

"I say I don't own a dirtbike," Luke said lightheartedly, "so I think that means no."

Damon leaned back and outstretched his arms. "No worries, man! I've got a friend who owns four or five of 'em. He'll let me borrow one."

"You're sure?" Luke asked. "I don't have anything to haul it with."

"Not a problem," Damon said. "You leave that to me."

Luke shook his head but grinned. "Alright, what time?"

"Well, the race starts at eight," said Damon. "So, what do you say we meet there 'bout seven-thirty? You know where the festival is, right? Just west of Richmond in Glover's Field? You could probably walk there from your house. There's a dirt track out there—"

Sarah coughed and stepped away. "Not to be rude, but I've gotta get to work. So if you two—"

"Aw Sarah, my bad!" Damon said. "Is it cool if I pick you up a little after seven tomorrow night? I'll be drivin' my truck this time."

"Damon," Sarah said lowly, "I *am* off tomorrow, but I'd kinda like to just—" She looked over Damon's shoulder. *What's he doing here?* He walked up behind them and smiled at her.

"Sarah? Sarah," said Damon. "Did you hear—"

"Hey Luke," Chris Scarlett said cheerfully. "Ready to eat?"

Luke turned around. "Chris! Right on time. How's it goin'?"

"Not bad, not bad." Chris shook Luke's hand. "How's your day been?"

"Pretty good so far," Luke said, smiling. He glanced at Sarah. "Chris, this is Sarah...and that's Damon. We're goin' to the festival tomorrow night. Do you wanna come with us? I guess I'll be racin' a dirtbike."

Damon seemed to jump. "Luke, I'm not sure if that's—"

"Sure, that'd be great," said Chris. "I was wantin' to go this year, but I didn't have anyone to go with."

"Well, now you do," Luke said. He looked up at the menu board. "Alright, I'm starvin'. Do you wanna eat with us, Damon?"

"No. I mean...no thanks, Luke." Damon shook his head. "I gotta get goin' as soon I get my food. Sarah, I'll see you tomorrow?"

"Um, yeah...see you tomorrow." Sarah glanced at Chris and Luke. "You guys have a good day."

Chris nodded. "You too, Sarah."

Luke just looked at her and smiled.

Oh brother. She rolled her eyes as she turned around, and walked to the nearest register to clock in. She scarcely had a chance to skim her shift's paperwork when she felt three excited tugs on her shirt sleeve.

"Sarah, Sarah, Sarah! Do you close tonight?"

She recognized Jenny's voice but did not look up.

"Yeah," Sarah exhaled, "I do."

"Yay! Me too!" Jenny said. "So was that your boyfriend?"

"What?" Sarah asked. She looked up from her paperwork. "What boyfriend?"

"You know, the tall guy with the ponytail," said Jenny. "The one that was here yesterday, *remember*? I liked his tattoo because it was scrumptious."

Somebody shoot me now. "No, Jenny. He's not my boyfriend," Sarah said. *Be nice, Sarah. Be nice. Don't take it out on her.* She laid her paperwork down. "I went out with the other guy...the one that gave me his phone number yesterday. He's got blonde hair and—"

"The pretty boy?" Jenny wrinkled her nose. "Eww! He looks like a prissy model. You need some dating help, A-S-A-P."

Sarah looked at the ceiling and took a deep breath. "Jenny, I'm not having a very good day, please don't—"

"Don't worry, Sarah," Jenny said. "We've got all night to talk about it. I'm a great advice-giver-person when it comes to boys. You'll see." She twirled on her heel and skipped to her register to take a customer's order.

Sarah walked to the drive-thru and slowly ran her hand down her face. *I am not gonna make it.* She glanced toward the lobby.

Chris and Luke sat at a small table by one of the floor-to-ceiling windows that formed the lobby's outer wall. Chris's back was towards her, but Luke faced her.

He does look different today. His unkempt scruff was gone. His face was clean-shaven, except for the neatly trimmed hairs on his jawline which led to the goatee around his mouth. He wore a black and blue plaid shirt that fit him nicely, and his jeans did not have one single hole in them. *Even his eyes seem different.* A faint ring of the lightest blue rimmed the pupils and gradually faded to silvery gray at the edges. She had never seen eyes so—

Luke looked up at her.

She caught her breath and spun, pretending to busy herself with reading the drive-thru monitor.

"I saw that!" Jenny giggled.

Sarah felt the warm blush upon her cheeks as she whipped a paper bag from one of the canisters.

It's going to be a long night.

CHAPTER 11

Leone's Inn was exceptionally quiet for an evening, but Luke welcomed the unexpected calm within the tavern.

The four log tables which ran the length of the room were empty and bare, with not one person sitting upon the benches or a single tankard of ale resting on the tables. A small fire crackled in the stone fireplace at the far end of the tables, illuminating the immense bear rug on the dirt floor, but the fire's rustling whisper was the only steady sound within the room. Luke could feel the soothing heat warming his back as he took a bite of his veal trencher and looked up.

Christoph sat across from him at their secluded table against the outer wall, and Christoph bit into his veal trencher as well, licking the meat's juices from his lips. Luke chewed his morsel slowly, savoring the seasoned flavor as the tender meat fell apart in his mouth, and glanced over Christoph's shoulder.

The rustic tavern bore the marks of forest and men. Hunting knives and animal skins decorated the walls, while archery bows and deer antlers hung from the rafters overhead. Clumps of dirt clung to the legs of benches and tables where mud-caked boots had once rested. A waist-high, wooden counter traversed the opposite end of the room and guarded the way to the kitchen, which was hidden behind the wall that served as the tavern's bar. Towering with shelves from floor to ceiling, the wall was stocked full with barrels of spiced ale and jugs of water.

Luke swallowed his food and craned his neck. He leaned to his right, taking a quick peek at Christoph to make sure he was not watching him, and looked towards the bar.

There she is.

He met her gaze for only a moment before she looked away and whirled to face the wall. A little blonde-haired girl said something and grinned, while Sarah yanked a cloth sack from one of the lower shelves.

Luke smiled when he saw it. Sarah's cheeks matched the color of her tunic.

Christoph coughed suddenly. "I think someone needs a bucket of cold water dumped on his head."

"What?" Luke asked, startled. He hurriedly averted his gaze. "Water? No sir, thank you. I've a whole cup right here." He whisked his tankard from the table and gulped eagerly.

"That you do," Christoph said, "but I didn't mean—"

An untimely inhale and a hurried swallow flooded his lungs with water, and Luke flew forward in his chair, choking. He slammed the tankard on the table and pounded his chest with his fist.

Christoph slapped his knee. "Seems I don't have to dump that water on you after all!" He laughed. "You've done it to yourself."

"No, I wasn't—" Luke coughed. "I was lookin' at all those barrels and drank too quick."

"Barrels? Is that what you were starin' at?" Christoph glanced back over his shoulder. "Barrels, aye. Lots of them. And a beautiful woman as well."

Luke casually reached for his tankard. "What woman?"

"What woman?" Christoph chuckled and turned around. "Do you think me blind?"

"Blind? No." Luke sipped some water to hide his smile. "Perhaps confused...."

"Aye." Christoph grinned and shook his head. "Well, let me tell you about her. She wears a red tunic."

"So you say."

"Her hair is the color of chestnuts, and wavy."

"Is it?"

"She is full of youth. Lovely to look upon."

"An angel, mayhaps? I would remember if I saw such a creature."

"I believe they call her Elizabeth." Christoph sighed. "But it would seem I was wrong. I doubt if I should mention that she has the eyes of a doe."

"No, she doesn't," Luke said. *How could he be so mistaken?* "Her eyes are blue...a deep blue, with not one speck of brown in them. And her name is Sarah, not Elizabeth. Have you forgotten already?"

Christoph wrinkled his brow. "You're certain of this? I thought for sure her eyes were brown."

Luke shook his head. "No. I've looked into her eyes plenty of times to know what color...." It was only then that he noticed the amused expression on Christoph's face.

"Please, do go on," Christoph said. He leaned back in his chair and waved his hand. "Tell me more about this woman that you don't know."

"Alright, alright." Luke smiled and glanced over Christoph's shoulder. "Perhaps I do know her."

Christoph picked up his trencher with both hands. "Have you spoken to her then?"

"Who?" Luke suddenly felt nervous. "Sarah?"

"No...Elizabeth." Christoph took a bite of his food and looked at him.

"Oh." Luke smiled, a little embarrassed. "No, I haven't spoken to Sarah. I'm not sure she...that is, I don't think she's very fond of me."

"What makes you say that?"

Luke exhaled and looked at the table. "I treated her poorly yesterday when I brought back my trencher. And more than just that—I was cruel to her. Today, when she saw me at first, she looked...well, she remembered. I could see it in her eyes. But she has every right to be angry with me."

Christoph shook his head. "But did you beg her pardon? Tell her you acted foolishly?"

"No," Luke said gloomily. "I'm not sure I can face her. It was a struggle just to say hello to her, let alone ask for her forgiveness. You heard how I stuttered when I tried to speak. I felt like a fool. And besides, she's courting Damon now, so what good will an apology do?"

"Let me tell you something, Luke," Christoph said sternly. He gestured with his scarred hands as he spoke. "Aye, 'tis true that seeking forgiveness may make you feel like a fool. No one likes to admit fault, but that makes no matter. If you've wronged someone, it's up to you to seek their forgiveness, no matter how wounded your pride might be." He smiled a little then. "And I think you may be surprised at how Sarah will react. Don't assume she won't forgive you. And don't assume she's courting Damon either."

"You truly believe she'd forgive me?"

"Aye. I do."

Would that I could be so certain. Luke shook his head doubtfully. "But how do you know she's not courting Damon? He asked her to come with us tomorrow night."

"That does not mean they're courting," Christoph said. "Did you see the way she acted around him? She seemed uncertain when he asked her to come to the festival."

"I thought it was because of me." Luke frowned and nudged his tankard distractedly. "After the way I spoke to her yesterday."

Christoph shook his head. "No, it was because of him. She made a grave mistake by choosing Damon. And she knows this."

What is he saying? Luke looked at Christoph carefully. "How do you know Damon?"

"I've known Damon for many years now," Christoph said. The look on his face was terribly serious, and so was his voice. "He and his kind serve Prince Leone, while my father is a Rovenian who fights against the Prince. My father sent me here to save the people from Prince Leone and lead them to Rovenia, but Damon and others like him are constantly working to thwart my father's plan. I've had many encounters with Damon throughout the years."

"Your father is from Rovenia?" Luke asked. "You're a Rovenian?"

Christoph nodded. "Aye, my family's citizenship is in Rovenia, across the Abyss, and my purpose in Terra Caligines is to bring as many people to Rovenia as possible. Much of my family is here with me now in Terra Caligines, spreading the word of my father's kingdom. This is the reason Damon didn't want you to invite me to the festival tomorrow night. He fears my presence may influence you."

Eddie. He feared you as well. And Damon...the scowl on his face when I asked you to come with us. Perhaps their fears are justified. Luke hoped his face did not betray his thoughts. He looked Christoph in the eye. "Do you see Damon often?"

"I saw him today...before I came here."

"Truly? Where?"

"As I told you before, I serve my father and fight the fires of this world." Christoph wrapped his scarred hand around his tankard and leaned forward intently. "There are times when, in order to do my father's work, I must confront the Prince. That is where I was today when I saw Damon and Sarah."

"Damon took Sarah to meet the Prince? But why would—"

"Leone Mortuo, the Prince of this world, is a very cunning man. He wishes for everyone to stay with him in Terra Caligines, but he especially desires those with potential. Sarah has potential, and Prince

Leone recognizes this. He will do everything within his power to make certain that her potential is used for his purposes. So the Prince is using Damon to bring Sarah to him. I went to see Prince Leone today so that I might disrupt their meeting, and Damon and Sarah left before the Prince could speak to them further."

Luke studied Christoph suspiciously. The leathery scars pocked his beard and disfigured his forehead, but his eyes appeared clear and truthful. His cream-colored tunic, faded breeches, and worn boots added to his seemingly genuine character. *But can I trust him? Why should I? Most people would deem him a liar and a fool.*

"What is it, Luke?" Christoph asked. "Do you doubt my words?"

Yes. Luke searched for a somewhat honest answer. "No, not entirely. But how do you...forgive me, but who are you that you know all these things?"

Christoph folded his maimed hands together and laid them gently on the table. He looked Luke in the eye. "I am Christoph the Scarred. I serve King Omnideus of Rovenia. I fight the fires of this world and battle against Prince Leone, my enemy. You know who I am. Every word I've spoken is the truth, but you must decide whether you believe me."

Luke listened but shook his head. "I believe you, Christoph, but I cannot condone your disloyal conduct. If you wish to live in Rovenia and serve King Omnideus, then so be it. But do not force your ideals upon me. I choose to live in Terra Caligines. Yet even so, I don't serve Prince Leone. I serve myself and do what is best for me."

"And in so doing, you ultimately serve Prince Leone."

"What? No, I—"

Christoph held up his hand. "May I ask you something, Luke?"

He means to persuade me. Luke nodded. "Go on."

"How did you get that mark?"

Luke felt his chest tighten. "What mark?"

"The one on your shoulder."

"My cross tattoo?" Luke calmed a little but still kept his guard. He shrugged. "I was rebellious and defiant as a young man. One day, a man in the village offered to tattoo my arm, and I chose the cross symbol because I knew it would displease my parents. I made a mockery of their Rovenian beliefs by getting that mark on my arm. Why do you ask?"

"You see, Luke," Christoph said, "your tattoo is a symbol of your desire to be apart of this world—to fit in, to do what you will. Prince Leone applauds that kind of attitude. But far worse is the mark upon your heart, a mark which destines you to an eternity of hellish torment."

You're mine. Forever.

A demonic lion with two red eyes flashed within his memory, but Luke ignored the disturbing image and glared at Christoph instead.

"There is no such mark upon my heart," he said lowly. He could feel his anger surging.

Christoph shook his head sternly. "No, Luke. You yourself know that is a lie. I see your mark, even now. It burns within your heart, aching with a soreness too painful to bear, though day after day you try. Each person in Terra Caligines carries that mark, that wound, and the only way to be rid of it is to journey to Rovenia, where King Omnideus will heal you. Only he can remove the mark and take away your pain."

How dare he. How dare he condemn me! He has no right! Luke clenched his fist and thrust his forefinger toward Christoph. "You are covered in marks! Perhaps blemished from head to toe! I ask you then, how can you be so quick to judge?"

"My marks are not the consequence of a sinful nature," Christoph said calmly, "and therein lies the difference. Many years ago, someone I loved was trapped within the flames of a raging fire. He cried out for my help, and I ran into the flames to save him, willing to give up my life for him. I saved his life from the fire, but the flames had already left their mark upon me—upon my feet, my hands, and my face. And so, it is because of love that I am scarred, for love that I was wounded."

Luke was overcome with shame. *I've scorned the man who saved my very life. What an arrogant fool I am!* He could not bring himself to look at Christoph, and so stared at the table. "I fear...that is, I've done you a great injustice, Christoph. I will leave you to your supper."

"No, Luke. Please stay." Christoph held out his hands beseechingly as Luke rose from his chair. "I wish to speak with you still. Please, sit."

"What?" Luke stopped. "I don't understand. I've insulted—"

"There is one more thing I wish to speak to you about." Christoph smiled and beckoned toward Luke's chair. "Come now. Sit."

Luke sat down as he was bid. *Who is this man?* He watched silently as Christoph took a drink and set the tankard firmly on the table. After a moment, Christoph looked up at him.

"Luke," Christoph said, "why did you ask for water instead of ale?"

I see where this may lead. Luke shrugged. "I wanted water instead of ale. What of it?"

"Is that the only reason?"

It's as if he can read my thoughts. Luke snorted and shook his head lightly. "I suppose I didn't wish to offend you."

"Why did you think I'd be offended?"

"Because you seem...different," Luke said. He looked at the table for a moment. "And I want to be different...to change from who I was last night. I've had my fill of ale over the years. Time for some water."

"Aye, very good. And have you thought about what I asked you yesterday?"

What do you believe, Luke? The question shot to the forefront of his mind. Luke slowly nodded. "Yes...all morning. But I'm no closer to the answer than I was last night." He looked up at Christoph. "I know I want something more, but I don't know what that something is. Can you understand how that feels?"

"Aye, I do understand," Christoph said solemnly. "To merely exist from day to day and to struggle without any purpose or direction is hopeless. That is not what you were meant to do."

"What am I supposed to do then?" Luke asked, genuinely searching for an answer. "How do I decide what to believe? And how to live? I need a reason to keep going, and right now I don't have one."

"You are asking the right questions, Luke." Christoph abruptly rose from his chair. "I know of a place which will answer those questions, if you're willing to listen and follow me. Tomorrow morning, would you come with me to—"

"Church?" Luke made a face. "Is that what you were going to say?"

"Aye," Christoph laughed, "it was. Is the word so repulsive to you?"

"No, but my mother and father...." *Tried to make me go.* Luke exhaled. "I don't enjoy being preached at for hours on end."

"This man won't preach at you," Christoph said. "He will give you the truth—the truth you are so desperately seeking. And the service lasts for only an hour, so your torture will be brief." He smiled. "Will you come with me?"

No. I won't. He's trying to pull me in, just as Eddie warned. But then...what if he's telling the truth? Could it hurt to find out? Luke rose from his chair. "Yes. I'll come. But only this one time. Because of what you did for me."

"Aye." Christoph clasped Luke's hand in his own and shook it gladly. "I'll meet you in the village square in the morning, and we can walk to the church together."

I hope I don't regret this. Luke gripped the scarred hand and nodded once. "Alright. Tomorrow then."

"Aye."

The two men separated and walked beside the log tables to the front of the tavern. They were almost to the door when Luke stopped suddenly.

Christoph paused in the doorway. "Luke?"

"I'm afraid I haven't been...what I mean is...." Luke glanced at the floor and tightened his hands into fists. *Why is it so hard to say?* He looked up at Christoph. "Thank you. I wish to thank you. For all."

Christoph looked him in the eye and bowed his head, then turned and walked out the door.

Instead of following him and leaving the tavern, Luke took a deep breath. He moved from the door and approached the wooden counter.

"Sarah?"

The young woman in the red tunic and black tights smiled when she first looked up, but her kind expression vanished as soon as she saw him.

"Aye?" Sarah asked. "What do you need?"

Luke swallowed. "Forgive me, I believe I've...rather, I know I've—"

Sarah crossed her arms.

Run fool, run! Luke lowered his gaze to the floor. "My manner toward you yesterday was cruel and unwarranted. I am truly sorry and beg your forgiveness."

She made no reply.

Luke could not bring himself to look at her. He hurried to the door, clumsily bumping into the doorframe as he rushed outside, and fled the tavern.

CHAPTER 12

This Sunday morning was a sleepy one, and the view outside her living room window made her feel the morning's weariness.

Gray, overcast skies draped the trees in a dreary haze, and the roofs of the houses across the street were dark with slick wetness. Murky puddles rippled steadily in the street, while a few confused security lights glowed in the unusual dimness. The leaves on the trees drooped and dripped, and the birds' usually chipper morning song was silent and still.

Nature itself did not want to move on this rainy Sunday morning, and neither did Sarah.

She'd successfully wandered to her couch, where she'd been lying for the past hour, but the short jaunt had exhausted what little energy she'd woken up with. Last night had been a long night, much like the night before, but it was halfway over by the time she'd gotten home from work and collapsed into bed.

Everything that could have gone wrong at work *did* go wrong. Two of her workers did not show up, so she'd run her shift shorthanded. A little while later, the electricity had flickered just enough to shut down the cash registers, so she was forced to reboot the entire computer system in the middle of her dinner rush. Chaos had ensued and customers had been infuriated by the delay. Finally, after she'd regained some control of her shift, the dishwasher had broken. And despite her repeated tweaks and kicks, she'd been unable to fix it, so she'd instructed Jenny to wash all of the dishes by hand. Already an hour behind, she'd finished her paperwork for the night, helped Jenny with the dishes, and left the restaurant after one in the morning.

The last time she'd seen her alarm clock before exhaustion closed her eyes, the green numbers had read 1:54 AM. So when her eyes had opened and the glaring digits had glowed 7:08 AM, she'd whipped the covers over her head and rolled onto her side.

She'd had no idea why she'd woken up so early. She had no plans this morning and no reason to get up before noon, and she'd been looking forward to sleeping in on her day off. Since she'd gone to bed in the morning, she'd had no intention of getting up in the morning. But the sleep she'd longed for would not return, and she'd tossed back over and tugged the sheet beneath her chin.

The clock had greeted her with 7:21 AM.

She'd groaned and squeezed her eyes shut, snuggling roughly into her pillow. She'd tried to get comfortable, tried to relax, tried to slow her breathing. Nothing had worked. All the while, one persistent thought would not let her rest, and she'd repeatedly done the math in her head.

Five hours. Five hours of sleep and I'm wide awake.

Several minutes of irritated tossing and turning had followed, but Sarah could not find sleep anywhere in her tousled bed. The sheets had tangled uncomfortably around her legs, and the pillow had bunched at the wrong angle beneath her neck. Flicking her eyes open and flopping onto her back, she'd stared at the ceiling and exhaled her displeasure. Then she'd turned her head slowly towards the clock.

7:59 AM.

"It figures!" she'd yelled, throwing the covers from her body. "The one day...the *one day* I get to sleep in," she'd swung her feet over the side of the bed, "is the one day I *can't* sleep!"

She'd stomped from her bedroom into the bathroom, ranting and muttering the entire way. She'd complained to the toilet about her night at work, and she'd mumbled something about a stupid dishwasher to the mirror when she'd brushed her teeth. The stairway had gotten to hear just how much she hated her job, and the blinds in her living room window had felt her fury when she'd twirled the wand to open them and jerked the cords to pull them up. After she'd thrust the window upward, the couch had felt the exclamation point at the end of her tirade when she'd plopped angrily onto its cushions and crossed her arms.

"And that's that!" she'd said to her TV.

The TV had not replied.

She'd reached for the remote on her coffee table and thumped the red power button with her thumb. She'd pressed another button. She'd hit it again. And again. And again.

An hour of channel surfing later, Sarah remained in the same drowsy position on the couch, lazily watching the rain pour outside. A cool yet humid breeze drifted through the window and flowed over her skin, while the TV cried out the dialogue of a lover's quarrel. She heard the passionate conversation but gazed distractedly out the window.

"How could you do this to me?" a woman cried.

"Me!" a man shouted. "I did nothing to you! *You're* the one who left."

She whimpered. "You don't love me, do you?"

"Love?" He snorted. "You wouldn't know love if it bit you in the—"

Sarah rolled her eyes and glanced at the TV. The woman smacked the man across the cheek, and the man dove in for a kiss.

"Of course he would," she said bitterly. She reached for the remote and changed the channel.

A well-dressed salesman crammed as many vegetables as he could into a glass pitcher and demonstrated how to use his new and improved Blasto Blender.

There is nothing on. At all.

Sarah groaned and propped herself up with a pillow against the arm of the couch. She yawned and pulled her legs beneath her, while the upbeat salesman continued to pitch his dynamite product. Tapping the remote impatiently against her thigh, she debated what channel she should try next.

Or I could text Damon, I guess.

Damon. The name cut into her thoughts like a jagged shard of glass, painfully reminding her that her Sunday evening would be spent by his side. The only reason she wanted to text him was to tell him she was sick. Then she could stay home and would never have to see him again.

The clever ruse was a lie, yes. But in a way, if she considered the deception from a slightly different perspective, she honestly was sick.

Sick of Damon.

At some point yesterday, Sarah had realized that she'd made a mistake. The awareness of her blunder had not set in all at once, and she could not be certain when she'd first known. But now, as she sat on her couch and considered everything that had happened, there was no doubt in her mind.

Damon Jefferies is a mistake.

What a fool she'd been to fall for his charms and good looks. Yes, Damon was handsome. Any girl could see that and would not blame her for finding him attractive. His sky blue eyes, his alluring smile, his athletic build, his clean-cut appearance—everything about him reeked of wonderful and perfect. Even the mere sound of his voice evoked a feeling of trust in anyone who listened to him speak. It was as if

Damon possessed the power to enchant any female, whether she was stubbornly resilient or hopelessly vulnerable, and do with her as he pleased.

And although she would never be able to prove it, Sarah knew in her heart that Damon had drugged her. Her Friday night with him had been nothing more than a classic example of date rape. He'd taken her to a bar, where he'd suggested she order alcohol and repeatedly encouraged her to drink more. She'd started to feel a slight buzz about halfway through her margarita, but it was not until *after* she'd come back from the bathroom that the room had started to spin. At the time, she'd thought nothing of it. But now, in hindsight, she could not believe she'd been so stupid as to leave her drink with him.

"Can you watch my drink for me?" she'd asked him.

"Sure, no prob," he'd said. He'd pulled the drink closer to himself.

She'd come back from the bathroom and taken a few sips. *"Mmm, it tastes even better than before...like sweeter or something."*

"Must be 'cause it's melting," he'd replied casually. *"The alcohol gets watered down and you can taste the fruity flavoring better."*

All the signs of her perilous situation were shamefully obvious now. Not only had Damon slipped something in her drink when she'd gone to the bathroom, but he'd also sat back and watched her consume the poisoned beverage. Once she'd imbibed the tainted slushy, it had been too late. No longer able to stand or walk or defend herself, she'd been at the mercy of his carnal desires.

So the fact that Damon did not consummate his depraved plan mystified Sarah completely. He'd had her right where he wanted her—on his bed, defenseless. Why had he not gone through with it? What had stopped him? There'd been no one there to help her, no one there to prevent him from hurting her. But yet, he had not touched her. Why?

She'd asked herself the question over and over again, but no answer would come to her. *Why* Damon had not raped her, *why* she'd arrived home physically unharmed, *why* she'd been protected—nothing made sense to her.

He meant to assault me. I should have been raped. That much I do know. Someone must have been looking out for me. But who? An angel?

"An angel." Sarah laughed aloud at the thought. "Right."

Damon himself was certainly no angel. He may have been good-looking, charming, and sweet, but there were times when he was ugly, obnoxious, and cruel. Perhaps even threatening. And as if drugging her had not been enough, he'd also lied to her, ordered her around, belittled her, and flat out treated her like dirt. But all of those offensive actions were not the worst part.

The worst part of all was that she'd let him do it.

It's your fault. Your fault for trusting him. Your fault for allowing him to take advantage of you. Your fault for putting yourself in the position to get hurt.

Your. Fault.

Sarah pursed her lips and glanced out the window, trying to hold back the emotion that suddenly welled in her eyes. It was not her fault, no. But then...yes. Yes, it was.

She had flirted with Damon when she'd given him a large fry instead of a medium. *She* had jumped at the chance to go out with him and agreed to go to a bar. *She* had ordered a margarita. *She* had been dumb enough to leave her drink with him. *She* had drunk the margarita, even when she'd known she should have slowed down. *She* had hung out with him yesterday, despite her suspicion that he'd drugged her. *She* had let him drive her around town all afternoon. And *she* had agreed to go out with him one more time, in spite of everything.

Your. Fault.

A single tear escaped over her eyelid and slid down her cheek, but Sarah quickly brushed the wet stream away. *I'm not going to cry, and I'm not going to text Damon either.* She'd told him that she would go tonight, and that was exactly what she would do. *One more time and never again.* Whether she would actually tell him it was over or just stop communicating with him after tonight, she had not decided yet. But one way or another, Damon would know that it was indeed over.

Sarah exhaled sullenly. The Summer's End Festival had always been a fun-filled event that she looked forward to every year. Carnival rides, fair food, games, crowds, laughter—it all took place on the last weekend of summer, right before autumn officially began. This year, Sunday was the only day that she could go because of her work schedule, and Damon was the only person who had asked her to go.

But Luke and that Chris guy will be there too, so maybe it won't be that bad. And I won't ever really be alone with Damon, except on the ride there and back. That made her feel better. *But I don't even know Luke or Chris. So I'm basically hanging out with two guys I don't know and one guy I wished I didn't know.*

She groaned and rubbed her forehead. "Stop thinking about it, Sarah!"

She was stressed. Her mind always ran away with her when she was stressed. *But I'm right.* She shook her head lightly. *I don't know Luke or Chris, and what little I know about Damon is more than enough.*

But Luke and Chris and Damon all seemed to know each other. What a strange coincidence that' all three of them could be linked together, and in such random ways as well.

Luke and Damon had worked with each other at a construction job, Chris and Damon currently worked for rival companies, and Luke and Chris were connected somehow as well, though she did not yet know the story behind their friendship. And oddly enough, she'd met all three men within the past two days.

"Weird," Sarah said to herself. *We all know each other, but we all don't really know each other.*

Out of all three men, Chris Scarlett was the one she knew the least about, but the one she felt she could trust the most. She'd seen him twice yesterday, the first time in Mr. Morten's office and the second time in the lobby of Leon's Grille. During both brief instances, Chris had conducted himself in a polite, humble, and respectful manner. His appearance had been plain and unassuming, and the scabrous scarring upon his face and hands had been his most striking feature. But a quiet strength had shined within his eyes, and a rare genuineness had emanated from him.

"You too, Sarah." They were the only three words Chris had spoken to her, but she would never forget the way he'd said them. She'd told him to *have a good day*, a polite phrase she'd forced herself to recite to every customer whether she'd meant it or not. Yesterday's recitation had been no different, as she'd simply rambled the words out of habit, but Chris had responded with those three trivial words: *you too, Sarah.*

The words had been more than just words, more than just a kind response to a cordial sendoff. Most customers typically ignored her courteous farewell or usually just recited some short salutation back to her. But his voice had been tender, and his eyes had looked into hers. He'd truly wanted her to have a good day, though she could not figure out why since she'd never met him before. Chris had *meant* what he'd said, and Sarah had believed him.

Luke Porter, though, had tripped over every word he'd attempted to say to her. He'd barely been able to look her in the eye, and when he had managed to meet her gaze, she'd been certain she'd seen the faintest tinge of pink flush his cheeks. As tall, strong, and rugged as he was, Luke had been intimidated by her.

And the way he ran into the door after he said he was sorry....

Sarah smiled as she remembered the scene. He'd seemed so shy, so scared, so nervous when he'd stepped up to the front counter and tried to get her attention. She'd been annoyed at first when she'd recognized him, but rightfully so. *He* was the one who had been condescending and obnoxious to her just a day earlier, and she was not about to hide her indignation and pretend she'd forgotten. After the way he'd spoken to her, he'd deserved to see and feel her scorn.

So when Luke had looked away from her uncomfortably, Sarah had been floored by the unexpected apology which had tumbled from his lips.

He'd dashed out the door then before she'd had a chance to recover or think of something to say. All she'd been able to do was grin when he'd run into the doorframe and bumbled outside like a little boy escaping the gaze of his secret valentine.

Poor guy. Maybe I shouldn't have been so hard on him.

Sarah smiled and gazed out the window. *He's not that bad-looking, actually.* And she *did* notice him the first time she saw him, just before he'd been rude to her. She'd noticed his scruffy complexion and sad eyes, his broad shoulders and thick arms, and his long legs and rough hands. She'd noticed everything about him, even more than she'd noticed Damon, but Luke was not at all her type. *He's a bad boy. I can tell by just looking at him. Damon is more clean-cut.*

But Luke had done something that Sarah knew Damon would never do. Luke had apologized to her. And he'd meant it.

Well, he still needs a haircut. Either way.

She could picture him, even now as she watched the rain fall outside her window. His hair was pulled back into a ponytail, his face was mostly clean-shaven, and the thin beard upon his jawline made him look quite gallant, especially when he wore that black and blue plaid shirt and those jeans with the black belt and those boots—

"Ooh, stop it!" She looked away from the window when she felt the blush warming her cheeks. "Damon, Chris, Luke—they're all men and men are all—"

The TV remote slipped from her hand and fell to the floor. The salesman and his blender instantly vanished from the TV screen.

"—the way, the truth, and the life, my dear brothers in Christ!" the man in the suit proclaimed from the TV. "And notice if you will, that

Jesus does not say, 'I am *a* way, *a* truth, and *a* life.' No! In the book of John, Jesus tells us that He is *the* way, *the* truth, and *the* life. It is only through Him that you can receive eternal life and be saved from your sin. Only Christ can cleanse your blemished heart and give your life meaning and hope. He knows you better than you know yourself because he created you, and he has a plan for your life...."

Sarah picked up the remote but listened for a moment, her finger hovering over the channel button. *I know that verse.* It had been one of Mrs. Thompson's favorites when she'd attended the Sunday School class at that church so many years ago. *What was the rest of it? Something like no one comes to the Father except through me?*

"—tells us about that plan in His Word," the pastor continued. "Please turn in your Bibles to Jeremiah twenty-nine and follow along with me as I read verses eleven through thirteen. This text is a portion of a letter written by Jeremiah and sent to the Israelites, who had been taken to Babylon as captives. What the Lord promises to the Israelites during their captivity can be applied in our lives today.

"Please read with me: *'For I know the plans I have for you,' declares the Lord, 'plans to prosper you and not to harm you, plans to give you hope and a future. Then you will call upon me and come and pray to me, and I will listen to you. You will seek me and find me when you seek me with all your heart.'*

"Today, I leave you with this verse, my friends, and challenge you to seek the Lord with all your heart. For when you do, the Lord promises that you will find Him, and He promises that He will listen when you pray to Him. And remember, not one of all the Lord's good promises to the house of Israel failed; each one was fulfilled. Please pray with me. Heavenly Father...."

Sarah watched as the pastor closed his eyes and bowed his head, while the camera panned over the auditorium and showed the congregation doing the same. When the pastor finished praying, the screen faded to black and a colorful commercial suddenly lit up the TV.

She glanced at the clock on her DVD player. The green numbers read 9:59 AM, exactly two hours later from the time she'd first stomped out of bed. She still needed to shower, get dressed, find something to eat, and run some errands all before Damon came at seven to pick her up.

And I don't even want to go.

Sarah pressed the power button on the remote and silently watched the TV screen go blank. Laying the remote on the coffee table, she forced herself from the couch and trudged upstairs to her room, where she grabbed a set of clothes to wear for the day. She walked into the bathroom and quietly closed the door.

Damon Jefferies. Chris Scarlett. Luke Porter. And me. She sighed as she stripped out of her pajamas. *Why in the world did I agree to hang out with three men I don't know?*

She turned the knob in the shower and waved her hand through the ensuing stream of water. When the water was hot enough, she hopped in.

As the soothing warmth washed over her body, a familiar ache tugged within her heart.

I know the plans I have for you...plans to give you hope and a future.

She suddenly remembered that Mrs. Thompson had liked that verse too.

What a coincidence.

CHAPTER 13

The small brick church stood assuredly along the quiet street and welcomed all visitors with its two great white doors. Since the rain had stopped and the overcast sky had begun to clear, both doors were open.

After a little hesitation upon the threshold, Luke strode beneath the archway and followed Chris into the sanctuary, where they scooted into the third pew from the back of the room.

It's a good thing he didn't decide to go all the way up front. Luke sat down at the end of the pew, right next to the center aisle, and laid his elbow on the wooden armrest. He leaned forward then sat back. He crossed his legs and uncrossed them. *Why did I agree to this?* He drummed his heels on the carpet and looked around the room.

The church was not extravagant or fancy, but it was not colorless or archaic either. Ten rows of wooden beams soared overhead and supported the lofty cathedral ceiling, and each beam descended from the ceiling's peak to the sanctuary's white walls. Luke counted five elongated, frosted windows evenly spaced along both sides of the room.

The sanctuary was carpeted in maroon and divided into fourths by two intersecting aisles. Twelve pews lined the front quadrants, while eight pews lined the back quadrants. *Forty pews. Not too big, not too small.* A wooden pulpit stood upon the stage at the front of the sanctuary, and an old upright piano hid in a small niche to the left of the stage.

Luke stopped drumming his heels and craned his neck. A little, white-haired lady wearing a plain blue dress shuffled along the wall to the stage and hobbled up three steps to the piano. She laid a book on the piano's music rack and fanned through the pages.

"That's Denise," Chris said lowly. He leaned into Luke's shoulder. "She's been the pianist here for over fifty years."

"Wow," Luke blurted. "Dang."

Chris chuckled. "This church was actually built in 1814. It's been repainted and remodeled in places, but the original building is two hundred years old. I saw you lookin' around, so I figured I'd tell you."

"Holy—I mean, wow," Luke said. "That's old."

"Yup," Chris said. "Sure is."

Luke smiled nervously and cleared his throat. *I've got to watch what I say!* He'd already let two other words slip on their walk to the church. *I can't cuss now that I'm actually here.* In his mind, for whatever reason, churches seemed to demand respect and veneration from all who dared to step inside, as if the building itself had eyes and ears to judge and assess.

No wonder this pew is so uncomfortable. He squirmed again.

He'd even attempted to dress up, though his best outfit was the one he'd worn yesterday when he'd eaten dinner with Chris. But he'd decided that the black and blue plaid shirt would have to do, considering all of his other shirts were either dirty or inappropriate for a church setting.

"Relax Luke," Chris said quietly. "It's just a building. The true church is more than wood, bricks, and paint. And Jesus doesn't look at the brand name on your pants. He looks at your heart."

Luke made a face and glanced at Chris. "How'd you know I was thinkin' about—"

Majestic piano music suddenly filled the room. Luke jumped as the unexpected song struck his ears, and he bumped a hymnal from the pew rack with his knee. The hymnal fell to the floor and landed in the shape of a tent, its pages spread and crinkled.

Chris bent forward and picked it up. "That's what happens when Denise starts playin' her music." He slid the hymnal back into the rack. "Even the hymnals can't sit still."

"Sorry," Luke whispered.

Chris just grinned and shook his head. He looked towards the stage then, while the piano's harmonious chords continued to ring throughout the sanctuary.

Luke watched him bob his head in time with the marching beat of the song. He even stretched his legs and crossed them at the ankles, while he folded his hands and laid them in his lap. He smiled too.

Luke tilted his head in surprise. *He actually likes this kind of music?*

The yellow work boots, worn blue jeans, and dark green flannel shirt that Chris was wearing had caused Luke to assume incorrectly. *I thought for sure he'd like country music. But classical music? Isn't this stuff older than classical music?* Even the white T-shirt peeking out beneath the unbuttoned collar of Chris's shirt had suggested that he was a country boy.

But the scarred man kept smiling and listening and hummed right along. Luke could not believe it.

The final measures of the chorus signaled the musical finale, and Denise held the keys in place for one momentous note and lifted her hands at once. The enduring tone ceased and a reverent stillness filled the room.

Luke raised his hands to clap, but he clumsily crossed his arms instead when he realized that nobody else was clapping. He watched Denise as she turned the pages in the hymnal. As if on cue, a young man rose from a pew up front and walked to the stage.

The young man wore a white dress shirt and black slacks. Luke noticed a familiar book in the man's hand as the man stepped behind the pulpit.

"My! I don't think I've ever heard 'Onward Christian Soldiers' played so spiritedly! Denise, you make me want to march off into battle right now," the man said. He rifled through his hymnal's pages. "Oh, and for those of you that don't know me, my name's Samuel. Rick isn't feeling well, so I'll be your music leader for the day.

"Let's start off this morning with hymn number one thirty-six. Please stand with me and let's sing with our hearts this morning! Denise, if you could give us the introduction...hymn number one thirty-six!"

The entire congregation rose and took their hymnals from the pew racks as Denise played the first few chords of the song. Luke followed Chris's lead and pulled a hymnal from the rack. He flipped through the pages until he saw the bolded number 136.

On Denise's musical signal, Samuel and the congregation began to sing, their voices blending into one melodic language.

Luke squinted and raised the hymnal closer to his face. He moved his lips occasionally, but no sound escaped his mouth. He listened to Chris sing. *He's actually pretty good. Not bad at all.* He watched Chris for a moment, but he never saw him look at his hymnal. *He's even got it memorized. Maybe there's more to him than I thought.*

The next thirty minutes of the church service went by faster than Luke had anticipated, and he was startled by how much he enjoyed those minutes.

The next two hymns started to grow on him, and the special music by a young boy playing his guitar impressed Luke because he himself had always wanted to play the guitar but never did. After an older man read some scripture from the Bible, the offering plates were passed around, and Luke tossed in a couple of dimes and a quarter, since that was all the change he had in his pocket. Another man then stepped up to the pulpit and led the congregation in prayer. Luke bowed his head but left his eyes open as he listened to the man's words.

"—and speak through Pastor Matthias today, dear Lord, and use his words to draw us closer to you. If anyone seated here this morning does not know you as his Lord and Savior, I pray that you would work in his heart and bring him to you. Help him to listen to your voice. Help us all to listen to your voice and to seek you with all our hearts. In your precious name, amen."

Luke raised his head as the man stepped down from the pulpit, and a different man came forward.

This new man was stout and of an average height, and he wore a gray suit which hugged his rounded belly. His black hair and beard were both streaked with gray, and he wore a pair of wire-rimmed glasses. With the leather-bound book tucked beneath his arm, the man very much looked like a professor.

Pastor Matthias, I bet. Luke remembered that the other man had prayed for him just a moment earlier. *Yup. Sure looks like a Matthias.* He watched him lay the book on the pulpit and smile over the audience. *And he definitely looks like a pastor too.*

"Good morning," Pastor Matthias cheerfully greeted the congregation. Several murmured *good mornings* hailed from the people as the pastor opened his Bible. "What a beautiful day it's turned out to be. I thought it was going to rain all day by the way it looked out there earlier. Well, it's the last Sunday of summer already, can you believe it? But I have a feeling it's going to be a great day, so let's get started. Our study will begin with the last book of the Bible. If you would, turn in your Bibles with me to Revelation 12:12."

The crinkling of a hundred pages being turned at the same time echoed throughout the sanctuary. Chris reached for his Bible and flipped through its pages, while Luke watched and waited for the pastor to continue.

"Here," Chris said lowly. He held his Bible so Luke could see it. "We can share."

"Oh. Thanks." Luke took the left half of the book in his hand, while Chris kept hold of the right, and searched the pages for verse 12.

"Okay, Revelation 12:12...is everyone there?" Pastor Matthias asked. "I don't hear anymore pages turning, so you all must be waiting on me. Now, be sure to pay close attention to the last part of this verse. See if you can pick up on something. Something which I think is very important.

"Revelation 12:12 says: *Therefore rejoice, you heavens and you who dwell in them! But woe to the earth and the sea, because the devil has gone down to you! He is filled with fury, because he knows that his time is short.*

"He is filled with fury, because he knows that his time is short," Pastor Matthias said steadily. "I would like us to focus on this sentence for a moment. Several things about this verse stand out to me, but one word in particular grabs my attention: *fury*. The devil is filled with fury. Notice that the Bible doesn't say the devil is mad or upset or annoyed. No, rather he is filled—and not just halfway or somewhat or kind of—but *filled* with *fury*.

"Does anyone know what the definition of fury is? According to my dictionary at home, the word *fury* is defined as wild or violent anger. Think about that for a moment. Have you ever seen wild anger? How about violent anger? Can you picture it? A feeling of rage so vicious and fierce that it consumes the person exhibiting it—*that* is the kind of fury the devil is filled with.

"So why? Why is the devil so infuriated? The answer is given in the latter part of the verse. He is infuriated because he knows that his time is short. He knows all too well what will happen to him at the end, and he knows his end draws near. Turn with me just a few pages over to Revelation 20:1."

Chris pinched the Bible's pages between his thumb and forefinger and turned them towards Luke. Luke looked down at the enlarged number 20 and read silently.

"Chapter twenty in Revelation is about the Millennium," Pastor Matthias said, "which takes place after the Rapture and the Tribulation. I will be reading verses one through three.

"And I saw an angel coming down out of heaven, having the key to the Abyss and holding in his hand a great chain. He seized the dragon, that ancient serpent, who is the devil, or Satan, and bound him for a thousand years. He threw him into the Abyss, and locked and sealed it over him, to keep him from deceiving the nations anymore until the thousand years were ended. After that, he must be set free for a short time.

"Well, that's not so bad, is it?" Pastor Matthias asked. "Yes, Satan is thrown into the Abyss, but he is released after a thousand years. Now keep in mind, Luke tells us that the Abyss is a place so terrible that the demons beg not to be sent there. So, Satan's thousand-year sentence will not be a pleasant experience. But after that time, he is released. So why should he be so enraged? After all, he will be set free." He paused and held up his finger. "But, *only* for a short time. Let's look a little further.

"Verse ten of chapter twenty reveals Satan's ultimate doom. This verse reads: *And the devil, who deceived them, was thrown into the lake of burning sulfur, where the beast and the false prophet had been thrown. They will be tormented day and night for ever and ever.*

"Ah, now we learn why Satan is so infuriated! He is doomed, doomed for all eternity to be tormented day and night. The word *torment* means extreme mental or physical pain and is synonymous with such words as *anguish, misery, suffering, harassment,* and *torture.* Satan will experience all of these things—and probably much worse than our limited vocabulary can describe—forever and ever. Not for a thousand years, not for a hundred thousand years, not even for a million years...but *forever.* There will be no end to Satan's torment.

"So in the meantime, what does Satan do?" Pastor Matthias asked. "He knows his fate cannot be changed, and he knows that no matter what he does, he will end up in the same place. He is doomed—condemned and sentenced by the Great Judge himself, God the Father. So what does Satan do? How does he react to this knowledge? Please turn a few pages back to 1 Peter 5:8."

Chris moved the Bible to his lap and flipped several pages back to a new book. He held the Bible between himself and Luke and laid his finger on the little 8 beneath the big 5. Luke nodded and scanned the print.

"Be self-controlled and alert," Pastor Matthias read aloud. *"Your enemy the devil prowls around like a roaring lion looking for someone to devour."*

Luke narrowed his eyes and read the verse again. Something about the words struck him.

"This, my brothers and sisters in Christ," Pastor Matthias said, "is what the devil does while he waits to be cast into the lake of fire. He stalks his prey restlessly, searching and seeking for someone to devour, to destroy. To bring down with him. That is his ultimate goal.

"Driven by his raging fury, he will take as many people with him into the lake of fire as he possibly can. Imagine what vengeful, sadistic motivation drives him. His sole mission is to make you trip, cause you to stumble, lead you astray, and ultimately separate you from God forever. He wants you to suffer just as he will suffer. Satan hates Christ and all who follow Him, and so the devil and his demons—his soldiers, if you will—will do all they can to keep you from giving your life to Christ and living for Him.

"In 2 Corinthians 11:14, Paul tells us about this ongoing, deceitful plot by Satan and his demons. Listen closely as I read verses fourteen and fifteen: *And no wonder, for Satan himself masquerades as an angel of light. It is not surprising, then, if his servants masquerade as servants of righteousness. Their end will be what their actions deserve.*

"These verses state very clearly that Satan and his demons—his servants, his soldiers—disguise themselves with goodness in order to deceive the world. Satan's demons are always working against you whether you know it or not. You may not be able to see them, but they are there, scheming and plotting behind the scenes...using people and worldly things to lead you away from Christ. This constant conflict between God and Satan is also described in detail in the Bible. Turn in your Bibles to Ephesians 6:12."

Chris fanned through the Bible until he found Ephesians, and Luke watched as Chris skipped through two or three pages to chapter six. Luke leaned forward attentively.

"For our struggle," Pastor Matthias said firmly, *"is not against flesh and blood, but against the rulers, against the authorities, against the powers of this dark world and against the spiritual forces of evil in the heavenly realms.*

"Beyond the physical and earthly aspects of this world, an unseen realm exists and directly influences our lives. This spiritual world is a very real place, although you and I cannot see it with our own eyes. Satan and his demons are there, striving to prevent men and women from coming to Christ and also doing their best to trip the believers who have already found Christ. But God our Heavenly Father is there too, and He is the one in control, not the devil. Christ and His angels—His soldiers—fight Satan's forces and protect all who belong to Him.

"If you belong to God's army, if you are one of His children, then the devil can do nothing to harm you. Satan and his forces have no power or authority in your life. However, the devil will do his best to make you stumble in your walk with God. Satan will tempt you, trip you, play on your weaknesses, and do everything he can to hinder you from living your life for Christ.

"But the Lord does not leave us to fend for ourselves. Not only does He promise us that He will be with us through everything, but

He also gives us instructions for how to defend ourselves against Satan and his demons. If you look at the very next verse after Ephesians 6:12—verse thirteen—you will see these instructions."

Luke looked down and found the little number 13. *Therefore put on the full armor of God....*

"*Therefore*," Pastor Matthias said, "*put on the full armor of God, so that when the day of evil comes, you may be able to stand your ground, and after you have done everything, to stand. Stand firm then, with the belt of truth buckled around your waist, with the breastplate of righteousness in place, and with your feet fitted with the readiness that comes from the gospel of peace. In addition to all this, take up the shield of faith, with which you can extinguish all the flaming arrows of the evil one. Take the helmet of salvation and the sword of the Spirit, which is the word of God. And pray in the Spirit on all occasions with all kinds of prayers and requests. With this in mind, be alert and always keep on praying for all the saints.*"

Pastor Matthias stepped around the pulpit, bringing his Bible with him. "Every person who believes in Jesus Christ as their personal Savior is equipped with this armor and can use it to defend themselves against the devil's attacks. Truth, righteousness, the gospel of peace, faith, salvation, the Bible, prayer—all of these things are a believer's tools to stand firm in Jesus Christ and weapons to ward off Satan's temptations."

Walking back to the pulpit, Pastor Matthias closed his Bible and quietly laid it on the pulpit. Luke bent forward, resting his elbows on his knees, and clasped his hands in front him. He watched the pastor expectantly.

What about me? What am I supposed to do? What if I don't know Christ? You haven't answered my questions! If what you're saying is true, then how do I—

"For those who do not know Christ, the Bible also has a message for you," Pastor Matthias said. "If you have not given your life to

Christ and have not accepted Him as your personal Savior, your soul is in great peril. Heaven and Hell are very real places, just as the spiritual world we've been discussing today is quite real. Life does not simply end when you die. Your soul lives on for eternity, and every person who dies without believing in Jesus Christ will be banished to Hell, where they will wait to be cast into the Lake of Fire with Satan and his demons.

"But the Lord does not want anyone to perish, as Peter tells us in the New Testament. Rather, Christ wants everyone to come to repentance. He wants you to believe in Him because He loves you, because He created you. And so, God made a way for us to come to Him, a way for us to be saved."

Luke felt the burning ache within his heart and yearned to know more. He clasped his hands more tightly. All his thoughts, all his senses, all his feelings—his entire world—hinged on one question.

What must I do to be saved?

"There is only one way to salvation," Pastor Matthias said, "and only one hope for this world. That hope, our salvation, is Jesus Christ. He is the only way, the only truth, and the only life. No man comes to the Father except through Christ.

"Satan will do his best to keep you from Christ and will use whatever means necessary to distract you from the truth. As the prince of this world, the devil is an expert in the world's vices and depravities. Alcohol, drugs, sexual immorality—these are just a few of the world's pleasures which ultimately lead to death and destruction, but Satan wants you to partake of them. He wants you to enjoy these things and thrive in your sin, to drown your emptiness with alcohol and numb your pain with drugs. He wants your life to be filled with overwhelming hopelessness, just like his.

"Our Heavenly Father, though, is the one who is in control. And despite all of Satan's subversive efforts, one hope remains."

Pastor Matthias stepped around the pulpit and walked down the three steps from the stage to the sanctuary's floor. He strode to the center aisle and quietly surveyed the congregation.

Luke watched and waited, frozen in his attentive stance.

"One verse," Pastor Matthias said gently. He held up his forefinger. "One verse in the book of John tells us the story of our hope and how to receive this hope into our lives. For God so loved the world that He gave His one and only Son—Jesus Christ, our hope—that whoever believes in Him shall not perish but have everlasting life. And the following verse, which many people tend to forget, reminds us that God did not send His Son into the world to condemn the world, but to save the world through Him.

"And in Romans, Paul writes that the wages of sin is death, but the gift of God is eternal life in Christ Jesus our Lord. For *all* have sinned and fallen short of the glory of God, but God demonstrates His own love for us in this: while we were still sinners, Christ died for us. For it is by grace we are saved, through faith. And we cannot earn this grace on our own or by our own works. No, it is a gift from God, so that none of us can boast.

"So what must you do to be saved? Believe. Believe in the Lord Jesus Christ, and you will be saved. God loves you so much, with a love that we humans can't even begin to fathom, that He sent His Son, Jesus Christ, to die on the cross for you.

"You see, you are blemished by your sin, stained and marked by your iniquity. The penalty for your sin—the payment—is death. So in order for you to be saved, someone had to die in your place. Christ was that someone. He took your sin upon Himself and bore the weight of that sin upon the cross. By giving up His life, He took your place and paid the price for your sin. And through His resurrection, He conquered death once and for all, proving His divinity and securing your hope.

"All you must do is believe in Him. There is nothing you can do to earn your salvation or work your way into Heaven. Simply seek

His forgiveness by asking Him to cleanse your heart of sin, and invite Christ into your life. Accept His gift of salvation. Leave your life of sin behind, and let Him be the Lord of your life. Let Him be your hope.

"If anyone would like to give their life to Christ, please come to the front of the sanctuary, and I will meet with you and we can pray together. Don't be afraid or nervous. If you feel Him knocking on your heart, don't ignore Him. Let the Lord in. For He knows the plans He has for you, plans to prosper you and not to harm you, plans to give you hope and a future. Let us pray."

Standing at the front of the aisle, Pastor Matthias bowed his head and closed his eyes. "Heavenly Father, we come to you today...."

Chris quietly laid the Bible in his lap, likewise bowing his head and closing his eyes.

Luke could not move. He struggled to maintain his composure.

His heart raced and his limbs trembled, while his mind reeled with indecisiveness. Emotion welled in his eyes, but he blinked back the unexpected tears. The faint tugging within his heart became an unbearable wrenching.

I've got to go forward! But no, not with everyone watching! I don't have to do this. Not now. My life is fine. Right?

"Denise and Samuel, if you could lead us in a closing hymn."

Luke glanced up. Denise scooted out the piano bench while Samuel walked up to the pulpit.

"Hymn number two fifty-seven, everyone. Please stand with me."

The congregation rose on Samuel's command, and Denise played the song's introductory chorus. Pastor Matthias waited in the aisle as the people's voices rang as one.

"Lord, I come to Thee with an aching heart."

Gripping the back of the pew, Luke forced himself to stand. He pursed his lips and inched his left foot into the aisle.

"I confess my guilt, and with sin I part."

His right foot followed. Then his left. Then his right.

"I forsake the way I am walking in."

One step at a time he labored down the aisle, neither looking to the left nor to the right.

"Save me now, I pray, from this load of sin."

He reached Pastor Matthias, who had been smiling at him the whole way, and firmly shook his hand. The pastor led him to the front pew.

Luke collapsed and broke into tears.

"Son," Pastor Matthias asked earnestly, "what is your name?"

"Luke," he choked. "My name is Luke."

"Let me pray with you, Luke," Pastor Matthias said.

A light bump shuddered within the pew, and Luke felt an arm wrap around his shoulders.

Pastor Matthias leaned over Luke and laid his hand on Luke's head. "Heavenly Father, Luke is seeking you now...."

Though his tears blurred his vision, Luke could see the scarred hand gripping his own.

Jesus, I don't know what to say. My life is broken. I've done so many wrong things and messed everything up. Forgive me. Please take my life and change it. I give my heart to you....

CHAPTER 14

An eerie calm engulfed the rocky plateau, as if nature itself was holding its breath in quiet anticipation.

The ancient trees beheld the scene like wooden statues, and not one leaf quivered on their petrified branches. Pebbles scattered to either side of the stone ledge, nervously fleeing the narrow path that led to the precipice. The raging river foamed against piles of driftwood and rushed around boulders, and the constant whooshing of its thunderous flow was the only sound high upon the cliff. A steamy fog rose from the depths where the river plunged and fell, tumbling like an endless waterfall into the black pit and disappearing into darkness forever.

The gap was wide and the gap was deep, unbridgeable and unfathomable. Stretching for miles and falling for eons, the infinite chasm eternally separated all from hope and offered only one remedy for the desperate at heart.

Death.

He'd stood here once before, gazing into the vast emptiness as he'd teetered on the brink, welcoming the death that would end his wretched existence. Everything about the grim place looked exactly the same, just as he'd remembered it. But standing here now, for the second time in his life, he recognized that one thing was eminently different.

This time, I am not alone.

Luke held Christoph's scarred hand and inhaled slowly to allay his pounding heart. Every muscle in his body trembled with anxiety, but every fiber of his being quivered with eagerness. Tears welled in his eyes despite his efforts to stay strong, and he pursed his lips as he took one final step toward the edge.

The Abyss yawned beneath him like the mouth of an immense beast, breathing wisps of white fog from its cavernous throat. The longer he looked, the more he hesitated. Doubt seeped into him, and fear gripped his heart as the fog crept around him. He swallowed and squeezed his eyes shut, firmly shaking his head to strengthen his will.

He clenched Christoph's hand more tightly. He forced his eyes open and looked straight ahead.

Far in the distance, almost so far that Luke could not see, a lofty mountain ascended beyond the reach of the Abyss and towered majestically over the void. Hues of blue and gray and green dappled the sides of the mountain, while its snow white peak sparkled in a brilliant shaft of light.

The kingdom of Rovenia shined through the gloom like a distant star in a black sky. For the first time in his life, Luke could see the land that he'd never believed existed. The beacon of hope reached out to him, calling to him from across the Abyss.

And all I must do is believe.

He took a deep breath and fixed his gaze upon the mountain, neither looking to the left nor to the right. He raised his foot from the ledge.

"I will not let you fall," Christoph said.

He locked his leg at the knee, like a soldier marching into battle, and tilted forward.

"Put your faith in me, Luke."

He squeezed Christoph's hand.

"I will never let go of you."

Luke dove over the edge as his foot sliced through the air, and the darkness soared to seize him.

Thump.

The unexpected collision of his boot with the ground lurched through his leg and pitched him forward. He staggered ahead and flailed his arms in front of him.

A strong embrace caught him just as he tripped, and he fell into the open arms. He clasped the scarred hand as he struggled to regain his footing.

"Easy, Luke! I have you," Christoph said.

Luke stood and looked around blindly. "We've...we've arrived? Is this—" He jogged ahead a little and then spun. "Christoph, is this—"

"Welcome to Rovenia, my son." Christoph walked to Luke and laid his hand on Luke's shoulder. "Your faith has saved you."

"Rovenia," Luke said quietly. He gazed upwards for a moment, but then looked at Christoph suddenly. "But how...I should have fallen. How did we cross?"

"If you had attempted to cross the Abyss by your own doing," Christoph said, "you would have fallen. But you did not come here on your own. I brought you here, just as I promised I would. Your decision to put your life in my hands enabled you to reach the other side."

"I know I wouldn't have made it without you," Luke said. "I believe you. But once I was there, and now I am here. What happened in the midst of those things?"

"The gift of salvation is an awesome thing, Luke," Christoph said, "and the crossing of such an immense separation is beyond human understanding. I am the way across the Abyss, and no one can come to Rovenia except through me. When you took my hand and believed in me, the void was spanned and your foot landed on solid ground. That is the simplest way I can explain it."

"But if this truly is Rovenia, where is everyone? And everything?" Luke asked. He looked around. "I don't see...I can't see anything, Christoph."

The entire land was white, with no definite shape and no distinct outline. The Abyss was gone, vanished as if it had never existed, and Terra Caligines was nowhere to be seen.

The only thing Luke could see was Christoph. He stood within an obscure world of white, and his green tunic, brown breeches, and black boots and belt shown distinctly from his white surroundings.

"You truly see nothing, Luke?" Christoph asked.

"Aye, I swear!" Luke said. "It's as though the whole world's gone white. I can see you, but nothing else. What's wrong with my sight?"

"Once you were blind," Christoph said. He suddenly stepped closer. "But now you *see*."

Luke lurched backwards. *What is he—oh my.* He stared in wonder.

Christoph glowed in a radiant light that fringed his entire body. The golden aura gleamed from his every limb and every fingertip. Gone were the pink scars and taut skin from his face. His beard was full and brown, and his skin was soft and healthy. Even his eyes seemed bright and aglow.

"Your scars, Christoph...your face," Luke said slowly. "You're healed. You—"

Christoph suddenly raised his hand and pressed it squarely over Luke's heart.

Luke gasped as the blazing heat poured into his heart. The terrible sting seemed as though it might last an eternity, but Christoph quickly pulled his hand away, and the fiery current ceased.

Luke clutched his heart. "What have you done—" *The heat. It's still there, but it no longer burns.* He rubbed his chest gently. *It soothes?* "My heart no longer aches. What is the reason for this?"

Christoph nodded towards Luke's chest. "See for yourself."

Luke hurriedly unlaced his tunic's collar and pulled the cloth apart. When he looked down at his chest, something like fish scales fell from his eyes, and he could see clearly.

The black, ragged *X* which Veneo had carved over his heart was gone. The wound was completely healed, and the flesh unscathed.

"Your heart has been made new, Luke," Christoph said. "I have removed the blemish from it."

Luke looked up at Christoph in amazement. "But how did...forgive me, I don't—"

The bright glow from his own hands distracted Luke, and he slowly raised them to his face. As he held his hands before his eyes, he recognized the same radiance upon his own skin as was on Christoph's.

"My spirit, my glory is within you now, Luke," Christoph said. "And when my father looks at you, he no longer sees your flaws and imperfections. He sees me."

Luke yanked up his tunic's sleeve distractedly. *My cross tattoo is gone as well.* "Your father?" He looked at Christoph then. "Who are you?"

Christoph smiled. "In your heart, you know who I am. Your eyes are no longer blinded by the shroud of your iniquity. You can see." He stretched out his right hand. "Look, Luke. Behold the kingdom of Rovenia."

Luke turned just as the light shifted through the clouds. The white veil dispersed, and he filled with awe.

From high above the kingdom, as if upon some great mountain peak, Luke surveyed the lush valley below. Sparkling blue rivers meandered through the green paradise, which went on for as far as the eye could see. Flowering fields and verdant forests rolled upon the hillsides and ascended the valley's walls to the blue-green mountains above. Turquoise ponds and lakes speckled the landscape, while animals and creatures of all kinds roamed freely throughout the countryside.

He could see thousands of white mansions scattered throughout the kingdom. Each mansion was fashioned from stones of pearly marble and looked to be at least two stories tall. Great glass windows sparkled within every wall, while the ivory stones of the terraces and walkways seemed to glisten endlessly.

The most magnificent spectacle of all, though, was not located upon the valley floor, Luke saw. Instead, it towered at the edge of the valley's farthest border, where the mountains blended into the blue firmament beyond, and gazed down upon the kingdom.

The castle of King Omnideus soared into the heavens, hiding most of the celestial structure from view. Its colossal golden gates, enormous marble stones, immense alabaster towers, and insurmountable white walls all vanished within the highest clouds.

Luke kept on looking, but he could not find the one edifice he'd truly been searching for. *Surely it is here.* He'd expected to find it at the center of the kingdom, in the very heart of the valley. *I'd imagined there would be more than one, no less than fifty at the least. Perhaps a hundred.* But the longer he looked, the more he was certain it was not there. *Not even one.*

"Where are all the churches?" Luke asked.

"There are no churches in Rovenia," Christoph said from beside him. "All of the church buildings are in Terra Caligines."

Luke looked at him, confused. "But it's widely known that King Omnideus holds the churches in high regard. Why then would he choose not to build them in his own kingdom?"

"Remember what I told you, Luke," Christoph said carefully. "The true church is more than wood, bricks, and paint."

"The true church?" Luke asked.

"Aye, the true church. Let me help you understand," Christoph said. "The church building is a place where people gather to worship

King Omnideus. But the building itself—the roof, the walls, the seats, the floor—these are not what makes the church." He paused a moment, as if he was thinking, and then held up his hand. "Consider this, Luke. A prison has a roof, a dungeon has walls, a tavern has seats, and a deadhouse has a floor. What difference is there between a church and these structures?"

Luke looked at the ground uncertainly. "What the church...holds?"

"What does the church building hold?" Christoph asked.

"People?" Luke looked up at Christoph. "Aye, it holds people. People worshiping King Omnideus."

"Aye. There is your answer, Luke," Christoph said. "Though the church buildings remain in Terra Caligines, the true church is here, in Rovenia. And this," he swept his hand over the valley, "is the *true* church."

No sooner had the words escaped Christoph's lips than a great multitude of people, too numerous to count, appeared in the valley. Rovenia suddenly teemed with life, like a giant bowled anthill alive with ants. Men and women of all ages and races walked along the cobblestone walkways and strolled among the trees and fields. A few people swam in the ponds and sailed in the lakes, while others hiked through the forests.

But even with the profuse populace, the valley seemed more than spacious enough to hold everyone. Not one area was overcrowded, and not one region was too densely inhabited. Most of the immense land was unoccupied, with infinite room for many more.

"The Rovenians are the church," Luke said quietly. He turned to Christoph. "But how do you know this?"

Christoph smiled at him. "Look, Luke." He glanced over Luke's shoulder. "Look at them."

Luke quickly turned around and gazed across the stony plateau.

A man and woman stood before him on the ridge, with a familiar crowd of people gathered behind them. The crowd sang joyfully while the man and woman walked towards him.

The man was dressed entirely in gray and wore a pair of wire-rimmed spectacles, and both his hair and beard were black but streaked with gray. The woman was a little shorter than the man, and her hair was white as snow. Her simple blue gown draped her small frame as she shuffled towards him.

"I know them," Luke said. "I'm certain of it." *But what were their names?*

"His name is Matthias," Christoph said from behind him, "and her name is—"

"Denise!" Luke said. "I remember."

Matthias and Denise both glowed with the same joyful light that illuminated Christoph and himself. The congregation was imbued with the light as well, but one person seemed to be missing from the jubilant group.

"Where is Samuel?" Luke asked.

Christoph stepped beside him and looked over the congregation. "In order to belong to the true church, to become a citizen of Rovenia, a person must believe in me. Many people attend churches in Terra Caligines and act as though they are apart of the Rovenian kingdom, but they have not truly put their faith in me and crossed the Abyss. Their minds know all about me, but their hearts do not believe. Samuel is one of these people." He turned to Luke then, a look of seriousness etched onto his face. "There is nothing you can do to earn your way to Rovenia. Going to church will not enable you to cross the Abyss."

Luke looked from Christoph to the congregation. *It does seem much smaller than I remember.* Many faces he'd once glimpsed within the rows of the church were not present now. "Why do they seem so happy then?" he asked. "If so many have been left behind, why do they sing?"

"We rejoice for you!" Matthias said. He walked straight to Luke and wrapped him in a mighty bear hug. "You were once lost, but now you've been found."

That was unexpected! Luke was startled by the strength in Matthias's arms, but he hugged him back happily. "Why would you sing for me?"

Matthias released his hold on Luke and held him at arm's length. "Because you have been saved, Luke. And when even one person crosses the Abyss, the whole kingdom rejoices." He clasped Luke's hand fervently in his own. "Welcome to Rovenia, my dear brother."

Luke smiled. "Aye, I'm honored to be here." He glanced at Christoph then but suddenly felt a little sad, as if he'd just remembered something was wrong. "What about the others? The people still in Terra Caligines." He let go of Matthias's hand and stepped toward Christoph. "What happens to them?"

Christoph shook his head as his eyes filled with sorrow. "If the people of Terra Caligines will not repent of their evil ways and give their lives to King Omnideus, then they will be doomed for all eternity, along with their leader, Prince Leone."

"Doomed?" Luke asked. "But surely you won't just leave them there. You must show them the way." He seized Christoph by the arm. "Someone must!"

"Aye, Luke. And someone will." Christoph calmly turned and walked away from him. "Come. I wish to show you something."

Luke took one last look at the valley and the congregation, then hurried to Christoph's side. "I don't understand, Christoph. You said King Omnideus wishes that none should perish, but how can the people of Terra Caligines know the way unless someone shows them? How can—"

"Your citizenship is in Rovenia now," Christoph said, "and this kingdom is your home forever. Nothing can take away your citizenship. But you must go back to Terra Caligines for a time and tell them. Tell them all that you have witnessed, and live your life so that they might see me in you. Share the way of salvation with them. Bring them to me, and I will lead them across the Abyss."

"But what will I say?" Luke asked as he walked with Christoph. "How can I persuade them? They may not believe me, or they may not want to come at all."

"Your words alone will not persuade them," Christoph said. "They will hate you because of me, and you will be a stranger in a foreign land because you are a Rovenian. I will give you the words to say when the time comes, and I will work in the hearts of those you speak to.

"You are free to travel between the two kingdoms, to come to Rovenia for rest and to renew your strength. But you must go back to Terra Caligines and be a light in the darkness. I promise that I will never leave you or forsake you."

"I will go back," Luke said firmly. "I trust what you say. But please, there is one last thing I must know."

Christoph stopped walking and turned to him. "What is it, Luke?"

"This doom you spoke of earlier," Luke said gravely. "You said the people of Terra Caligines are doomed. What exactly is their fate?"

"This is what I would have you see." Christoph raised his arm and pointed into the distance. "Look, Luke. See with your own eyes the fate of all who dwell in Terra Caligines."

Blinding radiance exploded across the heavens, and the dazzling flash flooded the Abyss with light.

A great bridge of white stones appeared before him. It seemed to hang in the air, suspended above the Abyss from nothing at all, and shot across the Abyss like a bolt of lightning. *The way to travel between the two kingdoms. Only Rovenians can see it.* The bridge began at his feet and ended—

A gasp caught in his throat. The sight beyond the bridge was too shocking, too horrific for his mind to accept. *No. It cannot be.*

Terra Caligines burned. All the land looked as though it had been spewed from the bowels of an unholy volcano.

The diabolical inferno ravaged every tree, every bush, and every boulder, leaving nothing untouched by the hellish flames. The soil was an ocean of dancing fire, and wave after wave of blazing combustion drenched the land. Lake Solardens was no longer a shimmering sea but a bubbling lake of fire. The cool waters of the Dedanima River were gone as well, and in their place a steaming river of lava oozed across the land and cascaded into the Abyss, where the waterfall of viscous fire plunged eternally.

Black plumes of smoke and ash erupted high above the trees and merged into one terrible cloud, while the stench of sulfur and burnt flesh saturated the air.

It burns perpetually yet never consumes. The fire seemed to blaze with an unnatural ferocity. Life filled the demonic flames, and they cackled and wailed and shrieked. Quivering black shadows leaped within the fiery fiasco, frolicking about the cremated landscape.

"Though the deadly fire rages all around them," Christoph said suddenly, "the people of Terra Caligines are blind to its flames. They cannot see their destruction. But you can, Luke. You must warn them before it is too late. The fire will not harm you, because my power flows within you, protecting you from its flames."

Terra Caligines is burning, Luke! If only you could see what we see! His mother and father's words burst into his memory as he gazed at the fiery devastation. *They were right all along.* Luke suddenly felt afraid. "Must I truly go back? They'll deem me a fool! How can I live in such a place? What will I—"

The black lion sprang from the flames and bounded to the edge of the Abyss, where it thrust its claws into the stony ledge to keep itself from hurling over.

"Malfera," Luke said lowly. "What is he—"

The lion threw back its head and roared with such fury that Luke felt the ground shudder beneath his feet.

A pale man then emerged from the forest, as if slowly materializing from the flames themselves, and moved to the lion's side. The lion sat down obediently upon its haunches, but it bared its fangs in a vicious snarl while its eyes glowed hot and wicked. The man smiled and gently stroked its head.

Veneo? Luke narrowed his eyes as he peered across the chasm. *No, not Veneo.*

The man was tall and gaunt, with skin the color of ash, but his hair was black and brittle. His black cloak shrouded his body and glowed orange where it dragged the ground, as if singed by the flames. His eyes were tiny red dots, like two bloody pinpricks, but fierce as lightning.

Prince Leone Mortuo.

The sinister eyes suddenly locked onto him, and Luke felt a voice breathe into his ear.

"You may no longer be mine, but she still is."

"Sarah," Luke said softly. He felt his anger surge. "No...NO! You can't have her!"

Prince Leone and the lion evaporated into the flames, but the Prince's insane laughter echoed long after they were gone.

CHAPTER 15

Glover's Field in Richmond, Virginia never changed.

The rolling fields, the groves of maples and poplars, the James River curving along the forest's border to the south—all of these features remained unaltered year after year. Even the rows of sunflowers standing along the riverbank seemed like they had not changed from last year, while the same chickadees and sparrows plucked at the seeds within the gigantic yellow heads.

The land endured, but time marched on. Autumn was coming, and with the autumn came the Summer's End Festival.

Once every year, during the last full weekend of summer, a carnival of gleeful commotion would arrive in Richmond and settle into the serene countryside known as Glover's Field. Fair rides and food stands, a petting zoo and a funhouse, and game booths and arcade machines all would gather for three consecutive days. During that time, Glover's Field would be transformed from a quiet, grassy meadow into a noisy, crowded fair.

The last day of this year's festival looked to be just as busy and lively as years past. Sarah had never seen the dirt parking lot packed with so many vehicles. *You'd think people would stay home.* She glanced up at the sky. *Especially since it looks like it's going to rain again.* The sun had finally shined in the afternoon, but now the sky was gray and overcast. A damp chill had settled in with the evening.

I should've stayed home. Should've ignored Damon when he knocked on my door. She shoved her hands into her hoodie's big pocket. The last day of summer felt more like the middle of autumn, though without the colorful leaves and frost-nipped grass. *And I should've worn that extra shirt under my hoodie too.* A gust of wind blew down her neck then, and she shivered as the cold air brushed her bare skin.

Oh well. Too late now. She balled her hands into fists within the pocket and pulled the purple hoodie tightly around her. The wind cut right through her jeans, and she shifted lightly from foot to foot. Her tennis shoes squished on the damp ground.

"You want my coat, Sarah? You look like you're freezin'."

The sound of Luke's voice startled her. *He's looking at me!* She quickly pulled her hands from the pocket and stood still.

"Oh, no. I'm okay, Luke," Sarah said as cheerfully as she could. She tucked a strand of hair behind her ear. "Just got a chill. Thanks, though."

"You're sure?" Luke asked. He took off his jacket and held it out to her. "I won't be wearin' this during the race, so you can wear it if you want. Just might be a little big."

Sarah bit her lower lip. The denim jacket looked heavy, and its fleece insulation looked warm. *Yes, I want it.* "Um, no...I'm—" She shivered again. "I'm good. Once we start walking, I'll warm up."

"Sarah Ryans." Luke shook his head and smiled. "Here. Why don't you go ahead and take—"

Sarah heard the truck's tailgate slam shut behind her. She turned just as Damon rolled the dirtbike beside her and put its kickstand down.

"She's alright, Luke," Damon said. He put his arm firmly around her shoulders. "If she gets cold, I'll keep her warm."

Luke and Chris stood across from them and seemed to glance at one another uncertainly. They might have passed for brothers, if Luke had not been so much taller and darker complected than Chris. Both of them wore faded blue jeans and dusty boots, but Luke had on a camouflage T-shirt, while Chris wore a green flannel shirt that was tucked into his jeans.

Sarah felt her cheeks getting hot. *It's okay. He'll let go soon.* It was all she could do not to squirm beneath Damon's arm. *He won't touch you for long.* She'd watched the three men unload the two dirtbikes from Damon's truck a few moments before, and Luke had rolled his dirtbike beyond her and stood it between himself and Chris. *I wish Damon would've done the same!*

Luke laid his jacket over his dirtbike's seat and looked on, while Chris slid his hands into his pants pockets. Neither of them said anything.

Damon suddenly guffawed. "Come on guys! It was just a joke." He wrapped both arms around her then and pulled her against him. "Sarah's a good girl. Can't you tell? She doesn't—"

Sarah pushed him away as hard as she could. The apple cinnamon smell on his clothes made her want to vomit.

Damon lurched backwards into his dirtbike, and it crashed onto its side before he could stop it from tipping. Sarah stepped back when he yanked it upright and cursed. He spun to face her.

"What is your problem?" Damon asked sharply.

Sarah pursed her lips as she looked at him. *He changed that quickly.* He stood spread eagle before her, with his big black boots planted solidly on the ground. His jeans bulged around his calves and thighs, while his red plaid shirt seemed to stretch across his chest. *He would be handsome, if he didn't look like he wanted to hit me.* His eyes were filled with hate, and his hands were clenched into fists at his sides.

"Don't touch me," Sarah said lowly. She swallowed and steeled her gaze. "Just don't, Damon."

She saw his eyes widen at that, and his nostrils flared. He raised his fist and pointed at her.

"Don't you tell me what to do," Damon said. He stepped toward her. "I'll touch you whenever—"

"Damon, that's enough!"

Chris was suddenly by her side. Then Luke was there too. Both men stood slightly in front of her, while Damon scowled at all three of them.

Sarah took a step back. *Oh no. Please don't.* She looked from Damon to Chris and Luke. *He'll hurt you both. He will.* But the two men did not move, never took their eyes from Damon. *Please.* She looked at Damon. He stood in the same aggressive stance as before, but now he seemed to be glaring at Chris and no one else.

"You," Damon said scornfully. "You wanted him to die, didn't you?"

Sarah quickly looked to Chris, but his facial expression remained unchanged, and he said nothing. *Wanted who to die?* She glanced at Luke. He looked as confused as she felt.

"What are you talking about, Damon?" Luke asked harshly. "You need to cool it, now. Chris didn't want anyone to die."

Damon suddenly smiled. "Oh yes, he did." He stood tall then and seemed to relax. "He wanted Eddie to die, so that's what happened. Eddie died."

Eddie who? Sarah almost asked the question aloud, but she stopped when she saw the look of shock wash over Luke's face.

"Dead?" Luke asked. He seemed upset. "No, he's not. I just saw him yesterday. Why would you say something like that, and now?"

"Just thought of it, I guess," Damon said. "It's the truth. A buddy called me this morning and told me." He shrugged. "I figured you knew already. He died last night."

Eddie who? "Um, who is Eddie?" Sarah asked. She glanced at Luke. "I don't think I know...knew him."

Luke exhaled slowly then met her gaze. "He was a friend of mine, I guess you could say. He had some issues." He shook his head and looked at the ground. "But then so do I. Last night, he asked me for money 'cause he said he owed a guy, but I wouldn't give it to him." He looked up at Damon then, almost angrily. "Is that why he died? Over some drug money?"

Sarah saw Damon nod.

"His life was worth more than fifty bucks," Luke said bitterly. "I should've just given it to him." He ran his hand down over face and looked away. "Maybe I should've gone with him. Tried to—"

"If you'd gone with him, you'd be dead too," Damon said. "Whoever killed Eddie wasn't the kind of person to show mercy. Eddie was stabbed and beaten so badly that his face was unrecognizable. I guess some homeless dude found him in an alley. You know how much Eddie lied. He owed a lot more than fifty bucks, so don't blame yourself."

"Don't blame myself," Luke said curtly. He turned to Damon. "So should I blame Chris? Since you said he wanted Eddie to die?" He made a face and crossed his arms. "Why would even you say something like that?"

"Because Eddie met Chris once," Damon said lightly. "Eddie told me about it years ago, though I'm pretty sure he didn't remember it for very long 'cause he was high at the time. Eddie said some scarred guy saw him smoking outside a bar and offered to give him a ride home. Eddie turned him down, but the guy kept talking to him...even started preaching at him. Eddie said he cussed the guy out, and then the guy left and never came back."

"So?" Luke asked. "You don't know if that was Chris. And what if it was? What does it matter?"

"Ask him then," Damon said. He nodded toward Chris. "Just ask him if he left Eddie there alone."

Sarah saw Luke purse his lips and glance at the ground, while

Chris looked on silently. Damon smiled. *He seems to be enjoying this.*

"Chris?" Luke asked after a moment. "Did you know Eddie?"

Chris nodded solemnly. "I did, yes. I saw him that night, like Damon said. And I saw him many other nights too. I reached out to him, offered him a way out, but he rejected me each time." He looked at Sarah and then at Luke. "No one here is responsible for his death. Eddie made his own choices, and it was his time."

"It was his time." Damon snorted and rolled his eyes. "Of course it was."

"Yes," Chris said sternly, "everyone's time will come." He turned toward Damon then. "Everyone's."

Sarah held her breath. *Oh no. Now he's done it.*

Damon cursed and made a fist. "Why you—"

"Sarah," Chris said calmly as he turned to her, "would you mind walkin' down to the track with me? I want to find a seat before the stands fill up. Then Damon and Luke can go sign in."

Sarah opened her mouth, but no words came out. *What?* She looked from Chris to Damon, and back again. "Um, sure. Yeah, that sounds good." She forced a smile but nervously glanced at Damon. "Is that okay with you guys?"

Damon glared at them but surprisingly unclenched his fist. "Yeah. I guess that's cool. Go grab your bike, Luke." He strode to his own dirtbike and roughly kicked the kickstand up. "There'll probably be ten or fifteen riders racing, so we should get down there and get signed in."

"Alright," Luke said.

Sarah watched him walk to his dirtbike and take his jacket from the seat. He held the jacket for a moment, as if he was studying it, and then turned toward her.

"Hey Sarah, do you think you could hang on to this for me?" Luke asked. He walked over to her with the jacket in his hands. "I don't wanna mess with it while I'm racing."

"Oh, okay. Sure." Sarah furrowed her brow a little but took the jacket from him. "Yeah, I'll hold on to it for you. No problem."

Luke started to walk away but turned back. "Oh, and it might be easier if you just wore it, then you wouldn't have to carry it everywhere." He shrugged as he took a couple of steps backwards. "But that's up to you."

Sarah glanced down at the heavy denim jacket and pressed it gently to herself. *After all that, he still remembered that I was cold.* She did her best not to smile when she looked up.

Damon was rolling his dirtbike past Luke just as he kicked up his kickstand.

"I'll meet up with guys after the race," Luke said. He gave the dirtbike a firm push and followed Damon. "By the stands."

"Alrighty then," Chris said. "That's where we'll be. Good luck."

"Yup, good luck!" Sarah said.

Luke grinned at her and nodded. *He does have a nice smile.* She watched him guide his dirtbike through the dirt lot and then cut through the field that led down to the racetrack. Both he and Damon had black helmets swinging from their handlebars, but their dirtbikes were not at all alike. Where Damon's dirtbike was black with red flames, Luke's was blue with white lightning bolts. *I like Luke's dirtbike better.*

"Well, are ya ready, Sarah?"

Sarah turned around. Chris stood quietly with his hands in his pockets and smiled at her.

Does he know I was watching Luke? Sarah smiled back shyly. "Uh yeah, I'm ready. Just let me put this on real quick." She swung Luke's jacket around her and slid her arms through the sleeves. After she pulled her hood from under the jacket, she held out her arms and looked down. "Oh dear." The jacket hung down to her thighs, and its sleeves drooped over her hands. *I could fit two of me in here.* She looked up when she heard Chris laugh.

"Well, I think it looks good on you," Chris said. He grinned and shook his head. "One thing's for sure, you won't be cold."

"That's true." Sarah bunched up the sleeves as she walked to him. "Hey look, I found my hands." She held them up and wiggled her fingers.

"It's a good thing," Chris said. "You don't wanna lose those."

"Now all I have to do is walk like this." Sarah held up her arms like someone had just pointed a gun at her, and moved past Chris. "That way I don't lose them again."

Chris laughed and walked with her. "What'll happen when your arms get tired?"

"Well...." Sarah lowered her arms to her sides, and the sleeves immediately fell over her hands.

"Guess that answers that question, doesn't it?" Chris asked.

Sarah grinned. "Yup."

They walked together quietly through the dirt lot and onto a sloping gravel road, but she glanced at him every now and then and wondered if he was doing the same. The pink splotches on his face looked so taut and raw that she could not help but feel sorry for him. Much of his beard was missing. *What happened to you?* She looked at his hands. The skin there matched his face.

He did not look that old, though, even with the scarring. *Maybe thirty? Not much older than me.* When she caught sight of the black walkie-talkie clipped to his belt, she wanted to ask him what it was for but did not want to seem nosy.

"That's my fire pager," Chris said. He smiled but kept looking ahead. "I'm on call tonight, so if there's a fire somewhere in the township, my pager will go off." He turned to her suddenly. "Oh, I'm a firefighter, by the way. Guess I should've mentioned that first, huh?"

Sarah smiled. "No, that's okay. Damon told me you were a firefighter. But he also said you work for your father?" She scooted closer to him as a car drove past them. "Is that why you were in Mr. Morten's office the other day?"

"Yup," Chris said. "I used to live in South Carolina, but I was transferred up here to Richmond's fire department a few weeks ago. I also do work for my father. He's the head of an overseas organization that rivals Mr. Morten's company, and sometimes he'll send me to Mr. Morten to protect our company's interests."

Sarah raised her eyebrows. "Oh, wow. You must be pretty important then."

Chris chuckled. "I s'pose you could say that."

"But you don't look important," Sarah said. *Oh, wow.* She winced when she heard what she'd said. "I mean, you don't act all important," she said quickly. "You look like an everyday guy."

"Most people don't think I look normal." Chris looked at her. "They don't see an everyday guy when they look at me."

"Oh." Sarah tried to smile but looked away instead. *I've got to stop staring at his scars. He knows what I'm doing.* She pushed the jacket's sleeves up her arms again. After a moment, she looked back up at him. "Chris, would it be okay if I asked...would you be mad if—"

"I rescued someone I loved from a fire," Chris said. He held his hands up where she could see them. "My hands, my feet, and my face all were burned severely, but the person I saved lived, so my wounds were worth it."

"Oh goodness," Sarah said. She stared at his hands. "But, you could've died, right?"

"Yes," Chris said.

Sarah suddenly wanted to cry, though she did not understand why. *What kind of man runs into a fire to save someone else? To give up his life for someone he loves?* She looked up at him and spoke quietly. "I don't know if I could do that."

"Oh, I think you could," Chris said gently. "You're stronger than you know." He glanced down the road then. "We go this way, right?"

Sarah followed his gaze. "Oh, yup. That'll take us around the midway and straight to the stands. We can avoid the crowds that way."

Together they both stepped up onto the sidewalk that wound around the outskirts of the fairgrounds. The raucous sounds and colorful lights of the carnival clamored to their left, while still more parked vehicles sat in the open field to their right, just beyond the gravel road they'd been walking on.

Sarah could see the silvery benches of the grandstand a little farther down the slope.

"You work at Leon's Grille, right?" Chris asked as he walked beside her. "Is that where you met Luke and Damon?"

"Mm hmm," Sarah said, nodding. "Would you believe I met both of them there just a couple of days ago? Friday, during our lunch rush, they both came in and ordered food." She laughed then and shook her head. "And we messed up *both* their orders. That was not a good day."

Chris chuckled. "I'll bet."

"Ah, the joys of fast food," Sarah said whimsically. "So how do you know Luke?"

"Ya know what," Chris said, "I actually met Luke on Friday too. I found a knife in Powhite Park while I was hikin' there Friday morning, and Luke's name was engraved on the blade. Well, I figured out where he lived and gave it back to him. We hung out last night at Leon's, and this morning Luke went to church with me."

"Church?" Sarah asked. She looked at Chris in surprise. "Luke goes to church?"

"He did this morning!" Chris said, smiling. "He gave his life to Christ after the sermon. It was awesome to be there with him."

"So what does that mean?" Sarah asked. "Is Luke a Christian now? He didn't seem like the kinda guy that—" She glanced ahead and suddenly realized they were next to the grandstand. *Wow, that was quick.*

The old grandstand in Glover's Field was not a typical grandstand, but a series of long, steel benches mounted into the hillside like an ancient theater. One after the other, the benches descended the hill like stair steps, until the hill sloped into the plain. The dirt racetrack was about fifty yards from the lowest bench, and the white finish line was centered with the middle of the benches.

"Where do you want to sit?" Sarah asked.

"Doesn't look like there's too many seats left," Chris said. "How about down there? There's a little room at the end of the row."

"Oh yeah, I see it," Sarah said. "That'll work."

She walked down the hill alongside the stands, while Chris followed behind her. When she reached the bench with the empty space at its end, she stepped into the aisle and shuffled in as far as she could. She sat down next to a big hairy man who was wearing a tank top and holey jeans, but he was talking to the man beside him and did not seem to notice her. *I should've let Chris go first so he could've sat by him.* She glanced at Chris just as he was sitting down and scooted back towards him.

"Do you have enough room?" Sarah asked.

Chris turned toward the edge of the bench and nodded. "Yup, I'm good. How about you?"

"I think so," Sarah said. She glanced at the hairy man beside her and inched a little closer to Chris. *He's probably a nice guy, but still.* She looked down at the racetrack then. "Oh, we're only three rows up! That's pretty good."

"I know!" Chris said. His shoulder bumped into hers. "I don't think I've ever got to sit this close to the track before."

"Me neither," Sarah said, grinning. "We must be special today."

Chris laughed. "Must be. Hey, I almost forgot. I didn't answer your question earlier."

Sarah looked at him. "What question?"

"You asked me if Luke is a Christian now, but I didn't get to tell you." Chris smiled and held up his hand as he spoke. "The answer is yes, he is a Christian, but not because he went to church. He is a Christian, a follower of Christ, because he asked Christ to come into his heart. Luke has given his life to Christ, and now he's saved. He has hope through Jesus Christ. And you know what?"

Sarah gazed quietly into Chris's eyes and shook her head a little.

"You can have that hope too," Chris said. "Jesus Christ died for you just like He died for Luke, and He can change your life just like He's changing Luke's. All you have to do is believe in Him with all your heart and give your life to Him. He has a plan for your life—a plan to give you hope and a future."

Wow. That's really...strange. Sarah narrowed her eyes as she looked at him. "You know, it's kinda funny, but I just heard that verse on TV today." *And I haven't been able to get it out of my head.*

"What a coincidence, right?" Chris smiled. "Maybe you can come to church with us sometime. I'm sure Luke would like that. You're more than welcome to join us."

Sarah smiled back. "Yeah, maybe I will."

"All riders to the starting line! Riders to the starting line!"

The announcer's voice echoed over the loudspeaker, and the people in the stands suddenly cheered. Sarah watched as several colorfully dressed riders rolled their dirtbikes from within the center of the oval track to the long white line.

"Looks like they're gettin' ready to start!" Chris said. "Do you see Damon or Luke?"

Sarah saw Luke's camouflage shirt and pointed excitedly. "There's Luke! He's wearing a number seven on his back, and Damon's the guy in front of him. Damon's number six."

She watched the riders steer their dirtbikes to the white chalk line, where each rider swung his leg over his bike's seat and mounted his two-wheeled steed. Luke and Damon were in the middle of the group, and they both removed their helmets from their handlebars and tugged them over their heads.

"Well folks, another festival has nearly come and gone," the announcer proclaimed over the loudspeaker, *"but we're not done yet! This year's motocross event features fourteen riders for a grand prize of $140 to the winner. Maybe we can get Jim here to throw in an extra ten bucks to make it an even one-fifty. What do you say, Jim? Why yessir, he said sure! Make that a grand prize of $150 to the man who completes five laps around the track and reaches the finish line first! Riders, start your engines!"*

Each rider immediately lifted his right foot and thrust downward. A few riders repeated the motion, then some again, while the hillside stadium filled with the sputtering reports of engines. Each dirtbike revved to life as the riders flexed their wrists around the throttles.

Sarah could feel the crowd's energy surge when a man carrying a black-and-white checkered flag strode to the edge of the starting line. The crowd roared with excitement, completely drowning the sound of the engines.

She watched the man extend the flag away from his body, towards the riders, and angle his arm upwards. The flag swayed at the ready.

"Riders, take your mark!"

The riders hunched forward simultaneously, each with one foot planted on the ground and the other foot cocked upon the foot peg.

"Get set!"

Sarah held her breath.

"Go!"

The flag whooshed downward.

Engines squealed and dirt flew as the line of riders lurched forward as one, tearing through the straightaway into the first turn. Around they went, each fighting for the inner lane, until six or seven riders emerged from the congested group and accelerated through the opposite straightaway to the second turn. The remaining riders brought up the rear, hastening through the straightaway to catch the lead riders.

"Here they come!" Chris shouted. "Is that Damon in second place?"

"I think so!" Sarah craned her neck as the lead group flew over the finish line. She looked quickly from rider to rider. "Where's Luke?"

"I don't know. I haven't—there he is!" Chris pointed as the rest of the riders crossed the line. "He's in the second group. Come on, Luke!"

"One lap down, and number nine is in the lead! Robbie Jackson is just flyin' around this track! But number six is right on his tail...Damon Jefferies! Don't count him out yet!

The two groups of riders dispersed into clusters of three and four as the lead riders sped through the opposing straightaway and rounded the second turn into the finish line. The bunched line of riders now stretched from the finish line back to the beginning of the second turn, where the last group seemed to be struggling to catch up.

"Three laps to go and Robbie Jackson is still anchored in first place! But Damon Jefferies is givin' him a run for his money! Numbers ten, one, and seven—you guys better get a move on!"

Blurring over the finish line, the last three riders zoomed through the straightaway into the first turn, while the lead group of riders was already racing into the second turn.

Sarah bit her lip. *Luke is in twelfth place!* She cupped her hands around her mouth. "Come on, Luke! You can do it!"

Chris whistled through his fingers. "Let's go, Luke! He's almost in last but—whoa! Look out!"

Sarah gasped as the first-place rider suddenly ricocheted into the middle of the track and skidded onto his side. Damon lurched to the inside but maintained control and accelerated through the straightaway.

"Oh man! Watch it, boys! Robbie Jackson is down...ho! Four more riders just hit the dirt! We've got a five-man pile-up in turn two! Seems I was wrong about numbers one, ten, and seven 'cause they're in second,

third, and fourth now after this shake-up! Looks like everyone's okay down there and gettin' their bikes up an' runnin'. Alright! Less than two laps to go!"

Sarah cheered as Luke sped safely across the finish line. He battled for second place with two other riders, who were on either side of him. Together they rushed into the first turn, but Luke slowed and cut to the inside, then accelerated, and cruised past the two riders above him. He sped through the far straightaway alone in second place, while Damon came out of the second turn and charged for the finish line.

Come on, Luke! Come on! Sarah pursed her lips and clasped her hands beneath her chin.

Damon streaked across the finish line. Luke flew out of the second turn. A trail of dust billowed behind each of them.

Come on, Luke! Sarah leaned forward anxiously. Then she broke into a smile.

Luke was closing the gap.

"It's the final lap! Number six Damon Jefferies has all but clenched first place...but wait! Here comes number seven! Who is that, Jim? Number seven...Luke Porter! Can Luke catch our leader before he runs outta track? It's gonna be close!"

Bolting over the finish line and through the straightaway, Luke shot into the first turn, not twenty yards behind Damon.

Sarah jumped up from the bench and raised her fists in the air. With Luke's jacket swaying all about her, she yelled at the top of her lungs. "Go Luke! *GO!"*

CHAPTER 16

The immense flames ravaged the hillside stadium and doused the plain in blazing reds and oranges.

Field after field rolled within the raging inferno, and tree after tree blazed within the intense wildfire. The groves of maples and poplars burned and smoldered, while tongues of fire lashed from their leaves like fiery bolts of lightning. The Dedanima River's burbling flux oozed to the south, a giant snake of lava slithering along the border of the Lumbrai Forest. Even the rows of sunflowers beautifying the riverbank were not immune to the festering flames, and the gigantic yellow heads exploded with virulent sparks.

All Glover's Field burned perpetually, consumed by the eternal fire which devoured Terra Caligines.

And Luke was right in the middle of it all.

"Hyah!" he shouted from the saddle. "Hyah, boy! Hyah!"

The white horse lowered its head and charged through the flames, while the thunderous tempo of its hooves hastened upon the dirt track. Puffs of steam rapidly shot from its nostrils.

Luke clenched the reins more tightly as the horse flew around the turn and galloped into the straightaway. He thrust his heels into the horse's flanks and vigorously snapped the reins.

"Hyah!" He snapped the reins again. "Hyah, boy!"

He raised himself from the saddle then and threw his shoulders over the horse's neck. Like a lion crouching before its prey, he gripped the reins with all his might and stared over the horse's lunging head.

The black stallion rippled within the fiery panorama, while a cloud of dirt and dust erupted behind it as it charged to the final turn. Its rider leaned hard to the left, and the stallion skillfully glided into the curve.

Luke did the same in an instant, his horse following on the stallion's heels.

We're close.

So close that he could taste the dirt in the air behind the stallion. So close that he could hear the rhythmic beating of its hooves upon the earth. So close that he could see the sweat shining on its black hair.

The stallion's rider quickly glanced over his shoulder, then scowled. He jerked his head back towards the finish line.

Damon? Luke had seen his eyes. They blazed crimson, glowing more fiercely than even the surrounding flames. *No, surely not you as well.*

Luke tightened his grip upon the reins and lowered his head. With one swift breath, he heaved his shoulders upwards and slammed his arms downward.

"HEE-YAH!"

His horse bolted into the straightaway and flew through the flames, galloping to the side of stallion. Their hooves suddenly seemed to pound in unison. They were one horse now, black on one side and white on the other.

Luke could see the white line rushing towards them, ever closer, ever nearer with each thunderous stride. It waved languidly behind a drifting curtain of reds and oranges.

He felt his rapid heartbeat slow to a prolonged thump, like a low drumbeat gradually dying within him. The cheers from the hillside swelled until they filled his ears. He floated with his horse, no longer lurching headlong but gracefully leaping forward.

Th-th-th-thump. He felt the hooves steadily hit the ground beneath him.

Luke rose and tilted forward, reaching for the finish. He saw the black stallion stretch its neck, while the white line glided beneath his horse's nose.

Then the line fell away behind them, as if someone had yanked it backwards. Luke glimpsed the black-and-white checkered flag whoosh downward. The crowd roared with excitement.

Luke dropped onto the saddle and pulled back hard on the reins. He turned his horse into the wind as the dust blew past him, and circled away from Damon.

"This way, boy," Luke said. He tugged the reins and gently tapped his horse's flanks. "This way." His horse trotted back towards the finish line.

The crowd's cheering intensified. Luke wanted to smile but would not allow himself to. *Who is it that they cheer for?* He turned in the saddle and glanced over his shoulder. Damon rode behind him, waving proudly to the crowd. *He thinks he's won.* Luke turned back and felt his heart sink. *No, he knows he's won.*

A young boy stood on the wooden stage in the inner circle of the track and waved a black flag embroidered with blood red flames. Thirteen other flags hung like banners over the stage's front railing, and the first of these bore three white lightning bolts upon a blue field.

"The black stallion is fortunate to have such a long nose," the herald shouted from the stage. *"For without it, he would not have been able to cross the line ahead of the white horse! Damon, we are honored by your victory. Come forth to the stage and grant us the pleasure of bestowing upon you the reward you've rightfully won. Terra Caligines, behold your champion!"*

Luke heard the galloping of hooves coming behind him. He halted his horse just as Damon flew past, a blur of red upon a black streak. Damon raised his fist above his head and punched the air as his stallion charged towards the stage. The crowd cheered them the entire way.

Luke wiped the sweat from his brow on the back of his arm. He looked on for a moment, quietly letting a breath escape from his lips, and then let go of the reins. He gripped the saddle horn and swung himself down. His boots thudded upon the ground at once, kicking up little wisps of dust. Without looking back at the stage, he slipped his fingers beneath the bridle and gently brushed his hand along his horse's nose.

"You did good, boy," he said. "Second place isn't so bad."

The horse huffed through its nostrils.

Luke smiled and patted its cheek. He turned his horse then and led it across the track, gazing silently at the rowdy stands. *Christoph and Sarah are somewhere up there.* He tried to see their faces in the crowd, but there were too many people on the hill. *Did Sarah cheer for me or Damon?*

He was almost to the edge of the hillside when a shrill neigh caused him to look back.

The black stallion reared majestically before the stage, and Damon waved to the crowd from high in the saddle. His red cape flapped proudly behind him like a flag upon a mast, while his black breeches and boots seemed to blend into the stallion's dark hair. *It's as though he and his horse are one.* The crowd roared once more.

"Ladies and gentlesirs, I give you your champion!" the herald bellowed. *"Damon! The victor of the Summer's End horse race!"*

The crowd's exuberant cries resounded through the hillside and echoed over the plain. The black stallion still reared, pawing the air with its hooves, and Damon still waved to the crowd.

Luke stood beside his horse, watching. He turned to the crowd and searched their faces. He looked across the rolling fields to the forest and river beyond. He could see everything.

But these people see nothing.

The fire was everywhere. It consumed the stage, flooded the racetrack, engulfed the hillside, ignited each banner and every pennant. It ravaged the land all around. And yet, no one seemed to notice.

People walked through fire and sat in fire. They laughed as the flames lashed at their faces, and they smiled while the sparks danced at their feet. They drank and reveled, deliberately blind to the nearness of their peril. They seemed to thrive in their unseen hell while living as though nothing would ever harm them.

Luke could see the black smoke wisping from heads and limbs, and gobs of ash covered the people from head to toe. But remarkably, none of the people actually burned. The flames did not touch one person. Not one.

Not yet.

Luke recognized the light of Rovenia shining through the flames. *There is still hope. The flames shrink back from the light. They are held at bay.* A handful of people in the crowd radiated the same glow which protected him. Not a hair on the heads of these people was singed, not one speck of ash dusted their clothes, and not one wisp of smoke floated around them.

"It is my great honor, on behalf of the entire Kingdom of Terra Caligines, to bestow upon Damon the accolades of a victory justly earned!" The herald reached into his tunic and pulled out a leather pouch, which he held up for the crowd to see. *"In this purse are fifteen silver coins—one from each of the riders and one from our patron, James Glover. Damon, may these coins buy you a few drinks and many pleasures!"*

The herald turned to Damon then, who yet waited upon his stallion, and gave him the pouch. Damon placed the pouch in his palm and untied its strings, and the pouch fell open. Even at such a distance, Luke could see the silver gleaming in Damon's hand.

"Until next year, my friends!" The herald waved to the crowd as they dispersed from the stands. *"Enjoy the rest of the festival!"*

Luke stroked his horse's neck and looked on. "Don't mind him, boy. It was only a race." *But a race we might have won.* He turned to his horse and smiled halfheartedly. "We did all we could. Just came up but one step short."

Someone moved behind him. He started to turn but felt a hand slipping into his.

"You did well, Luke," a voice said softly. "And if your horse could talk, I'm sure he would tell you much the same."

Luke felt a rush of excitement. *Sarah.* He squeezed her hand and tried to control the grin he felt sweeping across his face. He turned to look at her.

"You truly think so?" Luke asked.

Sarah smiled at him. "Aye. I do."

She wears my cloak. He nearly laughed when he saw how big it was on her. The sleeves would have fallen over her hands if she had not bunched them up. *But even so, it cannot hide her beauty.* She wore a pair of black tights, which accentuated the length and slenderness of her legs, and a pair of plain boots. Her hooded purple tunic fitted her figure down to her knees, while its filigreed neckline widened to reveal the graceful lines of her collarbones. She wore her hair down, and the auburn waves fell all around her shoulders.

He gazed at her, unable to take his eyes from her, but uncertain what to say. *I must tell her.* He glanced over her shoulder, then at the ground. *The fire is all around her, but she sees not one flame.*

"Luke?" Sarah asked. "You truly did well. Christoph said so himself."

Luke looked up at her. "Oh, I...that is, I'm not—"

"Aye, I did say so!" Christoph walked up behind Sarah and stood beside her. "You had us both on our feet at the end."

Where did he come from? Luke extended his hand and grinned. "Christoph, you startled me. How is it that you appear out of nowhere?"

"Appear out of nowhere?" Christoph narrowed his eyes as he shook Luke's hand. "I fear you are mistaken. I walked not very far behind Sarah all this time. Mayhaps you were a little distracted?"

"Distracted?" Luke glanced at Sarah, who happened to be looking at him. He quickly looked back to Christoph. "Uh...no. I fear...I fear it is you who are mistaken."

"Aye?" Christoph asked. He seemed to hold back a smile. "How so?"

Luke felt his cheeks getting warm. "Well, you said—" He ran his hand over his head. "That is, I meant—" He looked at Sarah. *Her cheeks are red too.* He smiled then but looked at the ground. "Aye. Mayhaps it'd be best if I talked to my horse from now on."

He heard Christoph and Sarah both laugh at that, and he could not help but laugh a little himself as he looked up at them. *What a family we make. Christoph could pass for my brother, if he was taller.* Christoph wore brown breeches and black boots just like he did, but Christoph's green tunic was long-sleeved and tucked into his breeches. His own tunic was woven with the browns and greens of the forest. *And Sarah.* He watched her laugh within the folds of the heavy cloak. *She looks even more beautiful now.*

"Oh goodness," Sarah said between laughs. "Luke, pay Christoph no heed. He has no right to make fun, but I'm afraid he has no manners."

"So says the girl who laughs heartily." Chrisoph grinned and looked at Luke. Then he looked back at Sarah suddenly. "Why Luke, I can't tell whose face is redder—yours or hers."

Luke glanced at Sarah just as she put her hands over her cheeks. *Hers are red, but mine feel hotter.* He tried to seem serious. "Hers is most certainly redder. Aye, I'm sure of it."

He saw her eyes widen at that. She started to open her mouth but crossed her arms instead.

"I see where Christoph gets his manners," Sarah said. She turned her head but seemed to be looking at him out of the corner of her eye. "Or lack thereof."

Luke chuckled. "Forgive me, m'lady." He swept his hand in front of him and bowed. "It was not my intent to offend."

Sarah tilted her chin higher. She peered down at him but said nothing.

Luke saw a slight smile on her lips. *She enjoys this.* He stood up before her. "What must I do to win your—"

The galloping of hooves thundered towards him. Luke turned just as Damon's stallion shrieked and reared beside him. The stallion danced on its hind legs while it pawed the air with its hooves. Suddenly it flew forwards, slamming its hooves onto the ground, and Damon swung himself down from the saddle.

"Fifteen silver coins!" Damon said. He held out the leather pouch and shook it by its strings. "Listen to them sing. They might have been yours, Luke, were it not for your little pony."

The white horse stamped at the ground and snorted. Luke gripped the reins and patted its cheek. "Easy, boy. Easy. You're alright."

"Dumb horse seems madder than you, Luke." Damon laughed. "I spoke only in jest. It was a good race. You nearly had me."

Very nearly. "Aye, it was a good race," Luke said. "Well done, Damon."

Damon guffawed. "Well done? Is that the best you can muster?"

"Aye, 'tis," Luke said. *He means to start a quarrel.* "The race is done. You've earned your victory. Let's not—"

"You leave him be, Damon," Sarah said. She took Luke's hand in her own once more. "The only reason you won is because your stallion has such a big nose."

Luke saw the anger wash over Damon's face. *Sarah, what have you done?* He squeezed her hand and stepped a little in front of her.

Damon glared at her. "Is that so?"

"Aye," Sarah said. "You ought to have lost."

Luke watched Damon's eyes. They were blue now but seemed to flare the faintest of reds around the iris. They swept over Sarah, gradually moving down until they stopped and stared.

What is he looking at? Luke followed Damon's gaze. Then he saw it. *He stares at us. At her hand in mine.*

"So," Damon said lowly, "*this* is who you choose?" He closed the fingers of his right hand around the leather pouch and slowly looked up. "You wear his cloak and hold his hand, I see."

Luke felt Sarah lean into him and grip his hand more tightly. She nodded.

"So be it," Damon said. "Then I have but one last thing to give to you."

"Luke, let us go on from here," Christoph said. He moved around Sarah and beckoned him away. "Leave Damon to quarrel with himself."

Luke looked at Christoph steadily. *I've already lost the race. Must I walk away now as well?* He shook his head. "No, we will finish this first." He turned to Damon. "What is it that you have for her? I warn you, if—"

"I am indebted to Sarah for her services," Damon said lightly. He held the leather pouch in his palm and untied its strings. "After all, each person must be compensated for work done, whether that work was done poorly or well." He removed a coin from the pouch and held it out toward Sarah. "Next time I'll be sure to choose a better whore."

The word triggered something terrible inside Luke, as if a dam had burst within him. Rage flooded his chest and rushed down his arm. He let go of Sarah's hand and plowed his fist into Damon's face, hearing the crunch of bone on bone but feeling no pain.

Damon lurched upwards as the blood sprayed from his nose. He landed on his back hard in the dirt and flames, and the pouch of coins flew into the air. Fifteen silver raindrops fell from the sky and scattered upon the racetrack.

"You will never speak to her again!" Luke shouted. He took two strides and stood over Damon. "Do you hear me? *Never again!*"

Damon scrambled to his feet. He stood there, glaring and breathing heavily, while the blood dribbled from his nose and trickled through his chin beard. He cupped his hand over his mouth and nose and swiped downward, casting a stream of dark blood to the ground. Then he balled his hands into fists at sides, and charged.

Luke heard Sarah gasp behind him. He raised his fists, braced his feet, and turned his body all in one quick movement. He saw Damon widen his eyes and cock his arm.

"Enough!" Christoph bellowed. He was there in an instant, between Luke and Damon. "Damon, you will gather your things and leave this place at once."

Luke saw Damon halt immediately, as if an invisible wall had risen up in front of him. Damon scowled but lowered his fists, and after a moment, he backed away and snatched the leather pouch from the ground.

The coins are silver no more. Luke glimpsed the bloody smears on each one as Damon picked them up and dropped them into the pouch. When he'd found them all and shoved the pouch into his pocket, Damon moved to Luke's horse and pulled a rope from its saddle bag. He tied the rope to its bridle and led the horse to his stallion, which he swiftly mounted.

Luke never took his eyes from him. *Damon looks more a monster than a man now.* His eye was nearly swollen shut, while his mouth and nose were covered in blood. Luke watched him take the leading rope in one hand and tug the reins with the other.

The stallion turned and approached Luke. Christoph yet stood by his side, but Luke stepped in front of him, to within arm's reach of the stallion's nose. He glared up at Damon defiantly, but Damon paid him no heed.

Luke saw him smile. *A wicked, bloody smile. What does he find so amusing?* He watched Damon raise his arm and curl all but one of his fingers into a fist. The extended, bloodstained forefinger pointed over Luke's head.

"*You,*" Damon rasped. "You will regret this, I swear."

Luke whirled. *Sarah.* She stood behind him, clasping the cloak about her shoulders and staring up at Damon. She looked close to tears.

He heard Damon laugh and turned back. The black stallion bolted onto the racetrack, while the white horse galloped close behind. They left behind a swirling trail of dust as they crossed the track and raced into the fiery field.

Luke watched them until they vanished from sight. He tightened his jaw. *If I ever see him again.* He clenched his fist and felt a pain shoot into his wrist. When he glanced at his hand, he saw the blood upon his knuckles for the first time. *His blood. Not mine.* Even so, he wiped his hand on his breeches.

"Luke?" Sarah asked.

He turned. Christoph was standing beside her, with his arm around her shoulders, and she was crying. He went to her.

"Are you alright?" Luke asked. He took her hand in both of his. "Damon will not harm you. We won't let him."

Sarah shook her head. "So you say, but he—" She wiped the tears from her cheeks. "You don't know him. He's cruel. If only I'd known before, I would never have—"

"What's done is done, Sarah," Christoph said. "Though Damon may have fooled you at first, he will never do so again."

He fooled me as well. "You were right, Christoph," Luke said. *I gave in to Damon's heckling, and now look what's become of it.* He let go of Sarah's hand and shook his head angrily. "If only I'd listened to you."

Christoph laid his hand on Luke's shoulder. "Aye, I'd hoped you would. But, as I said, what's done is done." He turned to Sarah. "What would you have us do, Sarah?"

Though her head was bowed, Luke could see the blush upon her cheeks. When she looked up at Christoph, her eyes seemed wet and glossy.

"Take me home," Sarah said quietly. She looked at Luke. "Please. It's not far."

"Let me take her, Christoph," Luke said. "It's the least I can do, after the trouble I've provoked. I promise no harm will come to her."

Christoph nodded slowly. "Very well, as you say. I'll see you to the edge of Glover's Field, and then we'll go our separate ways. After what has taken place this night, Damon will not dare hurt her with you by her side. But you must still be on your guard."

Luke nodded once, like a soldier going to battle. *I will.* He turned to Sarah and held out his hand.

She looked at it for a moment, then placed her hand in his. When she looked up at him, she was smiling.

Aye. Luke smiled back. *I will.*

CHAPTER 17

The western horizon was no longer streaked with the purples and reds of the setting sun but blended seamlessly into the night sky.

Millions of stars sparkled within the black canvas, and not one cloud shadowed the vast firmament. The night was so clear that the seldom seen stars shined radiantly, as if they'd been created that very night and were glowing for the first time.

All the air was still and cool, too chilly for the last day of summer but perfect for the beginning of autumn. Every now and then a light breeze would rustle the leaves, causing a few to fall to the sidewalk. Most of the trees were yet full and green, but some were trimmed with oranges or yellows on their utmost branches. The woodsy scent of fresh, dried leaves wafted ever so faintly through the air that it was almost undetectable, but it was there nonetheless, hinting at what was to come.

Security lights buzzed and crickets chirped. A car would occasionally drive by, temporarily flooding the pavement with light and drowning the quiet with its engine. But the light would dim and the noise fade as the car sped past, and the street would return to its tranquil stillness.

Sarah did not want the night to end. *Maybe I should walk slower.* When Damon had first threatened her in Glover's Field, all she'd wanted was to go home. *Lakeview should be bigger. Or farther away.* She glanced up at Luke as he walked beside her. *Then you wouldn't have to leave as soon.*

He looked at her, then smiled. *Oh goodness.* She smiled a little then looked down at the sidewalk. She slid her hands into the jacket's pockets and quietly balled them into fists. *Why am I so nervous?*

"You're awful quiet over there," Luke said.

Sarah kept her eyes on her shoes. "Oh, I was just thinkin', I guess." She looked up at him then. "That's all."

"I see." Luke grinned and looked up ahead. "Thinkin' about what?"

"Oh," Sarah shrugged, "nothin'." She heard him chuckle. *I wonder what he's thinking.* She saw him look at her out of the corner of his eye. He was still smiling. *Maybe he's thinking about me.* She smiled and looked ahead.

"So you're quiet and you think about nothin', huh?" Luke asked.

"Yup, I guess so," Sarah said. *He doesn't know what to say.* She glanced across the street. *Not that I do either.* "Soo, what are you thinking about?"

"Me?" Luke asked. "Nothin'."

Sarah laughed. "Hey, that's my line."

"I know," Luke said. "I just stole it."

"Well, that wasn't very nice."

"Sorry."

Sarah chuckled and kept walking. She focused on an intersection ahead of them as it came closer, while she waited for Luke to say something. *Maybe I should say something.* She stopped beneath the stop sign, and Luke stood beside her. *But what?* She looked both ways. It was clear. She crossed the street. He walked with her.

When she reached the other side and stepped up onto the sidewalk, Sarah glanced at Luke. His hands were in his pockets, and he seemed to be looking straight ahead, just strolling along. She felt a slight breeze upon her face, and she glimpsed his camouflage T-shirt drifting against his chest. *I think I can see his muscles.* She turned her head toward him. *Yup, I can definitely see his muscles.* She looked away when she felt her cheeks getting warm.

Sarah flexed her fingers within the jacket's pockets as she walked. *I hope he can't read my thoughts.* She chewed her lip and looked at her shoes again. *What must he think of me? I'm flirting with him, but I just went out with Damon a few hours ago.* She widened her eyes at that. *I hope he doesn't think I do this all the time. Why won't he say anything?*

Sarah looked up at him. "So Luke—"

"Sarah, are—"

She pursed her lips as she looked at him, trying not to laugh. Luke scratched his head, and then he grinned.

"Um, yeah," Luke said. "I'm sorry. You go first."

"Well, I was just—" Sarah tucked a hair behind her ear. "I mean, I just wanted to—" She glanced down. "Oh my, is your hand okay?"

Luke seemed to jump. "My hand?" He held it up quickly. "Oh wow, I'm sorry. It's not mine." He rubbed the red flakes from his knuckles. "It's Damon's. I should've wiped it off better."

Sarah winced as she watched. *He might have broken Damon's nose.* She looked a little closer. *His knuckles are bruised.* "Um, are you sure it's okay? Your hand looks swollen."

"Nah, it's good." Luke held his wrist and flexed his fingers slowly. He winced. "Well, maybe a little sore."

Sarah stopped walking and took his hand in both of hers. "Oh, it *is* swollen." She felt his hand with her thumbs, gently pushing here and there. "You should probably put some ice on it when you get home."

She wondered for a moment if he'd heard her, but then she thought he nodded.

"Okay," Luke said.

Something in his voice made Sarah look up. She ran her eyes over his hair, which was pulled back loosely in a ponytail, and she noticed that some of the strands hung behind his ears. She traced his beard along his jawline until she reached his lips, which were curved into a half smile. She looked to his eyes then. *They're so gray. But there's blue in them too.* They gazed at her.

She suddenly remembered that she was still holding his hand. She let go.

"Yes, ice," Sarah said. She quickly turned away and started walking again. "Make sure you put some ice on that."

She heard Luke chuckle just before he came up beside her.

"Okay," he said.

Sarah felt the blush sweeping across her cheeks. *It's a good thing it's dark out so he can't see how embarrassed I am.* She peeked once more at his hand as it swung by his side. The shadows made his knuckles look puffy and misshapen. *He did that for me.*

"Thank you," Sarah said.

"For what?"

"For standing up for me." Sarah looked up at him. "Thanks."

"Oh." Luke smiled. "No problem."

Sarah glanced at the ground. "You know, I've never had a guy punch someone for me before."

"Really?"

Sarah shook her head. "Nope. Never." *But I kinda liked it.* "I guess I never really needed a guy to punch someone for me, though." She turned toward him suddenly. "And I usually don't cry like that. Just so you know."

Luke laughed. "That's okay. You're allowed."

"Well, I just didn't want you to think I was a baby or something," Sarah said. "Like one of those girls that's always emotional and what not."

"One of *those* girls?" Luke asked.

"Yeah, you know," Sarah said. "Those girls that always cry—" She noticed for the first time that he was trying not to laugh. "Hey, I am not one of...I was just sayin' that—" She smiled and turned away from him. "Oh, go get a haircut."

Luke guffawed. "What? What's wrong with my hair?"

"It's too long."

"Oh, that's *right*," Luke said. "I remember you sayin' something about that the other day."

"What?" Sarah turned back to him. "When did I—" *The dude with the weird tattoo who needs a haircut.* She winced. "Oh. Sorry?"

Luke laughed. "You're fine. It does need cut. I let it get long after I got my tattoo awhile back." He glanced up at the sky and narrowed his eyes. "Yeah, that sounds about right. I was goin' through a rebellious phase then, and I guess I never quite grew out of it."

"Oh, well it doesn't look bad on you," Sarah said. "But I think you'd look good with it short." She held out her hand towards him. "I mean, not that you don't look good now. You do. I just meant—" *Good grief, Sarah! Stop talking!* She cleared her throat and tried to smile. "Um, yeah."

Luke just smiled then looked ahead.

Sarah watched him quietly. *He's so much taller than me.* "How old are you?"

"Twenty and seven years, to be exact." Luke turned to her. "Why?"

Sarah shrugged. "Just wondered."

"Oh. And how old are you?"

"Twenty-six. To be exact."

Luke chuckled. "That's a good age. Almost as good as twenty-seven."

"You mean *better* than twenty-seven, right?" Sarah asked.

"Hmm, better than twenty-seven?" Luke seemed to study the sky again. "Nope, sorry." He looked at her then. "Twenty-seven is better. Guess you'll have to wait 'til your next birthday to find out."

"Whatever," Sarah laughed. She stopped at another intersection, then walked into the street. "You'd better be nice to me, or I'll tell Chris on you."

Luke followed beside her. "Hey, don't do that. Chris might smack me."

"Oh, no he would not." Sarah stepped up onto the sidewalk. "Chris is too nice to do something like that. Now, I might smack you." She glanced at Luke and grinned. "But Chris wouldn't."

"You're probably right," Luke laughed. "You know, I've only known Chris for two days. But he's already saved my life twice."

"What?" Sarah made a face as she looked at him. "How?"

Luke smiled a little. "Well, he saved me when I was up on the A-Line Bridge, and it was because of him that I went to church and was saved."

"Wait, the A-Line Bridge?" Sarah asked. "What were you guys doing up there? I didn't think people were allowed on the bridge."

"They're not," Luke said. "I'm pretty sure the cops keep an eye out for teenagers or anybody that tries to cross it. But I wasn't trying to cross it." He pursed his lips then and seemed to look at the ground. "I was trying to jump. To take my life."

What? Sarah stopped walking and stared him. "You tried to commit suicide?"

Luke looked up at her and nodded. "Yes."

"But why?" Sarah searched his eyes for an answer. "Why would you want to take your own life?"

"Well," Luke sighed, "at the time, I thought I knew. I felt helpless and overwhelmed, like I was trapped. I didn't think my life was worth living anymore, 'cause everything seemed so pointless. Have you ever felt that way before? Wondered why you keep trying even though you know it's never gonna get you anywhere?"

Sarah nodded quietly. *Yes. More than once.*

"That's how I felt," Luke said. He shrugged and shook his head. "And I just couldn't take it anymore. There was this pain inside me, this pain of struggling each day to survive just so I could make it to the next day and repeat the process all over again. I had no hope, no reason to try anymore. I started doing drugs to numb myself, to help me relax, but I felt worse once the high wore off. And the alcohol didn't help either. So Friday night, I made my decision and went to the bridge."

Friday night? Sarah covered her mouth with her hand. "But...I saw you that morning. Friday, during lunch." *How did I treat him? I said so many terrible things behind his back! What if he heard me?* She laid her hand on his arm. "Luke, I'm so sorry. I didn't know."

"But how could you have known?" Luke asked. "I was just another rude customer bringing back his food. There's no way you could've seen what was going on inside me. As foolish and selfish as it was, ending my life was my decision. If I'd succeeded, it would've been my fault and nobody else's."

Sarah moved her hand from his arm and slipped it into her jacket's pocket. She glanced at the ground. *How could I have been so mean to him?* She looked up at him, sensing the guilt upon her face. "So...what happened?"

"Well, before I ran to—" Luke looked away from her and exhaled. He shook his head and turned back. "Eddie, my friend that was killed last night, he brought me my share of the drugs we'd bought the day before. And I snorted some right before I went to the bridge."

"Oh," Sarah said quietly. "Is that why you...."

Luke nodded. "Yeah, that was part of it. After I snorted the drugs, I felt desperate and almost paranoid. Like I just had to kill myself right then, right now. I've never craved death so bad as I did in that moment. So I ran to the bridge, and I jumped over the edge." He furrowed his brow. "Or at least I thought I did. I felt myself falling, but then something grabbed my shoulder and pulled me back."

"Chris?" Sarah asked.

"Yes, Chris." Luke suddenly smiled. "I don't know how long he'd been there or where he came from, but he saved my life that day. When we went to Leon's the next night—when Damon and you and me and Chris were all there, remember?"

Sarah nodded quickly.

"Well," Luke said, "me and Chris went there and ate supper, and he invited me to come to church with him. I told him I'd go, mostly because I felt like I owed him one, but also because I was curious. I knew I was missing something in my life, so I figured sure, why not? But when we went to church this morning, something in me changed. I felt—" He scanned the sky for a moment, then looked at her and smiled. "Different. I felt different."

Sarah narrowed her eyes. "What do you mean, different? Like, religious or something?"

Luke chuckled. "No, not religious. I just felt different." He held out his hand toward her. "See, I've always made fun of people who go to church. But as I sat in that pew, I found myself actually wanting to know more about Christ. When the pastor gave the invitation to come forward and receive Christ, I felt like my heart was going to explode if I didn't walk down that aisle. I craved Christ as much as I'd craved death not two days before. And I didn't realize it then, but the pull inside my heart was the Lord working to bring me to Him. So I gave my life to Him, and now I have hope. Eternal hope and a future with Christ."

Sarah caught her breath. *There it is again. A hope and a future. How many times have I heard that today?* She shook her head a little. "But how do you know it worked? Are you sure you're really saved?"

Luke smiled and began walking again. "You know, I asked Chris the same question when—"

"Hey Luke, that's my place." Sarah pointed to a duplex across the street. "We can cut across here if you want."

"Oh sure, my bad." Luke turned and stepped off the sidewalk. "You're probably wantin' to get inside since it's kinda cold out."

Sarah smiled as she followed beside him. "That's okay. I shouldn't have cut you off like that. What were you gonna say?"

Luke furrowed his brow. "Um, I was talking about salvation and giving my life to Christ. And you asked…what was it you asked?"

"How do you know you're saved—that was my question," Sarah said. "I've always wondered what it would be like to ask Jesus into my heart, or how you'd know it really worked. I learned about that stuff in Sunday School a long time ago, and for some reason it's always stuck with me. Sometimes a verse will even pop into my head. I could never figure out why that was."

"I know why." Luke looked at her and grinned. "He's pulling at your heart too."

Sarah smirked at him. "Who, Jesus?"

"Yup," said Luke. "He died for you just like He died for me, and He wants you to give your life to Him. Then you'll have hope and a future. You won't be lost and empty anymore."

"Yeah, I dunno," Sarah said. *Why should I give my life to Christ? What if He leaves me?* She stopped walking when they reached her doorstep, and she turned to Luke. "What if my life is fine the way it is? Maybe I'm doing okay without Jesus. Or, if I gave my life to Him, how would I know I'm saved? Does it really feel that different?"

Luke met her gaze. "It's not so much that I feel different, like lightning struck me or something. Physically, I *feel* the same. I don't think salvation is a feeling. Feelings can change depending on what mood you're in. Salvation is real, permanent. In my heart, I know that I am His, and I know He will never leave me or forsake me. I have that confidence in Him."

"I just—" Sarah shook her head and glanced at the ground. "I'm sorry, but I'm just not sure I need Christ." She looked up at him. "I've lived for twenty-six years and done alright. Why should I follow Him now?"

"That's what I thought too," Luke said, "until I was so broken that I couldn't go on any longer. Even though I wouldn't admit it, my life without Christ was hopeless and empty. I lived for myself and tried to find happiness in anything I could, but nothing would satisfy me. Now I know that Jesus Christ is the only true hope in this world.

"And He wants to be your Savior too, Sarah. All you have to do is believe in Him. No person is too far gone to be made new in Christ, and no sin is too big for Him. He will forgive you because He took your sin upon Himself when He died in your place. Without Him, you would go to Hell. But through Him, you can have eternal life, if you believe in Him and turn from your life of sin. Christ has changed my life already, and I never dreamed that would be possible."

Sarah looked into Luke's eyes, and she could see the sincerity shining within them. *He has changed. This isn't the same man who yelled at me during Friday's lunch rush.* She smiled.

"What are you thinking?" Luke asked.

"You are...different." Sarah narrowed her eyes as she studied his features. "You're...I don't know. At first I thought Damon was a lot nicer than you, but now I realize how wrong I was." She looked away. *So wrong.*

The touch of his hand against hers startled her.

"Sarah, look at me." Luke took her hand in his. "I want you to stay away from Damon. There's something about him, something...dangerous. I couldn't see it before, but I can see it now. I'm not sure if he would actually hurt you, but I know he wouldn't treat you right. So please, stay away from him. Please."

Sarah gazed up at him, suddenly feeling weak and vulnerable. *No one has ever spoken to me like that before.* She wrapped her fingers around his hand and held it tightly. *How could he care so much?*

Luke smiled and leaned closer. "I'll take that as a yes?"

"Mm hmm," Sarah said. "Yes."

Luke seemed to run his eyes over her face, but then he took a step back. "It's getting late, Sarah." He gently let go of her hand. "I should probably let you get inside before you freeze."

"Oh. Yeah, you're right," Sarah said. She stepped back too. "I forgot you still have to walk home."

"That's okay. It's not too far," Luke said. "Could you do me a favor, though, before I go?"

Sarah quickly nodded. "Sure. What is it?"

"This is my phone number, and Chris's is on there too." Luke handed her a little piece of paper with two sets of numbers scribbled on it. "If you need something, or if Damon comes around and bothers you, you can call either one of us."

"Oh, okay." Sarah slipped the paper in her pocket. "I will. Thanks." She turned towards the door.

"Hey Sarah?"

She spun back. "Yes?"

"Could I have my coat back?" Luke asked. He looked as though he was trying not to shiver. "It's gettin' a little chilly out for me."

"Oh goodness, I'm sorry!" Sarah hurriedly shimmied out of the jacket and handed it to him. "You should've said something earlier."

Luke grinned. "Nah, that's okay. I should've worn a heavier shirt anyways."

Sarah watched him swing the denim jacket around his shoulders and slide his arms into its sleeves. The jacket seemed to shrink as he pulled it around himself. *It looks better on him than on me, that's for sure.* She noticed the way his camouflage T-shirt peeked out from between the jacket's open flaps, and she liked how his jeans bunched around the tops of his boots.

"Well," Luke exhaled, "I better get goin'." He walked a little ways into the yard. "Have a good night, Sarah."

"You too." Sarah unlocked the door and opened it partway. "Hey, maybe I'll call you tomorrow morning? I work tomorrow night, but I'm not doing anything before that."

Luke nodded. "Sure, that sounds good. Maybe we can talk some more about Christ then, if you wanted."

"I'd like that." Sarah stepped into the doorway but stopped. She turned around. "Luke?"

He was still standing there, looking at her. "Yeah?"

Just do it. Sarah ran from the doorway straight to him. Laying her hands on his chest, she stood on her tiptoes and pressed her lips into his cheek. When she pulled away, he was staring at her.

"What was—" Luke touched his cheek, then quickly moved his hand and rubbed the back of his neck. "Um, what was that for?"

Sarah glimpsed the pink tinging his cheeks. *I've embarrassed him.* She smiled at that. "Just for...everything."

"Oh." Luke lowered his hand to his side and smiled. "You're welcome."

Sarah ignored the warmth upon her own cheeks and laid her hand on his arm as she looked up at him. *Should I kiss him again?* She searched his face for a moment, then let her hand slide down his arm and fall to her side. She grinned as she turned around and hurried to the door.

When she'd stepped inside the doorway, Sarah turned back for one last look.

Luke was walking across her yard to the street. His elbows were bent at his hips. *He must be cold. His hands are in his jacket's pockets.* When he reached the street, he looked back over his shoulder. She saw him smile then, and he turned slightly and waved.

Sarah waved back excitedly. *He's probably laughing at me right now.* She giggled a little and leaned against the doorjamb. When Luke had crossed the street, she closed the door.

The living room was dark, except for the pale glow of the security light beaming through the closed blinds. *What a night.* Sarah smiled and walked up the stairs, gliding her hand along the handrail. *I never dreamed it would end this way.* When she reached her bedroom, she slid her hand along the wall for the light switch.

Something moved behind her in the darkness.

She gasped and started to—

It caught her around the shoulders and pinned her against itself. She inhaled just as a damp cloth was clamped over her mouth and nose.

Acrid fumes stung her eyes and burned the back of her throat. She fought to wrench free, squirmed and twisted with all her might, but it held the cloth firmly upon her face.

Every fearful breath she took pumped the dizzying scent into her head. She seemed to struggle in slow motion, weakly and sleepily. All at once she felt exhausted. She could no longer hold her head upright, and it drooped to her chest.

Her entire body went numb, yet she did not seem to fall. She hung limply in the air, like a lifeless puppet dangling by its strings.

A presence hovered over her shoulder, and a hot breath tickled her neck.

"I told you that you'd regret it." Something moist, soft caressed her ear. *"Didn't I?"*

The rush of horrific recognition was the last sensation Sarah felt before the darkness overwhelmed her.

CHAPTER 18

Her eyelids fluttered. She could feel them quivering with groggy awareness. She forced them open.

A sliver of light pierced the darkness and exploded into her vision. She squeezed her eyes shut as the brilliant shock throbbed within her head.

She sucked her breath through her teeth. The pain faded slowly into the recesses of her mind. She coughed and shivered. Her fingers tingled. She balled her hands into fists.

Awake. I am awake. She felt dizzy, sick. She swallowed and raised her head.

Her eyelids lifted, then lowered. Then lifted again. Little orange waves rippled within the blurry panorama. She blinked.

The cone-shaped outline of a torch vibrated into focus. She could see the feathery cluster of flames dancing atop the torch's pitch-soaked head. The bright flames reflected from the golden sconce, into which the torch's wooden rod was inserted.

She blinked again. Two brass vines looped around the sconce's arms. Both vines were adorned with tiny golden leaves.

I know that sconce. The flickering flames illuminated the far wall and painted her bedroom with quavering, orange shadows.

Sarah saw her bed standing along the wall to her right, with its headboard just beneath and to the right of the torch. Her closet was to her left, next to the room's only window, and she knew her drawer chest sat behind her. *I'm in the center of the room.* The open doorway was directly in front of her.

And I'm sitting. Not on the wooden floorboards, but above. *In a chair.*

She looked down at her lap then and glimpsed something upon her waist and chest. It seemed to wrap around her, and tightly. She narrowed her eyes—

Sploosh...splash...sploosh.

The sounds sloshed behind her, somewhere over her shoulder, and each one was instant and distinct. Like water being rhythmically heaved from a pail, the sound seemed to be moving steadily from her left to her right, but always it was behind her.

Sarah turned her head and tried to stand up. Her body lurched but was immediately held in place.

What is this? She tried to twist, even began to thrash, but her frantic motions were barely noticeable. The chair itself did not move.

Oh no. She glanced down quickly.

Ropes. Everywhere.

Thick, rough ropes coiled around her chest and waist, binding her to the back of the chair and pinning her arms at her sides. Even more ropes wound about her legs, tethering them to the chair's posts.

Sarah felt her heartbeat quicken. *Who has done this?* Her breaths came faster and more frequently. *What do they plan to do with me?* She looked up suddenly.

What is that smell? The odor was sharp and toxic but sweet and pleasing at the same time. It saturated the room.

"Excellent," a man said behind her. "You've awakened. I had hopes I might be able to speak with you before I left."

Sarah caught her breath. *No. Not you.* She scanned the floor frantically, while she listened and waited. *What do I say to him?* She dare not try to move again.

A cruel chuckle came from over her right shoulder, and the wet sloshing resumed its regular tempo. *He is enjoying this.* A man gradually crept into her sight but always lurked behind her in the shadows. The swinging motion of his arms appeared to match the cadenced sound of the splashing.

Sarah tried to steady her breathing. *What is it he's doing?* She pursed her lips and forced herself to look.

He was almost to the corner of the room, just beyond the foot of her bed. His back was towards her. A red cape stretched across his broad shoulders, and his black breeches and knee-high boots seemed to lengthen his legs. His blonde hair looked darker as he hunched in the corner's shadows. *But I still know him.*

Sarah watched him rise to his full height and carry a large black bucket to her bed. He gripped the bucket by its rusty handle with one hand and held the bucket's bottom edge with the other. In one swift motion, he swung the bucket backward and pitched it forward.

Yellowish brown liquid spewed from the bucket's mouth and slopped the middle of her bed, soiling the lavender bed covers with an ever-widening, putrid stain. She watched the man cock the bucket and aim for her bed a second time.

"Damon, stop! Please!" Sarah shrieked. "What do you want with me?"

Damon halted his upward swing and calmly lowered the bucket to his side. He turned towards her and smiled. Sarah cringed. His smile gleamed with vicious hatred, as did his fiery blue eyes.

"I wanted you," Damon said lowly. "And I want you still, but it's clear you've made your choice." He raised the bucket and gently held it with both hands. Then he glared at her. "A very, *very* unwise choice." He heaved the bucket forward.

Sarah stared as the river of brown flew into the air and soaked the already drenched bed. *He is mad with rage.* She swallowed. *And I am the object of that rage.* "Damon, please. Why must you do this?" She squirmed within the ropes. "Untie me. Please, I beg of you!"

"Untie you?" Damon chuckled and lightly shook his head. "And why would I do such a thing? I have you right where I want you."

Sarah felt the dread rush through her like an unexpected chill, and she shivered with fear. Something in his voice terrified her. "What do you mean?" She could feel her eyes welling with tears, and her throat suddenly burned. "What are you going to do to me?"

Damon smiled silently. He came towards then, letting the bucket swing by his leg, and walked between the wall and the foot of the bed. When he reached her chair, he set the bucket on the floor and laid his hands on either of her shoulders. He brought his face to within inches of hers.

A puffy bruise ringed his right eye, while his nostrils were encrusted with blood. The bridge of his nose looked purple and swollen.

"What do you think I'm going to do to you?" Damon whispered.

Sarah turned away from him.

Damon laughed. "Sarah, don't be angry. Won't you even look at me?"

No. Sarah tightened her jaw.

She felt a hand clamp around her chin and jerk her head to the right, bringing her face to face with his savage scowl.

"*Yes,*" Damon said, "you *will* look at me."

Sarah held his gaze, trying not to wince. *Don't give him the pleasure of seeing your pain.* Damon glared at her and roughly released her chin. She watched him walk to the bed.

"Now that you know your place, we may talk." Damon sat down on the edge of her bed and looked at her kindly. "What was it you so desperately wanted to know?"

Sarah balled her hands into fists. *Hide your fear.* She looked back at him steadily. "What are you going to do to me?"

"I would think it's rather obvious," Damon said. A cruel smile spread across his lips. "Tonight, I am going to kill you."

Sarah gaped at him. *He...he is what?* She'd watched his lips move and heard the garble of speech, but the words themselves were just odd sounds. It was as though he'd spoken another language. *Surely not. No. He wouldn't be so calm if he truly meant it.*

Damon chuckled. "Shall I continue?"

Sarah lowered her gaze to the floor.

"As you wish," Damon said. "Allow me to explain the predicament you now find yourself in. While you were sleeping, I tied you up." He laughed a little. "No doubt you already noticed this. Afterward I—" All was quiet for a moment. "Hmm. No, I did not touch you in any vile manner. I certainly pondered it, aye. But I was not permitted to go that far this time. Your womanhood is yet whole, I promise you."

Sarah felt her shoulders drooping from the weight of his words. She trembled within the ropes but kept her head bowed so he could not see her face. *He must not see my pain.* A single tear fell down her cheek and dripped from the tip of her nose. She sniffled. The ropes chafed her wrists, making them feel as though they were burning. *I must be strong. He may yet change his mind.*

"Once you were bound, my task became quite simple," Damon said. He nudged the bucket with boot. "The liquid herein is...ah, how might I put this?" He paused. "A most lethal concoction, aye. I've poured it all over the lower levels of your shanty, as well as the staircase and hallway. But in this room, I went slowly around the edges and finished with your bed. This way, when the time comes, you will be able to watch."

He wants me to ask. Sarah raised her head and narrowed her eyes. "Watch what?"

She saw him glance towards the torch then, and he smiled when he looked back at her.

"I think it best that I don't spoil it for you," Damon said.

No, it cannot be. Sarah felt the horror surge into her chest. *"Nooo!"* She screamed at him and strained against the ropes. "You can't do this to me!"

Damon laughed. "But I can. And I will." He shrugged lightly. "Besides, if you could see what was truly taking place around you, you would know that you're already destined to burn. I am merely bringing about that end much sooner."

"You liar!" Sarah shouted. "There is no fire but for the one you plan to set. This is all your doing!"

Damon shook his head sternly. "No, Sarah. I may be the one who attacked you and tied you up, but ultimately you are here because of the choices *you* made. All you have done over the past few days has brought you to this moment. You chose to drink the ale at the Night's River, you chose to meet Prince Leone, you chose to accompany me to the horse race. But in the end, you chose Luke over me. So now, while you are yet within our reach, you must pay for your choices."

"Who do you think you are?" Sarah asked lowly. "You've no right to condemn me to suffer this...this torment! You alone are at fault! If it weren't for—"

"Terra Caligines is burning, you foolish girl!" Damon yelled. "And you are blind to its flames! Even now they rage all around you, and still you blame me for your peril.

"You have brought this upon yourself, Sarah. You ignored every warning and disregarded every sign of your doom. You rejected the only One who could save you and instead lived for yourself and others. You avoided the thought of death, refused to consider what might happen if everything came to an abrupt end. And yet here you are, facing that abrupt end. But it is too late for you. No one can save you now."

"You once told me the Rovenians were mad," Sarah said spitefully. "But now you sound just like them. You are nothing but a fool. Terra Caligines does not burn now and will never burn! It is you who should—"

Damon laughed wickedly. "One day, I will! And you will join me!" He slammed his fist into the bed and suddenly scowled at her. "You cannot begin to fathom the depths of my hatred for the Rovenians. I am not one of them, as you so accuse. When you look at me, you see a man. But your human eyes cannot see beyond this decaying flesh."

Sarah watched him clasp the front of his tunic and dig his fingers into the skin above his heart. He grimaced and looked at the floor.

"You don't know," Damon said. He looked up at her then. "You don't know what lies beneath this fleshly exterior...beyond this physical world. All the conflicts, the manipulating, the coincidences that take place in the obscure background of your life—you cannot know."

Wait. Sarah looked down at her own chest, unexpectedly reminded of the mark upon her heart. *He speaks the truth?*

"Ah, so you do believe me," Damon said. "Aye, you know of what I speak. That mark binds you to your fate more tightly than those ropes bind you to that chair. The wound upon your heart yearns to be healed, longs for something more to stop the pain. And the longing within you proves that there is life beyond this miserable existence. But you will not find that life. Not now. This is the best you will ever have."

"No," Sarah said quietly. She ran her eyes over the floor and pursed her lips. *There is a way. I remember.* She looked up at Damon. "I know how to find the life you speak of."

"What?" Damon narrowed his eyes and leaned forward. "What did you say?"

"I know the way," Sarah said steadily. "Christoph and Luke both spoke to me of—"

"They are both fools, just as you are!" Damon pushed himself from the bed. "Christoph himself is a scarred halfwit who claims to know the way, but he chooses to live amongst those who reject him! What better example of a fool is there?"

Sarah watched him pace about the room. He raised his arms and clenched his fists, scowling the entire time.

"For *years* we have waged war against Christoph and his father," Damon said furiously. "We have appeared to mankind in many forms throughout the ages, been called by many different names, all in an effort to bring mankind to us and lead them away from Rovenia. We despise the Rovenians because we know what fate awaits us...and what glory awaits them. We have no hope, so why should any of mankind?"

Glory? We? Sarah furrowed her brow. "What has Christoph ever done to deserve such hatred from you?"

Damon smirked. "You mean from us. It is not what he did to me alone, but what he did to *us* which evokes *our* fury." He strode forward and stood over her. "Christoph damned us—me and all the others. Damned us to an eternity of suffering and torment. He and his father, whose name is so abominable I will not speak it—together they banished us from Rovenia and condemned us to...to...."

"To what?" Sarah asked.

Damon sneered. "Everlasting destruction."

No. Christoph would never. Unless— "What was it you did?" Sarah asked curtly. "You must have done something to warrant such punishment."

"NO!" Damon swiped his hand before her face. "Christoph's actions are not justified, and our fate is undeserved. We followed Prince Leone and rebelled against the King of Rovenia because we knew that our Prince was a far better leader than the King could ever be. But the King squashed our rebellion and cast us from his presence. He exiled us to the realm of the dead, to the land of the shroud—the fiery pit of Terra Caligines."

Damon stormed to the doorway and stood with his back to her. She watched his shoulders rise and fall slowly, and he seemed to bow his head. When he turned back around, he crossed his arms and glowered at her.

"My brothers and I are doomed, Sarah," Damon said lowly. "And we know our time for revenge is short. The only way we can exact any sort of retribution upon the King is to steal that which he loves the most—people." He took a few steps towards her, and his expression appeared to soften. "Our sole mission is to take as many people with us into this fiery pit as we can. So we lure and entice and trick these fools to come with us...and they do!" He smiled then. "Humans are so easily swayed, so quickly seduced by the pleasures of this world. Why the King loves them so, I will never understand."

He truly is heartless. And utterly resolved to see this through. Sarah looked at him imploringly. "Why must you do this to me? I am only one person, hardly a threat. You can still let me go."

"Sarah, my dearest," Damon chuckled, "you truly don't understand, do you?" He walked to her and smiled sympathetically. "You are not just one person. You are the *only* person who is uniquely you. For as long as this world has existed, there has never been a Sarah Ryans just like you, and there will never be another Sarah Ryans just like you after you are gone. That fact makes you special, unique. Valuable."

Sarah saw him glance at the floor suddenly and narrow his eyes. His smile broadened. She watched him pick up the bucket by its handle and slowly tip the bucket with his free hand. A steady stream of brown spattered to the floor just beyond her boots.

"The King knows how much your life is worth, Sarah." Damon began to walk around her, one measured step at time, and kept the bucket tipped at his side. "But you humans are content to squander your lives on worthless things, to waste your lives doing whatever it is that pleases you at the time. You willingly debase the gift that has been given to you, and that devaluing of life plays right into our hands."

Damon vanished behind her left shoulder, but Sarah could still hear the constant spattering of wetness on wood. She listened to the sound, followed it as moved steadily behind her, until Damon reappeared on her right side. *What is he—* She gasped.

"You see, Sarah," Damon said lightly, "Prince Leone had hopes that you would stay here, in Terra Caligines. He knew your potential, and he wanted your skills to be used for his purposes."

Damon reached the beginning of circular, wet trail and stopped pouring. Sarah watched him set the bucket on the floor. Then he smiled at her. *No. Please, no.* Her heart began to race with fear.

"Damon, I beg you," Sarah said desperately. "Don't do this terrible thing. Please, untie—"

"As I was saying," Damon said, "Prince Leone sent me into your life to distract you, to keep you from going down a road that might lead you to Rovenia. He instructed me to interfere with your encounters of Luke and Christoph, to make certain you didn't get too close to either of them. But the scarred imbecile thwarted our plans...*again*." His face darkened and his eyes grew fierce. "Christoph interrupted us when I introduced you to Prince Leone, he accompanied you during the horse race, he encouraged Luke to apologize to you. Oh, Christoph ruined everything again!"

Damon cursed and flung the bucket across the room. Sarah thought to scream but he lunged at her before she could force the air from her lungs. He clamped his hands around her shoulders so hard that the chair scooted backwards.

Damon shoved his face into hers. "I saw you. Out there."

What? Sarah strained back against the chair. "Out...where? Damon, I—" When he opened his mouth slightly, she could see the saliva stretching between his lips.

"Outside on your doorstep. With him," Damon said. His voice was barely a whisper, but it was the only sound she could hear. "I saw you kiss him."

Sarah quivered as she stared at him. *Breathe. Just breathe.* If she moved her head at all, her nose would bump into his.

"You could have been mine." Damon looked into her eyes, but then seemed to gaze at her mouth. "But now you will never be his."

Damon dove forward as his eyes flared to red, and enveloped her mouth with his. Sarah pursed her lips and tried to turn away, but he pinned her against the back of the chair. She closed her eyes as she squirmed, but he would not stop. *Get off me!* She forced herself to open her mouth. When she felt his lip, she bit down with all her might.

Damon jerked backwards and laughed. "I always knew you had it in you! You just needed to be...awakened. Needed someone to light the fire within you." He touched his lip gingerly, then smiled and licked the blood from his fingers. "Aye. Permit me to light that fire for you."

Sarah stared at him as he walked to the doorway. *No. NO!* "You cannot do this to me!" She strained against the ropes until she could hardly breathe. "Damon! Don't leave me here!"

Damon reached for the torch and removed it from the sconce. He turned within the doorway and calmly bowed his head toward her.

"Don't be afraid, Sarah. We will not be parted for long," Damon said. He looked at her then, and his eyes were bright red. "After all, we have all eternity to be together."

He smiled one last time and walked into the hall, while the light from his torch flickered along the walls.

"Damon!" Sarah shouted. "Damon, please!"

He did not look back. She watched him stride through the hall and turn at the staircase, while his cape waved behind him. As he moved down out of sight, she listened to the stairs' descending creaks. Then all was silent.

Sarah trembled within the darkened room, fighting the urge to scream. *He won't do it. He won't.* She held her breath as she strained to hear the slightest sound. *He'll come back. He'll—*

A deafening whoosh exploded downstairs, as if a hundred trees had crashed to the ground at once. Flames erupted on the wall beyond the staircase, while orange shadows thrashed in the hallway.

Sarah smelled the smoke before she glimpsed it drifting through the floorboards. A door slammed somewhere beneath her.

"DAMON!"

The distant galloping of hooves and the vicious crackling of flames were the only replies to her screams.

CHAPTER 19

The night air seemed to have grown chillier during the short time it had taken him to walk from Sarah's duplex to the other end of town.

Luke flexed his fingers within his jacket's pockets and pulled the jacket snugly around him, shivering a little as he did so. *I wonder if I can see my breath.* He blew steadily into the air, but no fog escaped from his mouth.

Okay, so maybe it's not that cold. He hunched his shoulders as he turned the corner and followed the sidewalk onto another street. *But it's still cold.*

He looked up ahead as he walked, casually scanning the buildings and the street. *I can tell I'm almost home.* The tidy duplexes and immaculate homes of Lakeview were gone now and had been replaced by shabby apartment complexes separated by chain-link fencing. Most of the ground in front of the complexes was paved over, while the few plots of grass which remained were overrun with garbage and children's toys. Even the street itself was pocked with potholes and streaked with graffiti.

I really need to consider moving. Nine years is too long to live in such a place. The sights and smells of the streets suddenly evoked a terrible feeling of guilt within him. He exhaled slowly and looked down at the sidewalk. *How many times was I high or wasted when I walked out here? What about that one time when I—*

Luke squeezed his eyes shut and opened them, shaking his head lightly. *But I'm not that man anymore. Christ has changed me. He's taken all that away from me, right?* He raised his head and looked up into the sky. Millions, perhaps billions of stars sparkled within the darkened expanse, miles and miles above him, and not one cloud drifted anywhere in sight. *I never truly noticed how awesome it is. How huge, infinite even.* He swallowed the burning lump that unexpectedly gathered in his throat.

Lord, who am I that you would love me? That you would see me here, now, walking on this cracked sidewalk in this crummy neighborhood? Out of everyone in the entire world, out of all those people who can see this same sky right now, who am I? I'm no one. He glanced down as he walked, wiping his eyes on his sleeve, and smiled a little. *I'm an ant, pretty much. A little ant runnin' around down here, tryin' to figure out which way to go.* He looked up at the sky again. *Lord, where do you want me to go? Are you listening to me even now?*

The sudden brightness of a security light filled his vision, and he quickly looked away. He blinked and glanced at the pole as he walked beside it. *Huh, I never noticed that before.* Several wrinkled sheets of paper were taped all over the pole. Each paper seemed to be advertising a business or seeking information about a missing pet, but one paper in particular caught his eye.

"Jamie Cross Therapeutic Services," he read to himself. "You call me, I'll listen. No matter what."

Luke grinned. *Okay, Lord. That answers my question.* He kept walking and listened to the sound of his boots hitting the sidewalk. He lowered his head and hunched his shoulders then, but the chill he felt was not from the cold. He smiled. *I can't stop thinking about her.*

His cheek tingled as he remembered the warmth of her lips. *I never thought she'd—I just stood there and stared at her.* He rolled his eyes. *It's like I forgot how to talk.* He chuckled and shook his head. *But she was blushing too. Her cheeks were rosy. A pretty red.*

Luke sighed and rubbed the back of his neck. *Lord, I can't get her out of my head. Guard my feelings for Sarah. Help me to keep them in check, to treat her with respect. To treat her how you would want me to treat her.* He slid his hand back into his jacket's pocket and looked up at the stars. *You can see her right now. Watch over her tonight, Lord. I talked to her tonight about you. I'm pretty sure she wants to know more, but she needs you to show her the way. You know her heart and her thoughts. Keep her safe and bring her to you.*

A hazy yellow light washed over the apartments to his right, creating misshapen shadows which swept across the walls. Luke immediately looked up the street.

Two bright headlights crested the slope a short distance ahead and bounced through the intersection. He heard the vehicle accelerate as its headlights fell over him and the sidewalk. He raised his hand to his eyes, squinting into the oncoming brightness, and stepped back from the street's edge.

The lights seemed high off the ground, and the engine sounded low and powerful. *A truck.* He heard it squeal through the street, appearing to speed right for him. *I hope he shifts down soon.* Luke stared as the truck raced by, while the smell of burning diesel fuel chased after it.

Poor truck. He snorted and shook his head. *That guy better be careful or he's gonna blow the—*

Red lights flared and tires screeched. He watched the truck slide to a stop in the middle of the street, not twenty feet beyond where he stood.

What's he think he's doin'? Luke felt for his knife and moved out from the wall, always keeping his eye on the idling truck. It looked black in the darkness but could have been blue. *It's a Ford. An old one.* He could see the rust above the wheel wells and along the running boards.

The truck sputtered and chugged loudly, while wisps of white smoke shot from its exhaust pipe. Luke wrapped his fingers around the hilt of his knife and tightened his jaw. *Well, is he gonna get out?* He stepped back and braced his feet.

The driver's side window glided down.

"Luke!" a man shouted. "Luke, get in!"

I know that voice. Luke relaxed his hand and took a step forward. "Chris? Is that you?"

"Yeah, it's me!" Chris looked out the window and waved earnestly. "Come on, you need to get in!"

Something's wrong. Luke jogged to the window. "What is it? Why—"

"Sarah!" Chris said. "It's Sarah. Get in!"

No. Luke gripped the bottom of the window frame with both hands. "What happened? I just left her house—"

"Just get in! I'll tell you on the way." Chris shoved the truck into drive. "Move it, Luke! We don't have much time!"

Luke bolted from the window and raced around the front of the truck to the passenger door. He yanked it open and jumped inside. The truck lurched forward, and he slammed the door shut.

"Chris, what's wrong with her?" Luke fumbled for his seatbelt. "Is she okay? Is she hurt?" He pulled it across himself and clicked it into place. "Chris, tell me—"

"Her house!" Chris said. He braked and jerked the steering wheel to the left, and the truck careened onto the intersecting street. "It's on fire, Luke. Her house is on fire."

"What?" Luke stared at him. *No, I don't understand. He must be wrong.* "What are you saying?" He suddenly felt enraged. "Where's Sarah!"

Chris did not look at him. "She's inside, Luke," he said quietly. "Sarah is trapped inside."

Luke fell back against the seat. *No. No.* He slowly turned his head and stared out the window. Glowing streetlights and colorful houses streaked by his window in a wild blur. *No. It can't be.*

"But how—" Luke swallowed the emotion gathering in his throat. "Are you sure that—" He turned to Chris. "How do you know for sure?"

"My fire pager," Chris said. He braked again and spun the steering wheel to the right. "I'm on call tonight with the fire department. My pager went off a little while after I got home—couldn't have been more than ten minutes ago. The call was about a duplex on Lakeview West. Said the right side of the duplex seemed to be where the fire started, but the fire had spread and engulfed the entire lower half of the structure. The address is listed under the name Sarah Ryans. No one seems to be home in the left side of the duplex, but they're certain Sarah's in hers."

"Well, maybe she's not!" Luke said. He blinked back the tears that welled in his eyes. "Maybe she got out. I dropped her off and she went inside, but maybe she decided to leave—"

"Luke, no." Chris looked at him sadly. "They can...Luke, they heard someone screaming upstairs."

The brutal words smacked Luke in the face. *No.* He felt his mouth open as he stared at Chris, but he could not find any words to say. He turned back to the window as the tears began to spill from his eyes. *No, no, NO!* He pressed his fist to his forehead and squeezed his eyes shut, while the tears fell down his cheeks.

"Luke," Chris said. "Luke, it's not too late. She still has time."

Luke opened his eyes but glared out the window. "No. She's gone." His voice was low and bitter. "It could be worse for her if she was still...for her sake, I hope she's—"

"No," Chris said sternly. "No, it would *not* be better if she was dead. It would be worse for her—worse than you could ever imagine. Have you forgot your salvation already? We've still got time! The fire department is there now tryin' to save her. They're doin' their best to get to her. Don't give up hope so easily, Luke."

"I should've stayed with her." Luke forced himself to look at Chris. "I never should've left her alone."

Chris shook his head. "This isn't your fault, Luke. You couldn't have prevented this fire, even if you'd known it was about to happen." He moved his foot to the brake, and the truck began to slow. "What is intended for evil can be used for good. The Lord is in control of all things at all times, and what you think is a hopeless situation may just be the complete opposite."

Luke narrowed his eyes. "*Intended?* What are you saying?"

"This fire." Chris seemed to tighten his jaw, but he did not look at him. "It was no accident."

Damon. Luke slammed his fist onto the dash. "I'll kill him! He'll wish he'd never—"

"No, you won't!" Chris stopped the truck in the middle of the road and turned to him. "You've got to control your temper, Luke. Revenge is not yours to give. Damon will be held accountable for his actions, but not by you." He thrust the gear shift into park and yanked off his seatbelt.

"What are you doing? We're not there—" Luke looked out the windshield and caught his breath. *Yet.*

A sea of red and blue lights flashed incessantly less than a block up the street. A dozen or more police cars blocked the road from both directions, while three fire trucks formed a semicircular ring in the duplex's front yard. Dozens of firefighters and police officers moved throughout the yard and the street, while a gathering of neighbors and onlookers watched at a safe distance from all sides of the scene.

Luke saw two ambulances parked just outside the chaotic ring, like two beacons of hope patiently standing watch. But even the ambulances could not escape the quivering orange glow which overshadowed everyone and everything.

"Oh no," Luke breathed. "Oh—"

"Come on, Luke!" Chris yelled. "We don't have much time!"

Luke hastily unclicked his seatbelt and flung it to the side. He lowered his shoulder into the door as he pulled the latch, and tumbled outside. He heard the driver's side door slam shut.

Luke pushed his own door aside and ran. Chris appeared at the front of the truck and sprinted with him up the street.

The air isn't cool anymore. The closer Luke came to the police cars, the more he could feel the heat upon his face. He started sweating beneath his jacket. *Almost there. Faster, faster.* He ran behind the ring of emergency vehicles, staying close to the far edge of the street, but then stopped. Chris flew by him.

Dear Lord. Luke stood in the street, staring beyond the sea of red and blue lights.

Gone was the little white duplex. A mountain of fire blazed in its place and consumed every board, every door, and every window. Violently twitching flames leaped from the roof and clawed at the sky, while the burning home popped and snapped and whined within the inferno.

"Sarah," Luke whispered.

A strong hand gripped his arm and tugged him forward.

"Hurry!" Chris shouted.

Yes, hurry! Luke followed him between the police cars and jogged into the hectic circle. When he'd crossed the street and reached the front yard where the fire trucks stood, Chris stopped in front of him.

"Give me your knife!" Chris turned around and held out his hand. "Quick!"

Luke could barely hear him above the roar of the flames. "What? Why do you—"

"Just give it to me!"

Luke pulled the knife from its sheath and hurriedly handed it to Chris.

"Alright, you stay here," Chris said firmly. He slid the knife into his belt. "I'm goin' in after her."

What? Luke widened his eyes. "Are you crazy? You'll die!" He stepped to him and gripped his arm. "It's hopeless!"

Chris looked him in the eye. "There is always hope, Luke." He gently pushed Luke's hand away. "But you must have the faith to see it. I'm the only one who can save her now." He turned and ran.

"Chris, wait!" Luke shouted. He went after him. "You can't do this! You'll—"

"Sir, you'll have to step back, now!" The fireman cut in front of him and blocked his view of Chris. "Civilians are not allowed beyond—"

"I know the girl who lives here!" Luke said. He stepped around him. "And my friend, he's—"

A gloved hand clamped around his upper arm. Luke spun.

"I'm sorry, sir," the fireman said. "We're doin' all we can. But the fire, it's—" He exhaled and shook his head. "It's just spreadin' too fast. Some kind of accelerant must have been used for it to take over like it has. I've never seen anything like this."

Luke could hear it in his voice and see it in his eyes. "No, don't you give up!" He felt the lump gathering in his throat. "Sarah's in there! She might still be alive!"

The fireman looked at him sternly. "Sir, I know how hard this must be for you, but you've got to stay calm. We got here as fast as we could, but...I'm afraid it's too late. No one can get in or out. With her being above the fire when it started, the smoke probably got to her before the flames—"

"Don't talk about her like that!" Luke wrenched his arm from him. "She's not dead! I would know—I would feel it. But I don't." He moved around him and started running. "Chris! Chris!"

Luke saw him standing at the back of a fire truck. *Chris! Don't— Chris?* He was dressed all in fire gear and was strapping a black fire helmet onto his head. Luke watched him reach into the fire jacket and pull something long and gleaming from his belt.

"Chris!" Luke shouted as he ran towards him. "Wait!"

Chris took off towards the blaze, his arms pumping and his legs churning.

No! Luke stopped in the yard. "Chris, *wait!*" He squinted and held up his hand as the heat stung his eyes. "Don't go—"

The blow struck him from behind with such force that he did not have time to brace his fall. His shoulder dove into the ground while something heavy slammed on top of him.

Luke felt the air shoot from his lungs. He coughed as he struggled to roll over. "Get—get off me!" He kicked at the big rubber boot and shoved the gloved hand from his arm. "I said get—"

"Man, I don't know who you're yellin' for or what you think you're tryin' to do," the fireman said, "but there's no way I'm lettin' you run into that fire! Now just take it easy, and I'll let you up."

Luke nearly cursed. "I said get off me!" He elbowed the fireman in the gut and rolled from under him. "I've got to—*Chris!*"

The scarred fireman leaped through the flaming doorway and vanished into the man-made hell.

"*Nooo!*" Luke stretched out his hand desperately. "I can't lose both of—"

The fiery explosion consumed the lower half of the duplex and reverberated through the ground beneath his body. Debris blasted out the sides of the burning structure like pieces of shrapnel rocketing through a battlefield. The upstairs window shattered, shrieking as the glass fractured and burst, and a new torrent of flames erupted out the jagged opening.

"Get up!" the fireman yelled. "Get back, get back!"

Luke felt a hand pulling him to his feet. The heat was unbearable now, and he shielded his face with his arms as he stumbled backwards. He could hear nothing but the roar of the flames.

Help them. Oh Lord, please help them.

CHAPTER 20

It was only a moment.

Another second in the infinite spectrum of time elapsed. It was fleeting, like the life of a shooting star, but it was imperceptible, like the quivering of an eyelash in a faint breeze. So instant was the second that it was practically over before it began, nearly ended before it took place.

One second. Barely a moment.

She might have held her breath, might have squeezed her eyes shut, might have turned away if only she'd had more time.

But one second was all Sarah had.

She saw the blinding light and felt the mounting pressure just as her world slowed to a surreal standstill. Jagged flames froze in place and drifting smoke hovered in mid-air, while the slick sweat halted partway down her face. The relentless roar of the fire ceased, abruptly cut off by the swelling of an invisible force, and silence pierced the room.

The moment lasted for a lifetime, the second for what seemed an eternity. Time itself paused in anticipation of the escalating fury, waiting on the edge for that final push.

Sarah blinked.

The window cracked.

Time shot ahead like a newly fired missile. The white light flew forward and engulfed the room, slamming Sarah against the chair, while a blast like a sonic boom simultaneously exploded beneath her. Glass shattered, wood splintered, and metal snapped as a furious heat ballooned below. Fiery debris erupted through the floor like flaming cannonballs and crashed all around her, igniting the room in swaths of blazing orange.

A scorched chunk of rubble fell from the ceiling and slammed onto her bed, landing within an upheaval of sparks and ash. The bed burst into flames, incinerating along a maze of damp trails, and hissed and crackled until it caved at the center and dropped onto the floor.

A swirling cloud of sparks puffed from around the bed and scattered about the room like hundreds of glowing flies. They rolled, tumbled, and danced in all directions.

Sarah moaned groggily and shook her head. *Wake up! Wake up!* She blinked again as she watched the sparks rain down upon the wall at the foot of the bed.

Terror seized her throat. She remembered a splashing, a deadly liquid being poured all along that wall.

NO! Sarah tried to scream, but the smoke choked the cry from her lungs. She coughed uncontrollably as she glimpsed one spark drifting to the baseboard.

Countless flames sprouted from the single fiery seed and jetted all along the wall, racing around the room like lightning. The heinous whoosh of the flames filled her ears and momentarily deafened all other sounds.

Sarah looked around herself in sheer horror. A doorless prison of fire surrounded her on all sides. The walls of her bedroom had become four panels of flame, while the window by her closet was nothing more than a blazing hole, ever-widening as the fire ate at its edges. The ceiling rippled within the waves of heat and smoke, but she could see tiny flames nibbling through the plaster overhead, as if they were invading her room from the roof above. The floor creaked and groaned beneath her while tongues of fire lashed up through gaping holes in the boards.

"Help me!" Sarah strained wildly against the ropes. *"Please, help—"*

She choked as a whiff of black smoke shot into her nose. Her throat tightened immediately, and she gasped. She gasped again. The inside of her mouth felt dry and tasted chalky. She tried to cough. Her lungs began to burn.

Sarah jerked her hands upwards, but the ropes held them in place at her sides. She balled her hands into fists and bowed her head desperately, staring wide-eyed at the floor. The air looked clearer at her feet, but she could not reach it. The smoke was too thick, too deep.

She began to feel dizzy and lightheaded. She gasped over and over again until her heart felt so swollen she thought it might burst.

I am suffocating.

Sarah grimaced. *I don't want to die.* She bobbed her head back and forth, back and forth with each arduous breath. Her short breaths turned into labored wheezes.

It's not supposed to end like this.

The unbearable heat sweltered, writhed all around her. It matted her hair to her face and drenched her body with sweat. It charred the strings on her tennis shoes and singed her hoodie and jeans. It stung the bare skin on her hands and face like a thousand tiny irons branding her flesh.

But I'm cold. Sarah shivered deeply. *So, so cold.*

She could feel the life leaving her body, her own heat slipping into the flames and evaporating into the smoke. Her toes were numb, her legs limp, her chest constricted. She could no longer feel her arms. Her head drooped and her heartbeat slowed.

Sarah closed her eyes.

A glob of molten fire dripped from the ceiling and plopped near the tennis shoes, igniting the ring of fire around the chair. The flames raced around both sides of the circle, colliding behind the chair, and blazed mere inches from the body.

The two clenched fists relaxed, and the fingers languidly straightened. A hoarse sigh escaped the parted lips while the eyelids fluttered feebly.

Jesus.

A single tear slid down the rosy cheek.

Save me.

CHAPTER 21

The warm, russet sheen behind the closed eyelids dimmed until a pitch-black stillness settled within the void.

While the blistering heat intensified, its vicious sting upon the skin weakened as the body lost all ability to feel. The strident crackling of the flames crescendoed, ascending to a profane volume that swallowed the room, but the destructive noise fell upon deaf ears. Black smoke billowed and churned like a toxic storm cloud and swirled into the nose, but the poisonous fumes went undetected. Even the gritty taste of ash grating against the tongue and clogging the back of the throat dwindled to a bland tickle.

Life ebbed away, and death took its place.

"Saaraah."

The raspy voice moaned the name in the darkness, eerily prolonging the word. No other sound could be heard except for the ghostly utterance.

"Saaraah."

Again it called the name, beckoning to the poor soul who was known by that epithet. The voice was distant, barely a whisper, but seemed to reach across a great expanse and echo ever nearer.

"Saaraah!"

Gone was the soft voice with its inviting and pleasant tone, replaced by a harsh command demanding an immediate response. The force of the word shook the shadowy realm like an earthquake, and a crushing weight slammed against the dark space.

"Sarah!"

The worried shout burst into the void and pierced the blackness like a bolt of lightning. Life raced through the veins and filled the heart, while the lungs expanded and the mouth gasped. A constant tugging near the feet could be felt, and feeling rushed into the toes as a pressure fell away.

"Sarah, wake up!"

Something heavy dropped upon her shoulder and squeezed, swaying her upper body back and forth gently as it held her. The iron grip jostled her senses and sent a shiver through her spine. She lifted her head.

Sarah opened her eyes.

A hooded man stood beside her. He seemed to be hovering over her, and she noticed his hand upon her shoulder. She watched his eyes flit about her face. *He looks worried.* Her head suddenly felt much heavier than it should have, and she let it drop to her chest.

Sarah caught sight of the man's boots standing beside the chair. She saw them step closer. *Wait, no. That's not right.* She blinked, lightly shaking her head.

A ring of reds and oranges and yellows thrashed around her and soared several feet higher than the chair, but the black boots held their ground—*within* the flames.

She stared, unmoving. *How can this be?* The boots did not burn, the breeches did not smolder, and the hooded cape did not ignite. Not a single flame or wisp of smoke touched the man.

"Sarah, I'm here," he said. "You're going to be alright."

I know that voice. Sarah raised her head weakly and glimpsed the scarred hand by the man's side. *What is he holding?* She squinted. A long, luminous blade protruded from the bottom of the fist.

Sarah widened her eyes. "Christoph? What...are you—"

"Shh. I need you to be still now," Christoph said. He brought the point of the dagger beneath her chin. "Do not move."

Sarah caught her breath as the blade drifted by her neck. *Oh, what are you doing? I thought you were here to help me.* She could only moan in protest.

"I will not harm you, Sarah," Christoph said. "You must trust me."

Trust you? She felt his hand tighten around her shoulder. Christoph moved the dagger lower but seemed to stop near her chest. His eyes were stern and focused. *What does he mean to—* She felt a tugging, like something being wrenched back and forth. Christoph never blinked. She heard a light snap, then another, and another.

The coils of rope loosened all at once. Sarah fell into his arms like a helpless child and buried her face in his chest. She felt Christoph scoop her from the chair and rise. When she turned her head, the ring of fire appeared much closer.

He means to walk through it! "Christoph...no," Sarah whispered. She could feel the heat upon her skin. "Please, don't—"

"Be still, Sarah," Christoph said gently. "It will all be over soon." He held her more tightly and stepped even closer. "Keep your head against me. As long as you rest in my arms, the fire cannot harm you."

Sarah winced as she gazed at the flames. *He must be mad! He must be.* She bit her lip and looked up at him. *But his eyes are truthful, and he does not burn. And neither do I.* She swallowed. *Yet.* "But how can...this be? Christoph, I'm afraid—"

A flaming beam crashed through the ceiling and slammed onto the floor near what was left of the blackened closet. Fiery debris erupted on that side of the room, while a violent tremor quaked through the floorboards. As the ceiling sagged around the jagged opening, the floor began to pop and creak ominously.

"Sarah!" Christoph shouted. "You must put your faith in me! I am the only one who can save you. Do you trust me?"

Sarah buried her face in his chest and nodded fervently. *He truly is my only hope.* She clutched the front of his tunic with both hands. *My life is in his hands now.*

And then she heard it. The sound of ice cracking beneath a boot, of a branch snapping from a tree. It shrieked into her ears more intensely than the roar of the fire.

"Hold on, Sarah!"

The terrible lurch downward and the heart-wrenching stop tensed every muscle in her body. Sarah clung to his tunic as Christoph staggered backwards. *Don't fall, don't fall!* She held her breath and dared to look.

The doorway was a sheer wall of flame, but the floor buckled some three feet below the threshold. Broken boards and snapped timbers jutted out from the ragged seam where the floor had ripped away.

Christoph steadied his bearing and spread his feet apart, placing one boot slightly in front of the other, and crouched at the knees.

Oh no. Sarah quickly turned away and pressed her face into his chest. All at once she flew against his body. His arms tightened around her, and for an instant she felt weightless. But then she felt the jarring impact and heard the crunching of wood.

Yet Christoph stayed upright and steady, and his strong embrace never weakened around her. *I am truly safe, despite my doubts.* Sarah heard his boots beating the floor then and sensed that she was rushing forward. *He's running.* She held on to him as tightly as she could.

She felt Christoph turn swiftly and jump down, and he descended step by step by step to a lower level. He never stumbled or slowed. When he turned again, she felt him spin suddenly and pivot back. She heard a terrible crash beside her and felt a wave of heat wash over her. He bolted forward again.

Sarah eased her grip on his tunic as she listened to his breathing. *We should be out of the shanty by now.* Christoph seemed to be jogging at a gentle pace, with no more lurching or bumping. He had not turned for some time. *Why he is still running?* She could yet feel the heat upon her skin and hear the crackling of flames, but neither seemed as intense. *Perhaps he is taking me a safe distance away.* She raised her head and looked.

A great fire, fiercer than any she could have imagined, filled her vision. So dense, so impenetrable were its flames that she could see nothing else. *He runs right through them!* She watched the flames sweep over her one after the other, like waves upon the shore, and widened her eyes in fear.

Sarah tucked her head frantically into his chest and covered her face with her hands.*Oh Christoph, where are you taking me?* She squeezed her eyes shut. *What if you drop me? Or trip? Or grow weary?* Tears welled in her eyes. *I will die without—*

Christoph stopped running.

Sarah instantly stiffened. She opened her eyes but stared into the reddish dimness behind her fingers. She waited on edge, holding her breath, straining to hear above the fire's incessant roar.

"*Help meeeee!*"

The bloodcurdling wail pierced her ears at once, and she jerked her hands away from her face as her heart jumped within her chest.

"*Oh please! Help me!*"

She heard the miserable cry again, but it was closer this time and even more distressed. While the words themselves sought aid, the anguish in the voice seemed to beg for mercy and plead for relief.

"You denied me in life. Therefore, I must deny you in death."

Christoph? Sarah had felt the deep rumble of the words within his chest. *But he sounds so cruel...so heartless. Who would he speak to in such a manner?* She pursed her lips and forced herself to look.

Within the rippling veil of flames, a forest of ancient trees burned and smoldered before her. Upon the ground was a river of liquid fire, like molten lava, winding through the trees. The viscous river oozed and gurgled beside a long dirt path, which stretched deeper into the burning forest.

Christoph stands upon this path, but he faces the river. Sarah looked up at him. She cringed. *What has happened to him?* His eyes were cold and dark beneath the hood of his cape, and his face hard. *It's as though he's angry, yet he remains calm.* He looked straight ahead and never once blinked. She followed his gaze.

Sarah gasped and covered her mouth with her hand.

The deformed creature convulsing in the river's depths may at one time have been a man, but it no longer resembled anything human. Its flesh was charred and decomposed beyond recognition, and its eyes bled tears of crimson which streamed down its blackened cheeks. Strangely tall and sickly thin, its gangly limbs thrashed within the boiling sludge, but no matter what it did, it could not escape the river's torment. Like a drowning rat which would never completely drown, the creature seemed doomed to suffer eternally in its molten prison.

"Please, I beg of you!" it shrieked, clawing at its own face. *"Help me!"*

Sarah was overcome with sympathy. *It wants to die, but death will not take it.* She watched the creature drag its maimed fingers down its face over and over again, with increasing ferocity. It scratched at its eyes and tore through its flesh but screamed when the agony did not subside.

Sarah looked to Christoph beseechingly. *Why will you not help him?* She searched his face for compassion, for that kind expression she so admired, but no sign of pity could be found upon his stoic countenance. Only condemnation and reproach shone through his eyes.

"It is too late for you!" Christoph said loudly. "Your fate cannot be altered. Be gone from my sight!"

Sarah turned back to the creature and saw the look of horrified pain wash over its face. It screamed as it clamped its hands on the back of its head and doubled over at the waist, as if overwhelmed with indescribable grief. The river began to churn and roil about its thighs, swirling and bubbling uncontrollably.

Sarah gaped in terror.

Seven black hands bearing savage talons rose from the volatile depths. Long and grotesque the arms emerged thereafter, dripping with the glowing lava, and surrounded the creature on all sides. When the hands reached the creature's shoulders, they ceased their sinister climb and cocked, spreading their fingers and baring their claws. The creature uncovered its face then, and its eyes filled with dread. One last time it tried to scream, but the demonic hands lunged, thrusting their talons into the rotting flesh, and dragged the creature downward until its mouth filled with the searing liquid.

Sarah trembled as the creature's head vanished beneath the receding lava. She could not look away from the bubbles appearing on the river's surface. "Christoph, who...who was he?"

"A man, once," Christoph said. "But no more. He is nameless now."

Sarah looked at him uncertainly. *He shows no emotion whatsoever.* "But why—"

"It's not much farther now." Christoph looked down at her and turned toward the path. "Keep your head against me."

Sarah pressed her face into his chest and felt his arms tighten around her. When she lurched against him, she brought her hands beneath her chin and held on to his tunic.

She heard twigs snapping and leaves crunching at once. Christoph seemed to duck and leap as he ran, but always he went forward. He went on for awhile that way, moving swiftly like a deer through the underbrush, until Sarah heard his boots scuffing on stone. Then he seemed to slow, and his arms relaxed around her. She listened to the steady clomping of his boots and let go of his tunic. *He's walking now.*

Sarah raised her head a little. All was suddenly silent and still. *We've stopped.* The air in front of her was cool and gusty, but she could yet sense the heat of the flames somewhere behind her. *Have we made it?* She turned away from his chest and looked.

A great mountain soared into the sky an immeasurable distance away. Its peak was white and partially hidden among the clouds, but a resplendent shaft of light shone on its face and flecked its sides with blues, grays, and greens.

I must go there. I must. Something about the mountain called to her, beckoned to her like the light at the end of a dark tunnel. *But how?* She looked for a way—a road, a bridge, a river, anything. *Nothing touches it. It's as though we've been cut off from it.* The mountain seemed utterly unattainable, completely out of her reach.

Sarah narrowed her eyes. *Perhaps we could climb.* She leaned over Christoph's arms and looked down.

Down into nothing.

She felt her heart lurch into her throat. An immense chasm yawned beneath her—a black pit that seemed to go on and on forever. She gasped when she glimpsed Christoph's boots standing upon the stone ledge. *His toes are over the edge!* She clutched at his tunic and frantically pressed herself against him.

"Give her back! She belongs to me!"

Sarah trembled. *No. I know that voice.* She looked up at Christoph, but he kept his eyes fixed beyond the Abyss. *Did he hear? Why does he only stare?* He looked down at her suddenly and smiled a little, then turned around.

Sarah saw Prince Leone first. *It was he who shouted, I'm certain.* He stood at the edge of the fiery forest, draped in a long black cloak which glowed orange around the hem. His black hair looked brittle and unkempt, and his skin seemed paler than she remembered. But his eyes were red as hot blood. *And they look at me.* She glanced to either side of him. *They all look at me.*

A black beast sat at the Prince's right hand. It appeared to possess the body of a gigantic lion, but it bore the sneer of a demon. Blood dripped from its white fangs and sizzled upon the ground beneath its paws.

Malfera. Sarah had heard its name whispered in the village. Its eyes glowed like rubies now. *It looks wherever the Prince looks. And so does he.*

The man standing to the Prince's left wore black boots and breeches and a red tunic. His hair was blonde and cut short, as was his chin beard, and he looked strong. His fists were clenched at his sides, and he crouched threateningly.

Damon. Sarah gasped. His eyes were no longer blue but—

"She will *never* be yours, Leone," Christoph said lowly. "She is mine. *Forever!*"

With the wall of burning trees towering behind them, Prince Leone and Damon scowled at once while Malfera roared in fury. All three pairs of eyes glowed even hotter than before, and all simultaneously darted to Christoph.

"This is not the end, Christoph!" Prince Leone shrieked. "I swear to you, this is not the end!"

Sarah gasped when she saw him lunge forward. He reached the clearing in two quick strides, but as soon as his cloak touched the stone, a curtain of white steam shot up before him. He wailed and stumbled backwards.

"This may not be the end, Leone," Christoph said firmly, "but with every foul breath, *your* end draws nigh. Now, away from me!"

A plume of black smoke erupted from the forest floor and engulfed the red-eyed demons, swirling and swelling around them as they screamed. A single bolt of lightning flashed within the hellish windstorm. Then they were gone.

Sarah laid her head against Christoph and breathed a sigh of relief. "Where do we go—Christoph!" She felt him spin and clutched at his tunic. When he stopped, she was looking out over the Abyss again. *Oh no.* "What are you—"

"Do you trust me?" Christoph asked.

"Wha—what?" Sarah looked up at him anxiously. He was grinning at her. "I—" She swallowed. "I do, but—"

She felt her stomach fly into her throat as Christoph leaped over the edge. She tried to scream, but the rapid descent sucked the cry from her mouth. *I can't breathe! I can't breathe!* She closed her eyes and buried her face in his chest.

"Sarah," Christoph said.

What? Sarah shook her head and kept her eyes tightly closed. She could feel herself falling still. *If I look now, I will most certainly die.*

"Sarah," Christoph chuckled. "Open your eyes."

He laughs? Sarah raised her head a little. *Are we still falling?* She forced one eye open and squinted into the sudden light. *White. Everything is white.* She held up her hand to shield her face and opened both eyes.

"Where—" Sarah blinked and glanced down. *I'm standing up?* She looked around quickly. "Where am I?"

Christoph appeared at her side. "This land is my father's kingdom. It is now your eternal home." He took her hand in both of his. "Welcome to Rovenia, Sarah. Your faith has saved you."

"Rovenia?" Sarah asked. "But you jumped into the...I thought we—" She caught her breath. *Christoph?*

He lowered the hood of his cape and smiled at her, while a radiant glow emanated from his face. The raw, taut skin was gone from his forehead and cheeks. His beard was full, his face young and healthy, and his hands soft and unblemished.

Sarah found herself touching his cheek. "Christoph, where...are your scars?"

"My wounds are healed." Christoph laid his hand gently over her heart. "As are yours."

Sarah gasped as a terrible heat blazed into her chest. She pressed her hand over his and grimaced, nearly dropping to her knees. *Oh, make it stop! Please—* He pulled his hand away, and the searing current ceased.

"What have you done to me?" Sarah asked. She clutched her chest and stepped back, but then she suddenly felt odd. *What is that?* A soothing warmth had replaced the painful sting in her heart—a peace like none she'd ever felt before. "Christoph?"

"Your heart has been made new, Sarah, through my power," Christoph said. He nodded towards her chest. "The mark of Terra Caligines, the symbol of your doom, is no more."

Truly? Sarah unlaced the top of her tunic and pulled the cloth apart. When she looked down, something like fish scales fell from her eyes, and she could see her chest clearly.

The mark was gone. Her skin was completely healed.

"How is this poss—" Sarah caught sight of her glowing hands and gasped. "What's happening to me?"

"My spirit lives within you now," Christoph said. He moved beside her and took her hand in his. "When my father looks at you, he sees me because I have covered your blemishes with my glory. So behold, Sarah!" He swept his hand across the vast whiteness. "See with your own eyes the Kingdom of Rovenia."

Sarah caught her breath as the white veil dispersed and a heavenly light cut through the clouds. A magnificent valley appeared below her, teeming with lush vegetation, shimmering rivers, and abundant wildlife. A white castle towered above it all and ascended into the heart of the clouds above. *A paradise unlike any I could have imagined.* She covered her mouth with hand, suddenly aware of the tears in her eyes. *And it waits for me, just beyond the slope at my feet.*

"Christoph, it's so...so—" Sarah blinked back the tears and looked at him. "So beautiful. How am I fit to live in such a place? I don't deserve—"

She saw the bridge over his shoulder. *Where did that come from?* She placed her hand lightly on his arm and stepped around him.

The white stone bridge shot across the Abyss and ended in a world of fire and brimstone. *Terra Caligines. It burns.* She pressed her hand to her chest. *And so do all who live there.*

"You," Sarah whispered. "It's because of you that I am here." She gazed tearfully at the flames. "I should've died. I deserved to die, but you saved me when I cried out to you." She turned and looked up into his eyes. "Why? Why would you risk your life to save me?"

Christoph smiled at her. "Because I love you."

You love me? Sarah trembled as she searched his face. *You would die...for me?* A horrible guilt washed over her then, and she fell to her knees before him. She covered her face with her hands and wept.

"Do not weep. Your sins are forgiven. I have removed them from you as far as the east is from the west. Arise, my dear child."

Sarah felt something rest gently upon her head. She lowered her hands from her face and looked up.

Christoph was leaning over her, with one hand upon her head and the other held out to her. She smiled timidly and placed her hand in his. As he helped her to her feet, she wiped the tears from her eyes then leaped into his arms.

"Sarah?"

Luke? Sarah let go of Christoph and turned around. *Luke!* He stood a mere stone's throw away, looking at her. She stepped towards him.

Christoph caught her arm. "Sarah, wait."

Sarah stopped and looked up at him.

"There is one last thing I must tell you before you go to him," Christoph said. "You will not see me for a time, so you must listen carefully."

"What?" Sarah asked. *He is leaving me?* "Where are you going?"

"To my father's castle, to prepare a place for you," Christoph said. "King Omnideus, my father, has given me authority over all the realms to do this and many other things. In the meantime, you must return to Terra Caligines and tell the people about me. Teach them to obey everything I have commanded you."

Sarah held his arm with both hands. "Must you truly leave me? I'm not sure if I can—" She pursed her lips as she looked at him. "What will I do without you?"

"I will never leave you or forsake you, Sarah," Christoph said. "My spirit lives within you now. Though you cannot see me, I will be with you always, to the very end of the age." He pressed his hand firmly over hers. "I promise you, one day I will return. I will come back for you. For both of you."

Sarah embraced him earnestly. "Come soon, Christoph. Come soon." She let go of him then, and with all her remaining strength, ran straight for Luke.

CHAPTER 22

Luke could not take his eyes from her.

Sarah?

She had appeared a moment earlier within the burning doorway, with her arms held up before her face. He'd watched her leap through the rippling flames and tumble to her knees upon the blackened concrete step. She'd stayed there on all fours, appearing to catch her breath, but finally sat back on her haunches. It was then that she'd pushed herself from the ground, like a wounded soldier unwilling to admit defeat.

But she's not hurt. Anywhere. Luke stared at her as she stood boldly before the blaze. Not a hair on her head was singed or out of place, and her face looked smooth and soft but not sweaty at all. *Her cheeks aren't even red, and they're almost always flushed.* They were a light healthy color, just like her hands.

Luke stepped closer. *It can't be.* Her hoodie was still purple, with not a single speck of soot or ash upon it. Her jeans were clean and whole, and her tennis shoes looked brand new.

He saw her look his way, and a wonderful smile swept across her face. She jumped clumsily from the step and ran straight toward him.

"Luke!" Sarah shouted. "Luke!"

Luke took off as he felt the joy rush through him. He flew across the yard and reached her in an instant, and she leaped into his arms. *She's so light.* He held her tightly against himself, as if he'd never let go, and twirled her around in wild circles.

Sarah began to laugh giddily. Luke grinned as he pressed his face into the crook of her neck, and he felt her hands pressing upon the back of his head. He slowly stopped twirling and stood in place, embracing her still.

"I thought I'd lost you," Luke whispered. He raised his head and gently lowered Sarah to the ground. "I thought—" He cupped her face in his hands, suddenly trying to hold back tears. "I thought you—"

Sarah pressed her finger to his lips. "But I didn't." She laid her hands on his chest. "You didn't lose me."

Luke brought her face to his and kissed her fervently. When he closed his eyes, he felt her hand slide along his neck, and he took her in his arms.

"She's over here!" a man shouted behind him. "Right here!"

The nearness of the voice startled Luke, and he pulled away from Sarah and turned around. A fireman stood but a few feet from him, pointing at Sarah but looking back toward the street.

That's the guy who tackled me. Luke kept his arm around Sarah and pulled her close to his side. A group of paramedics and firefighters was jogging towards them from the street.

"Luke," Sarah said, "I don't need to go to the hospital. Tell them I don't—"

"Miss!" The fireman strode to them. "Miss, we need to get you to—"

Luke watched him stop in place, as if he'd just ran into a wall. The fireman opened his mouth slightly and raised his hand, but he furrowed his brow instead of speaking.

He's staring at her, just like I was. Luke glanced down at Sarah, and she looked up at him and shook her head earnestly. He chuckled a little and looked back at the fireman. "Sir, I don't think she—"

"It can't be," the fireman said softly. He seemed to look Sarah up and down. "You...you don't have one burn on you. Anywhere." He took his helmet off and stepped closer. "Not even one."

Luke saw Sarah hold out her hands and slowly turn them back and forth. She flexed her fingers as she gazed at them.

"He's right," she whispered. "Not even one."

She's just now noticing? Luke smiled and kissed her forehead. She laid her head against his chest.

"But how is that possible?"

Luke looked up at the fireman. "How is what possible?"

"Her, that's what." The fireman pointed his helmet at Sarah. "How is she alive? How did she—"

Luke heard the groan of snapping timbers and whirled just as the charred remains of the duplex collapsed to the ground. Plumes of sparks and ash erupted into the air while the burning heap continued to shift and crackle.

Sarah gasped and seemed to turn her head frantically. "Luke...Luke! Where is he?"

"Sarah, I'm right here," Luke said. He put himself between her and the fire and laid his hands on her shoulders as he looked at her. "It's okay. I'm right—"

"Luke, no," Sarah said earnestly. "Not you."

Luke felt the anguish wash over him. *Chris. How could I have just forgotten about him?* He let go of her and turned around.

Plumes of thick smoke rose from the dying flames, but nothing moved within the blackened mound. Luke noticed a group of firefighters blasting the fire with water from a long hose and took a step towards them. *Chris?* They were too far away to tell for certain.

"He was right behind me."

Luke felt Sarah lean against his side. When he looked down at her, he saw the tears in her eyes as she gazed at the flames.

"Sarah, it's not your fault." Luke took her in his arms and rested his chin on her head. "Maybe he—" His throat suddenly burned with emotion, and he swallowed quickly. "Maybe he got out. There's so many firefighters that any one of them could be—"

"No, Luke," Sarah said softly. "Wait. He said...he promised—" She lifted her head and looked up at him. "He told me I wouldn't see him for a time. But he told me he'd never leave me." She turned toward the fire. "So I thought...I thought he was coming out. I didn't even look back to see—"

"You mean there's someone else in there?"

Luke turned and saw the fireman standing before him. The way he was creasing his forehead made his face look worried and frightened at the same time. Several paramedics and firefighters stood around him, gazing wide-eyed at Sarah.

"Miss, please," the fireman said. "Did I hear you say that someone else was in there?"

"No, I don't think...I'm not sure," Sarah said. "My friend, he carried me through the flames and set me down in the doorway. I thought he followed me out, but I don't know where he is now."

Luke saw the fireman raise his eyebrows and glance at the paramedic standing next to him. A few in the group appeared to whisper to each other.

"Um, did you say—" The fireman took a step towards Sarah while he held on to his helmet with both hands. "Did you say you were carried through the fire?"

Sarah nodded. "Yes, he carried me."

"Who carried you?" The fireman nodded toward Luke. "This man?"

"No, not me," Luke said. *He doesn't believe her.* He slipped his arm around Sarah and pulled her to him. "It was the man I came here with. He saved her."

"Man?" The fireman nearly laughed. "What man? You came here alone."

What? Luke felt a twinge of anger. "No, I didn't. When you tackled me, I was yellin' at him. I was tryin' to stop him from running into the fire, but you tackled me. Even if you didn't see him, you had to have heard me yellin' at him."

"I'm sorry, sir," the fireman said. "When I tackled you, I had no idea who you were yellin' at. There was no one there with you. I thought you were in shock, and I was afraid you were gonna do something stupid." He put his helmet on his head and shrugged lightly. "You came here alone, and she came out of that house alone. Simple as that."

Luke glared at him. "I *didn't* come here alone. And she *didn't* come out of that fire alone." He took a deep breath and ran his hand over his head. "Why won't you believe us? Just look at her! She's proof enough that something miraculous has happened here."

Now the fireman smirked. "Miraculous?" He chuckled and looked over his shoulder. "Hear that boys? God's performin' miracles by burnin' houses down."

Some of the emergency workers laughed. Those who did not seemed to look at each other uncomfortably.

Luke clenched his fist at his side. *He gave up his life for her, and you laugh?* He felt the tears stinging his eyes. "He was my friend. He died for her. How dare you—"

"Luke," Sarah said softly. "Luke, look."

"Not now, Sarah." Luke kept his gaze squarely on the fireman. "I'm not going to let you mock—"

Sarah pushed away from him and ran.

"Sarah, what—" Luke stepped back, startled. "Sarah, wait! I'm sorry." He took off after her, following her across the yard to the back of a fire truck. She stopped behind it and stood with her back towards him. But then she bent down.

Luke jogged up behind her. "Sarah, are you alright? Why did you take off like that? You scared—"

"He did make it out," Sarah whispered. Her head was bowed and her arms bent at the elbows. She stood completely still. "Luke, he did get out it. And he'll never leave us, just like he said."

"What?" Luke asked. "What do you—"

Sarah turned around and held out her hands to him, palms up. When she looked up at him, she was smiling through her tears.

He did get out. Luke stared at the knife lying across her hands. Its curved hilt was raven black and wrapped with golden wiring, while its stainless steel blade bore a familiar name etched in golden lettering.

"It was here," Sarah said. "On top this fire gear."

When she stepped to the side, Luke saw the firefighter's uniform lying in a neat bundle on the grass. Two rubber boots stood beside the folded uniform, while a black fire helmet lay upon it.

"Here," Sarah said. "Take it. It's yours."

Luke watched her hold the knife out to him, and he wrapped his fingers around the hilt. *Twice he gave me back my knife.* He took it from her hands and held it up before his eyes, reading the name on the blade. *Twice he gave me back my life.*

"He's alive," Sarah said. "He really is—"

A light flashed beside them.

Luke glimpsed the newscaster and her cameraman just as the fireman appeared beside him.

"Get these people outta here!" the fireman shouted. He strode to the newscaster and wagged his finger toward her cameraman. "You two are not allowed beyond—"

"Miss Ryans! Sarah Ryans!" The newscaster side-stepped the fireman and held a microphone out to Sarah. "I'm Sherri Collins with WKRC Channel 3 out of Richmond. How were you able to save yourself from that fire?"

"I didn't," Sarah said. "I was bound, but he set me free. He cut my ropes with that knife. Then he carried me through the flames and saved me."

Luke watched the cameraman push past the fireman and hover over Sherri's shoulder.

"Who saved you?" Sherri asked intently. "Who saved you, Sarah?"

The fireman moved between Sarah and the microphone. "Enough! I want you two outta here! And I want this girl taken to the hospital and examined immediately. She may be suffering from shock. And her boyfriend too. Well, get a move on! Don't just stand—"

"Um, may I ask something?"

A paramedic stepped forward from the group of emergency workers which had gathered around them. She looked young, too young to be a paramedic, and was barely five feet tall. Her hair was brown and pulled back in a ponytail, and her build was very slight. She wrung her hands a little as she stood waiting.

She was one of the few who didn't laugh. "Sure," Luke said. He nodded kindly. "Go ahead."

"Well, I was just wondering—" The paramedic glanced at the ground and looked back up. "I was wondering what his name was."

"His name?" Sarah asked.

"Um, the man who saved you," the paramedic said. "I want...I'd like to know more about him. What was his name?"

Luke saw the fireman step back as Sherri thrust the microphone closer. The cameraman leaned earnestly over her shoulder, while the emergency workers looked on expectantly. Blue and red lights flashed in the background.

"Luke, would you like to tell them?" Sarah asked.

Luke felt her hand slip into his, and he glanced down at the knife in his other hand. *I will give you the words to say when the time comes, and I will work in the hearts of those you speak to.* He looked at Sarah. She was smiling at him. He squeezed her hand and looked up at the camera.

"His name is Jesus Christ." Luke turned to the paramedic and smiled. "We'll tell you how He saved us both."

9 780989 026444